MW00775360

OPEN SEASON

JONATHAN KELLERMAN

OPEN SEASON

AN ALEX DELAWARE NOVEL

BALLANTINE BOOKS

NEW YORK

Published in the United States by Ballantine Books,
an imprint of Random House, a division of
Penguin Random House LLC, New York.

BALLANTINE BOOKS & colophon are registered trademarks
of Penguin Random House LLC.

Hardback ISBN 978-0-593-49769-2
Ebook ISBN 978-0-593-49770-8

Printed in the United States of America on acid-free paper

randomhousebooks.com

2 4 6 8 9 7 5 3 1

First Edition

To Faye

OPEN SEASON

CHAPTER

1

The images were grainy and blurred. But they told a story.

The storyteller was a camera perched above the entrance to Westside Acu-Care Hospital on National Boulevard, a short stroll west of Robertson. The only active location on a grimy stretch of warehouses dominated by the concrete spaghetti of freeway overpasses.

The lens was a poorly placed witness, focused narrowly on a right-of-center slice of the hospital's circular drop-off area. Luckily, it had captured the basics.

Saturday, two fifty-three a.m.: A car, dark, compact, speeds around the outer rim of the circle and stops short, rocking back and forth.

Seven seconds later, the driver's door swings open and remains that way.

A man in a dark hoodie, pants, and gloves exits, runs to the rear right passenger door, and flings it open. Stooping, he reaches in and begins sliding something out. As the bulk of that something is brought outside of the car, it takes form.

Oblong, swaddled in something dark.

Bending his knees and lifting smoothly, the man slings the shape over his shoulder, totes it a few feet, and lays it down with no apparent tenderness.

Five seconds later, he's driven off and the thing, human-sized and inert, remains on the pavement.

Milo stopped the tape. "In answer to your next question, not for six minutes. The guard took an unauthorized bathroom break and didn't get back until then. Seventy-eight years old so I guess he gets some kind of pass."

His frown said not much of one.

I said, "Impressive security."

"Place was run by skeleton crew, a nurse told me they're probably going out of business."

He tapped his computer monitor. "Top of that, the camera's an antique, the techies couldn't tell a thing about make and model. And you saw the tags. As in none."

Removing license plates said careful planning. Likewise gloves and a face-blocking hood. Milo has the highest solve rate in the department. No sense mentioning any of that.

He rubbed his face. "Weird place. If there were patients, I didn't see them."

I knew the hospital's history.

Abortion mill morphing to a slip-and-fall physical rehab center then to one of those inpatient drug rehabs that promises everything and delivers nothing. Each transformation short-lived and polluted by missteps and legal wrangling.

The new owners, a New York–based health-care outfit with connections to New York senators, had tried switching to pediatric urgent care funded by government money. The location made success unlikely. So did several malpractice suits that had scared parents away.

But grant money kept flowing and now the place was tagged as a "neighborhood-based acute-care facility serving the greater, diverse community." With Cedars, Kaiser, and the U. within easy driving distance, it had no reason to exist.

I knew all of that because during the pediatric phase, I'd evaluated a nine-year-old boy whose broken femur had been set incompetently at Westside, leading to the possibility of a permanent limp.

My job had been to tell the court how that would impact a kid psychologically.

Not profound findings but the plaintiff's attorney needed someone like me to spell them out.

Milo said, "Any ideas?"

I said, "Rewind."

He relinquished his desk chair so I could manipulate the tape's stop-and-freeze. His office on the second floor of the Westside station is closet-sized and windowless and once he's on his feet he displays all the serenity of a bear in a trap.

Stomping out to the corridor armed with his cellphone, he turned right. Diminishing heavy footsteps said he'd walked a ways.

Then they stopped; none of the usual pacing. Probably calling the Coroner's. For the third time since I'd been there.

After my fifth viewing of the tape, I went out to the hallway.

Milo was thirty feet away, just standing there. A black eyebrow tented. He walked toward me. "Spot anything?"

I said, "Maybe the techies can get a more precise height estimate but he's good-sized—probably tall as you—and solidly built. The way he lifts and carries says he's strong and practiced, so he could work a job requiring muscle. Or he spends a lot of time in the gym."

His nod said he'd reached the same conclusions.

Twisted lips said he'd hoped for more.

I looked at his phone. "Any progress at the crypt?"

He smiled. "Good guess—scratch that, excellent intellectual reasoning." He pocketed the phone. "Nah, it was a busy night, she hasn't even been moved to storage. One promising development. Basia just came on shift, and she promised to facilitate."

Dr. Basia Lopatinski is his favorite forensic pathologist. Smart, hardworking, inevitably cheerful, she'd been a tenured professor in Poland, had finally gotten board certification in the U.S.

I said, "Go, Basia."

He said, "If I was oriented that way, I'd try to marry her. Let's get some coffee."

We took the stairs down to the ground floor, exited onto Butler, continued north to Santa Monica Boulevard then west along the weekend-quiet thoroughfare.

Warm, sunny Saturday. Beautiful weather always seems cruel when you're dealing with the loss of a human being. But that's L.A., seductive and perverse.

Milo's grimly set mouth set the tone: time to walk in silence.

He'd arrived at the death scene at three thirty and it was now just over seven hours later. His green eyes were sharp but the rest of him looked shopworn, pockmarked pallor clashing harshly with coarse black hair, dirt-gray windbreaker rumpled irretrievably, brown khaki cargo pants worn low and freed from the swell of his gut, sagging sadly.

New desert boots, though. Tan with pink soles. Likely a gift from Rick, who'd long given up trying to spiff up his partner's wardrobe. The exception: replacing boots defeated every few months by their wearer's bulk.

Only an hour had passed since Milo's call at nine forty-five but it felt like much longer. When my phone vibrated on the kitchen counter, Robin and I were finishing a late breakfast and sharing bits of omelet with our little French bulldog, Blanche.

Robin reached over, retrieved the phone, read my screen and grinned. "We squeaked through."

"Big Guy?"

"Who else."

I put the phone on speaker. "Morning. What's up?"

"Hope you're not busy."

Robin smiled, kissed me, and got up.

Before following, Blanche cocked her head curiously.

I said, "Promise you a walk when I get back."

As they left, they both had that knowing look.

I was behind the wheel of the Seville by the time Milo finished giving me the basics. Took Beverly Glen through Westwood over to Pico, hooked west to Butler Avenue, then south to the West L.A. station.

A uniform was waiting at the staff lot to card-key me in.

"Good morning, Doctor."

"Good morning."

Not for everyone.

Substantial time lapse between the discovery of an unexplained death and any sort of forensic analysis is the rule, not the exception. Unlike what you're fed on whiz-bang TV shows, processing a dead human is a painstaking process involving a small army of people who know tortoise beats hare every time.

Uniforms are the first to arrive, then detectives, then coroner's investigators and crime scene techs. Everyone knows the rules and waits their turn.

Last in line are the crypt drivers who bag and zip then *clickety-clack* the gurney open and roll the body smoothly into their van as the wheeled cart folds flat obediently. The duration of the ride to 1104 North Mission Road in East L.A. depends on where in the sprawl of L.A. County the crime occurred and, more important, the traffic situation. Just like any other commute.

The body's driven to the back of the Coroner's and eased onto a loading dock. No tasteless humor to be heard, just the mute ballet of people doing their jobs.

And the buzz of aspirational flies collecting at doors and windows. No matter how tightly the building is sealed, they never stop trying.

In a homicide, the case belongs to the detective but the body belongs to the coroner and it's hands-off until the coroner's investigator gives the okay. The C.I. this morning had already been to a shooting near Skid Row and didn't arrive until just after five a.m.

Milo had spent the time inside the hospital, interviewing nurses and doctors, all of them wide-eyed with shock and having nothing to offer. The flustered guard was located dry-retching in a bathroom. Because of his age and obvious frailty, Milo went easy on him.

Not that pressuring him would've made a difference. All Atkins Gillibrand knew was that after he'd seen "the bundle," he notified the white coats and watched in horror as they unwrapped it.

"They didn't do no doctoring, sir, not a bit. Checked for a pulse, said she was long-cold, and called 911."

Nossir, he didn't know her. No one else did, either. Pretty girl, though, couldn't be more than twenty, twenty-five.

Canvassing the neighborhood is basic procedure but in this case it was irrelevant because there were no residences or open businesses nearby, just shuttered industrial buildings and the freeway jumble. Homeless people often camp under the passes but no sign of any so maybe they'd fled at the sight of black-and-whites speeding by, light bars strobing the darkness.

Once Milo had learned all that, there was little for him to do. When the C.I., a retired RN named Gladys King, arrived, the same applied to her.

No pockets through which to rummage or labels to read, no obvious "defects."

"Probably an O.D.," she said.

Milo said, "She was dumped by a guy who sped off."

"Ah," said King. "Guess that makes it your business. Good luck."

2

Our silent walk covered three blocks before Milo hooked a thumb at a café with a tricolor Italian flag over the door.

Geppetto's was *Closed SATURDAYS until noon*. One person inside, a squat, aproned, gray-haired man sweeping. Milo rapped the glass, the man saw us and unlocked the door, beaming.

"The usual, *Comandante*?"

"Sounds good, Miro."

"You, signor?"

I'd had three cups of Ethiopian at home. "Decaf espresso."

We settled at a marble-topped table in the far corner as Miro fiddled behind the counter.

I said, "Miro. He's Spanish?"

"Croatian. Miroslav."

"Ah."

"Long story." Showing no inclination to tell it.

Miro returned with a double latte for Milo, a demitasse for me, and a plate that he set down in front of Milo.

"Some coffee" had expanded to an assortment of baked goods. Or maybe that was the intention all along.

"Today we got cannoli, amaretti, and frittelle." A finger-poke indicated each one.

Milo said, "Can't wait," and didn't.

When he'd finished the pastries and accepted two more cannoli from Miro, I told him what I knew about the hospital.

"You held off telling me because . . ."

"Didn't see it as relevant but now I'm wondering. At a typical hospital he couldn't have escaped detection. Maybe he's got a connection to the place. Or he's from the neighborhood and familiar enough to know security's lax. A third possibility is that he's actually dumped another O.D. there."

"I asked the staff about anything like that happening there and they said no."

"Given all the changes, the current staff probably hasn't been there long."

"Fine, I'll look into it."

Reaching for the cannoli, he bit down with fury, rained crumbs onto his shirt.

He finished everything Miro brought before throwing cash on the table, standing and stretching.

During the walk back to the station, his head canted forward as if primed for battle.

Resumption of silence.

That changed a block later when his phone chirped Mozart.

He listened, said, "Fantastic, kiddo. Could you email it to—you have? I *love* you."

Clicking off, he doubled his pace, long legs chewing up distance like a relentless mass of farming apparatus.

I said, "Basia."

"She ever quits, I'll need Prozac."

———

Within an hour of hearing Milo's plea, Basia had examined the body externally and confirmed the absence of wounds, x-rayed it anyway, and found no bullets or foreign objects internally. A blood draw submitted for a tox screen was followed by inking and printing ten fingertips and two palms.

The prints paid off.

3

Marissa Adrianne French, twenty-five years old, five-five, one seventeen, brown and blue, driver of a six-year-old white Accord.

DMV photos typically bring out the worst in faces but this face had managed to dodge the indignity.

Beautiful young woman with wide, sparkling eyes, the blue of her irises so deep they came across indigo. Broad, white smile, rosy cheek-bones, dimple on the right. "Brown" was chestnut laced with strands of ice blue, worn long and side-parted, with a flap that half concealed her left eye.

The address on her driver's license was a three-digit apartment number on Coldwater Canyon Avenue in Sherman Oaks. Milo pulled up a street view. Massive gray mega-unit between Magnolia and River-side.

Her prints were on file because Beverly Elms Gardens, where she worked as a Caregiver Level I, had required a background check. Milo looked up the facility. Olympic just east of La Brea, specializing in "Eldercare and Memory Rehabilitation."

He called and got put on hold. Switched his phone to speaker and muttered, "Wonderful," when too-soft rock began streaming. Returning to his keyboard, he entered his LAPD user I.D. and began searching databases.

Since the background check nineteen months ago, Marissa French hadn't accrued any criminal charges. Nor was she listed as a crime victim or a party to a civil suit.

Milo had just logged onto NCIC when the phone said, "Can I help you?"

Female voice, flat with boredom.

Marissa French's name elicited "Doesn't ring a bell."

"Your facility fingerprinted her."

"If you say so."

"She no longer works there?"

"That I couldn't tell you."

"Ma'am," said Milo. "She's dead and she listed you as her place of employment."

A beat. "Dead."

"Could you see if she ever worked there and if she left, is there a forwarding to a new job?"

"We don't keep that type of information . . . dead . . . an accident?"

"I'm a homicide detective, Ms. . . . ."

"Julie. You're saying murder."

"It's not a pretty situation, Julie."

Silence.

"Julie?"

"Okay . . . could she be a temp?"

He rolled his eyes. "Good question."

"I'm only saying because if she was a temp you need to talk to HR and they're over at corporate in Buena Park. Would you like the number?"

"I would, Julie, but if you could be a doll and just check your records that would be super-helpful."

"Not pretty, how?"

"You really don't want to know, Julie."

"Okay. Hold on."

We endured several more minutes of music beaten to a sodden pulp before a new voice came on. Male, deep.

"This is Truc. Marissa A. French worked here but as a float."

"Meaning?"

"She had no contract but agreed to be available when someone was needed to fill in on a shift."

"On-call."

"Yes."

"How often did that turn out to be?"

"No idea, sir. That would require going through like a year and a half of data."

"Giant hassle, huh?"

Truc said, "Let me see what I find."

"Appreciate it."

"Julie told me she got killed, I want to do what I can."

"Thanks, Truc. Here's my number."

When the line went dead, he turned to me. "A float. Okay, let's look at her social media."

I'd been working my phone and showed him the results.

He said, "Thank you, Oracle of Delphi."

The camera adored Marissa French and she reciprocated.

Her online presence was extensive and chiefly photographic. Hundreds of images, some selfies, some taken by others. Sometimes she'd posed with men and women her own age, the most common position, grinning, drink in hand, the background always a blurry crowd scene.

But most of the collection consisted of solos of Marissa French.

That might fit with not much by way of "friends."

Despite all the images, she'd named only four.

Tori, Beth, Bethany, Yoli.

Short blond hair, long blond hair, long black hair, a pile of red waves. Each woman svelte, pretty, wearing full makeup and clothing that advertised fitness.

Never photographed as a group. Each of them stood next to Marissa in party scenes. Center screen reserved for Marissa.

As I kept looking, I realized the same went for men. Always relegated to the sides.

People as props?

Milo screen-shot the four names along with accompanying photos and emailed the lot to his desktop. The computer began chiming receipt and we returned to examining what was shaping up as Marissa French's sadly brief legacy.

The photos fit into three categories.

Marissa posing on the beach in a bikini or topless with arms folded across her chest.

Marissa perched on sun-splotched hilltops in shorts and tees, hair blowing strategically.

Marissa crouching in what appeared to be a forest, looking entranced by pinecones, ferns, and stones and wearing tight western shirts, denim short-shorts, and boots with heels that mocked the notion of hiking.

What seemed to be modeling poses. But modeling's about more than beauty and for all Marissa's good looks, she projected a limited emotional range—smile or pout—and none of the results had produced anything better than what the DMV robot had accomplished.

A rare burst of prose followed the photographic display:

I'm available for movie work, here are my credits. xoxoxoxo *M*

No agency listed, just an email address.

Then the "credits."

During the past eighteen months, Marissa French had worked as an extra on four TV pilots and three low-budget horror flicks.

Milo said, "Heard of any of them?"

I shook my head.

"Same old story, poor thing."

I said, "Maybe she worked as a float to be available for auditions."

"Which never came through." He scrolled quickly through several more screens, came to the end, and was about to click off when his eyes widened.

The final photo was time-stamped Friday, eleven thirty-four p.m., and featured Marissa French in a minimal red dress with side cutouts that exposed a tight waist and a violin curve of hip.

Standing with a man. This time, not an age peer, not even close.

Mid- to late-forties and nothing prop-like about him. Unlike every other photo in Marissa's collection, she'd given up center stage and was edged so far to the right that her left arm was out of the frame.

Easy for her companion to fill space. He was tall enough to stand well above a five-five woman wearing four-inch heels, and broad, with piled-up shoulders and a muscular torso running slightly to flab.

Middle-aged but dressed younger, in a black, scoop-necked Pink Floyd T-shirt with high-cut sleeves that emphasized bulky arms. A diamond or something pretending to be glinted from his left earlobe. A chunky gold chain dangled to the hem of the scoop.

A pug-nosed, meaty face was improbably tan where it wasn't booze-flushed. A toothy, borderline-rodent smile was a tribute to the excesses of cosmetic dentistry. Black hair was buzzed nearly invisible at the sides, the top a curly thatch lubricated to gleaming. Framing the capped teeth were thick lips bottomed by a triangular, black soul patch.

His left arm was tattoo-sleeved. His right, un-inked, was slung over Marissa French's bare shoulders in a casual display of ownership. Nothing in her body language said she'd signed on voluntarily. Glassy eyes said she wasn't equipped for protest.

Both he and Marissa held oversized martini glasses filled with something red. His smile was triumphant. Hers, pathetic.

Milo said, "Joe Beef looks like he's bagged a trophy. She's not into it, why's she standing for it?"

I said, "Look at her eyes."

He studied the image. "Yeah, she is kinda hazy."

"His size fits the video and so does the time frame."

"Partying close to midnight and she's dead before three."

I said, "He takes her to his place or somewhere else where he can control the scene, makes sure she's incapacitated. She was dumped naked so he likely did his thing or tried to. At some point, she stopped breathing so he got rid of the problem."

Milo's eyes swept back and forth between the two faces, alternating between revulsion and anger. Ending with a long look at the grinning man and cherry-sized lumps running up and down his jaw.

"Bastard. Who *are* you?"

CHAPTER

4

Neither of us had noticed the older man anywhere else in the photo dump but we reviewed the images anyway.

Nothing.

Milo said, "All the other shots, she's the star of the show, loving herself. She lets down her guard for a sleaze like this?" He shook his head. "Maybe he's been criminally sleazy before, I'll send this to Brand Leary in Vice."

As he typed, I said, "No shots with other men during the past week."

"She and Beef had a thing?"

"Maybe not romance," I said. "She could've let down her guard because she thought he had something to offer."

"Like what?"

"A speaking part."

"The old fake-Hollywood-honcho deal? She could be fooled that easily?"

"Getting nothing but crowd scenes for a year and a half can sap your confidence. If he happened to show up when she was feeling vulnerable, who knows?"

"Sheep, say hi to Wolf." He frowned.

"Or," I said, "she'd already given up and decided to switch gears. To me he looks like a guy with a porn vibe. Washed-up actor turned producer, director."

"Hmm. I guess a girl with her looks could make some decent short-term money. So what, last night was an audition that went bad? Let's see what her besties have to say. At the least, maybe one of them knows how to reach her family so I can do what I hate."

Learning the full names of Marissa's female friends proved easy. She'd posted their names with links to their own social platforms.

Long blond hair was Victoria "Tori" Burkholder, twenty-five, an "aesthetician" at a salon in Sherman Oaks.

Short blond hair was Elisheva "Beth" Halperin, twenty-four, assistant chef at a French café in Encino.

Long black hair was Bethany McGonigal, twenty-five, administrative assistant to an unnamed boss in an unnamed location.

Red and curly traced to Yolanda "Yoli" Echeverria, twenty-four, staff assistant, again, no details.

DMV said Tori Burkholder lived in the same neighborhood where she worked, an apartment on Coldwater, four blocks north of Marissa's. Beth Halperin and Yoli Echeverria roomed together in Reseda, and Bethany McGonigal listed a flat in North Hollywood.

Milo said, "Buncha Valley girls, maybe that's where the parties were. Including the last one. And 818 *is* porn central, which would fit with Beef being from that world . . . lemme see if Leary got back— nope."

He tried the Vice detective's desk.

Brandon Leary said, "Hey, just got it. Sorry, don't know the dude. He rape and kill someone?"

"Looks like he O.D.'d a woman, did his thing, and dumped her body."

"Oh man, that's evil. Okay, I'll show it around, he does have that predator thing going on."

"Thanks."

"Anytime, Milo. Glad it's you not me dealing with it."

No home numbers for the four friends, but those of the salon and the café were public knowledge.

He tried Christopher Van Vliet Hair & Beauty first and asked for Tori Burkholder.

A slow-talking man with a nasal voice said, "She's not in today. Would you like me to book an appointment for tomorrow?"

"No, thanks, I need to talk to her." Milo identified himself.

The man said, "She's in trouble with the cops? I find that hard to believe."

"A friend of hers is in trouble."

"And you want Tori to rat the friend out?"

Milo exhaled. "The friend is deceased, sir. I'm gathering information."

"Deceased. Oh my. Hold on, I'll give you Tori's cell."

"Appreciate it."

"Deceased," said the man. "The world has gone insane."

Voicemail at Tori Burkholder's number. Milo moved on to Bistro Genial, talked to a harried-sounding woman and worsened her mood.

"We are *busy*."

"It's a police matter, ma'am—"

"Whatever. Quick, quick, what do you want?"

He began explaining.

Click, then static on the line.

He said, "She hung up on me?"

A soft, accented voice came on. "This is Beth. What is going on?"

Milo said, "This is Lieutenant Sturgis from the police department. Sorry to drop this on you but something bad has happened to a friend of yours—"

"What friend?"

"Marissa French."

"We're not so much friends," said Beth Halperin.

"I see. Well, I thought you might be able to help me with information."

"Information?" Hardened voice. "You are one of those—trying to get my data?"

"No, ma'am. Unfortunately, Marissa is dead and I'm the detective—"

"Dead!" A loud wail caused him to distance the phone from his ear. "No way!"

"I'm afraid so. She died last night—"

A gasp. "No!"

"Is there any way we could talk about Marissa?"

"Okay, yes, sure, yes," said Beth Halperin. "I will leave now, I cannot do soufflé like this—Marie-Claire? I am leaving . . . no, no, I have to . . . a friend has died . . . do what you *want*, I am *going*."

Milo said, "Where can we meet?"

"I'm going home." She rattled off an address on Amigo Avenue.

Milo said, "That's Reseda?"

"Do a GPS."

CHAPTER

5

We left just before two, hit merciful traffic on the 101, and arrived thirty-two minutes later.

Beth Halperin lived in a custard-colored cube with a low-peaked tar roof that evoked a five-year-old's drawing of a house. Gray pebbles in place of a lawn. No greenery visible beyond the cracked driveway hosting an older black Celica.

More of the same on the rest of the block. Bungalows built for aircraft workers in the fifties.

Milo said, "Amigo Avenue. You spot any signs of friendliness?"

During the drive, I'd found the property listed on a rental agency website. A thousand square feet on a cement lot three times that size. No garage but AC, hardwood floors, a granite kitchen, and cable-readiness.

Three thousand a month, six-month lease, and a month's worth of deposit required. The cost of being young and barely self-supporting in L.A.

Beth Halperin opened a flat gray door wearing a man's white shirt over black leggings. Since posing for her California I.D., short blond hair had expanded to long and pearly white.

A tattoo in some sort of foreign script ran along her right forearm.

The hand at the end of the arm trembled, as did its mate. She laced her fingers to still them and looked us over with huge, pale-blue eyes that lingered on Milo's olive-green vinyl attaché case. The irises were rimmed in red, a mascara blot smudged her left cheek, a pimple so rosy it had to be fresh had erupted on her chin like a nasty little volcano.

Despite the symptoms of stress, lovely. Same as the other three.

Maybe that had been part of the appeal. The pretty girls hanging together.

Milo introduced us but Beth Halperin didn't seem to be listening as she stepped back and let us into a small, low living room set up with a black, faux-leather sectional that screamed *by-the-month*. Aluminum-and-glass tables looked as if they couldn't withstand a breeze.

"AC" was an ancient louvered box sitting atilt in a window, "hardwood" was cheap gray laminate that extended into a gray kitchenette. Three framed posters hung on custard-colored walls. The Grand Canyon at sunset, adorable penguins huddled on an ice shelf, glossy towers on a beach. In the beach scene, *Tel Aviv* was emblazoned atop the skyline in wispy white letters meant to emulate skywriting. Or maybe a plane had actually left the message.

Milo said, "Elisheva. That's an Israeli name?"

Her frown said, *Here we go again.* "It's a Hebrew name. The original where they got Elisabeth. So call me Beth."

"Got it." He smiled.

Unimpressed, she sat on the shorter arm of the sectional. "What happened to Marissa?"

Milo said, "Can't get into details but she may have overdosed."

"Impossible. Marissa did not take drugs."

"Never?"

"Not since I am knowing her. She told me she took them in high school and it messed her up. She drank a Sea Breeze, that's all. Maybe sometimes another cocktail. But only one, she wanted to be in control."

"Sea Breeze."

"Vodka and cranberry juice, I think they are disgusting. Mostly she held them to look like she was drinking. She did *not* overdose."

Milo leaned forward. "Beth, I'm a homicide detective."

"Yes, I know that, I googled you."

"The point is she may not have known she overdosed."

A second of silence, then: "Oh."

Beth Halperin's hands separated and relaced around her right knee, bending her forward. She rocked a couple of times, stopped, sat up straight, and looked away from us.

"Stupid, stupid, I got . . . *mevulbal* . . . confused."

"Understandable, Beth. How'd you and Marissa meet?"

"She knew Yoli—my roommate—from high school."

"Which high school?"

"Here. Reseda."

"Did Bethany and Tori also go there?"

"Yes—you talked to them?"

"Not yet. Marissa listed the four of you as her friends."

"Okay. Yes. They were friends from a long time. I started rooming with Yoli and they didn't know me. But later they accept me."

"You earned your stripes."

Beth Halperin smiled. "Stripes I earned in the army. Three."

"You made sergeant."

"It's not hard. I ran a kitchen near the Lebanon border. That's where I met Oded. A guy. He was a lieutenant. After the army, we traveled and he came here to go to engineering school."

Her hands flew apart again and re-formed as white-knuckle fists. "Then he said bye-bye and I'm here, so I look for a place to cook and go to Sweet James in Canoga Park, Yoli is a waitress and her roommate left her with all the rent so I move in with her."

"We're talking a while back."

"Two years. I'm returning to Israel in August."

"So you met Marissa—"

"After that. Maybe . . . twenty months."

"What can you tell us about her?"

"Nice," she said.

I said, "But you weren't close."

Her lips screwed up. "She is dead, I don't want to . . . to say."

Milo said, "It could help us find out what happened to her?"

"I don't see—okay, nothing drama but she got more into . . . being an actress than being a friend. She did it in high school and thought she could do it for a job."

"Ah," said Milo. "And that made her . . ."

"Not here. For all of us."

"Busy."

"Yes," said Beth Halperin. "But more than that. Busy *here*." She tapped her head.

I said, "Distracted."

She was digesting that when the door opened and a beautiful olive-skinned, red-haired woman in a black cowl-necked sweater, black tights, and black flats stepped in and froze.

"Beth? What's going on?"

"Marissa is dead!"

"What!"

"Dead! They are police!"

Yolanda Echeverria's black eyes rounded. She dropped her purse to the floor and teetered.

We got up ready to catch her but she remained on her feet. I retrieved the purse and set it down on an iffy table.

"I . . . don't understand."

Milo said, "Why don't you get off your feet."

He guided her to the sectional, waited until she'd settled next to Beth Halperin. Then he explained.

She said, "O.D.? She never took anything."

Beth said, "That's what I tell him."

Milo opened his case and produced Joe Beef's photo. "This is the last person she was photographed with. Do you know him?"

The women looked at each other.

Beth Halperin said, "Maybe the producer?"

Yoli Echeverria said, "That's what I was thinking."

Milo said, "Marissa told you she'd met a producer."

Twin nods.

Yoli Echeverria said, "We told her be careful."

Beth Halperin said, "I think to myself it is stupid."

I said, "Stupid how?"

"What?" she said. "All the time she gets nothing except a few extras—"

"Non-union stuff," said Yoli. "Like no real money."

Beth said, "Exactly. Then she meets a producer and he's going to give her an actress job?"

"She was so so happy," said Yoli. "I didn't want to burst her bubble."

"I told her," said Beth. "She yelled at me. That's the last time we spoke."

"Oh," said Yoli. "Sorry."

They looked at each other again.

Tears flowed. Lots of them.

We spent a few more minutes, Milo asking the right questions, repeating some of them. Learning only that mention of "the producer" had come up a week before Marissa's death.

"First time we heard from her in like a week, two, I dunno," said Yoli.

Beth said, "She is telling us she is right and we are wrong."

I said, "When's the last time you saw her?"

Another ocular consultation.

Yoli said, "Two and a half weeks ago?"

Beth said, "About. Before she told us about him. It was an opening."

"Of?"

"A clothes place," said Yoli. "Mama Baba on Melrose. She said they needed girls for pictures but when we showed up, they took like one picture."

"Of her," said Beth. "Show them."

Yoli retrieved her purse and scrolled her phone.

One of the images we'd already seen. Marissa at the center, Yoli to the left.

Beth said, "We left fast."

"Crazy," said Yoli.

"Stupid," said Beth. Sharpness in her voice. She realized it and slapped a hand over her mouth. "Sorry. Not her fault. It's wanting something too much. But you don't do that."

I said, "Go to openings?"

"No, I mean him." Forming air quotes. "He say he's a producer so you just go? He killed her?"

Milo said, "We really don't know much yet. Anyone else you can think of who might want to take advantage of her?"

"Probably a lot of guys," said Yoli. "It's that way anytime you go out."

"Did Marissa complain about anyone?"

"Uh-uh." She looked at Beth.

Beth said, "Not to me."

Yoli said, "We always thought she was fearless."

"Okay, thanks—do you think Tori and Bethany would have anything to add?"

"Probably not," said Yoli. "We'll ask them. If they have something, they'll call you, what's your number?"

Milo handed out two cards.

Yoli said, "Homicide. Ecchh."

Milo said, "How can we reach Marissa's family?"

"There isn't one, not really. She never knew her dad and her mom died like . . . three years ago. Some sort of neurological thing, she didn't want to talk about it. There's an aunt, she mentioned an aunt. I'll see if Tori and Bethany know about her."

"I'd really appreciate that, Yoli. Thanks for your time."

We stood.

Beth Halperin said, "At the border I used to hear rockets explode. This is worse."

Out in the car, Milo said, "Fake movie producer, makes sense, everything's falling into place. When we get back I find out who her phone carrier is, put in the affidavit for the subpoena, see who she talked to before she died, and hopefully come up with a name. Once I get a name, I go back to the databases and if they don't tell me anything, I recheck with Leary because sleazy is sleazy, you never know, maybe the bastard got busted for something but didn't get charged."

Long oration.

He turned to me. "That's the plan. Comments?"

I was forming the word "None" when his phone rang.

The screen said *Petra*.

He switched to speaker. "What's up, kid?"

She explained.

"The plan" was now a thing of the past.

Detective III Petra Connor had a cool, confident voice and told the story with her usual economy.

Just after twelve noon, Oleg Karkovsky, an off-site manager for a real estate conglomerate headquartered in Las Vegas, had entered one of the eighteen buildings he oversaw in L.A. County. This one sat on Selma Avenue between Sunset and Hollywood, two blocks short of the street's termination at Highland.

Karkovsky's destination was a third-floor one-bedroom unit scheduled for inspection of a faulty water heater. The tenant had demanded immediate repair, irate and foulmouthed because of lukewarm showers. Despite being three months behind in his rent.

Karkovsky had knocked, received silence, used his master key to get in. Calling out and receiving no reply, he'd headed for a utility closet off the kitchen. Before he got there, something out on the unit's narrow balcony caught his eye.

Petra said, "I'm quoting verbatim, you add the Russian accent. 'The guy's lying there, I think idiot fell sleep, maybe out there all night. The fools I deal with in Hollywood are worse than in Moscow.' Anyway Karkovsky opens the slider ready to do a wakey-wake and sees the blood."

Paul Allan O'Brien, forty-three, had been shot once through the neck, the bullet nicking his carotid artery and his jugular vein before passing through cleanly and exiting through the back. Bouncing off an external wall behind him, it had landed on the floor and settled beside a long-dead potted palm.

Petra said, "Full metal jacket, .308, don't see those often. The techs confirmed it but I could see it myself, the cartridge was pretty much intact. I'm figuring the pass-through was due to the jacket being unmodified because something military—hollow point, a custom job— would've exploded inside him. Hopefully, the fact that it didn't go deep into the wall will tell us about distance and trajectory. The most likely origin—the only thing I can see—is it came from somewhere in the building next door. We're talking fifty or more units and two stories higher. But it's got a security door, no one answers my buttonpushes, and I haven't had time to seriously look for access yet. So why am I calling you? Because on the floor of O'Brien's bedroom is a skimpy red rayon dress with cutouts, lacy thong panties, five-inch-heel shoes, and a purse. Inside the purse is the I.D. of a Marissa French, a wallet with money and cards but no phone and no Marissa. I look her up and she's brand new on the murder list as one of yours. So here we are again, sir, pooling our talents. What's Marissa's story?"

Milo told her. "Does O'Brien fit my bad guy?"

"To a T. Big and muscular, one sleeved arm, soul patch, the Pink Floyd tee. Karkovsky knew nothing about him other than he owed rent and was a jerk. So looks like he took her home, overdosed her, did whatever he did to her, then dumped her over by you and came back here. Then someone shoots *him*. Beyond weird."

Milo said, "You gonna be there for a while?"

"Oh yeah."

"How about I come over and have a look."

"Great."

"Alex is with me."

"Even better."

We got to Hollywood just after five. Lots of traffic, lots of tourists on foot looking for something that didn't exist. The sky was graying irregularly now, sunlight putting up a brave struggle with insistent clouds as we made our way to Selma Avenue.

Petra was easy to spot in the crowd of uniforms and official vehicles blocking the front of a shabby, plain-wrap, five-story apartment building.

Young, athletically slender and pretty, dressed as always in a perfectly tailored pantsuit, Petra looks like anything but the senior detective she is. Her clean-jawed ivory face and black bob bring to mind Singer Sargent's *Madame X*. Everything about her suggests cool efficiency, confidence, elegance. A senior executive at some corporate unicorn.

Despite her relative youth, she'd worked Hollywood murders for most of her career, fast-tracked every step of the way, initially because the department wanted more female D's but soon after by earning it.

Hollywood Division stays busy even during low-crime periods but this wasn't one of them. Violence had risen all over the city courtesy of a district attorney allergic to prosecution. Morale at the D.A.'s office and among cops was low as too many crimes were brushed off as minor-league. But murders were still getting worked and homicide detectives are accustomed to intensely focusing and shutting out noise, so aces like Milo and Petra continue going about their business with a single-mindedness that borders on obsession.

One of the reasons I like working with them.

She saw us right away, came forward and lifted the yellow tape. Today's suit was charcoal with black velvet lapels.

She and Milo hugged then she shook my hand. "Any thoughts on the way over?"

Milo said, "Just that life seems to be getting stranger."

The coroner's van was still in place. I said, "Can we see the body?"

"You bet. There's an elevator but it makes too much noise for my taste. You okay with the stairs?"

"Sure," said Milo, touching his gut.

Petra held the front door open for us. No entry hall, just a corridor carpeted in dishwater-colored poly with walls painted an awful green. A single lift with a brown metal door to the left, stairs to the right.

I've seen Petra sprint several flights. This time she gave Milo a glance and took it slow.

The stairwell reeked, roach-cakes placed on each landing fuming camphor, mixing with rancid cooking grease and stale tobacco smoke.

Had Marissa French wondered about an audition in a place like this? Or had she been too far gone by the time she arrived?

We exited onto the ground-floor corridor's twin.

Milo said, "What did O'Brien do for a living?"

"Don't know yet," said Petra. "Obviously nothing lucrative."

A uniform guarding the entrance to Unit 305 moved aside to let us in. We followed Petra across a living-area-*cum*-kitchenette not radically different from the one in Beth Halperin and Yoli Echeverria's Reseda rental.

The sliding glass door to the balcony was open, letting in ethane-flavored breeze. The balcony floor was grubby concrete. A rusting metal railing ended at least a foot below current safety standards.

Paul O'Brien lay tucked in the left-hand corner, flat on his back, eyes open and matte, slack mouth affording a view of tooth-rimmed gullet. His left arm was curled up against his body, his right had been flung upward by impact and landed in a way that suggested a grotesque farewell wave. Blood glistened on the black T-shirt, splotching it maroon. A greater volume of blood spread around O'Brien's sizable body.

Neat hole just right of his Adam's apple, the edges blackening and curling.

Petra said, "No decomp, a bit of livor, rigor's come and gone, and he's cold. Given liver temp and cool weather until an hour after sunrise, C.I.'s guessing sometime in the early morning. When was he seen dumping poor Marissa?"

"Just before three a.m."

"Perfect fit," she said. "He goes home to celebrate getting away with it but someone has a different idea."

She pointed to the other end of the balcony where a hibachi with a grill that needed cleaning squatted. Just left of that were a pair of yellow plastic chairs and a matching table. On the table was a bottle of Casamigos Tequila. On the floor, a pair of unlaced black-and-orange basketball shoes.

"There was also half a hand-rolled joint near his body, techs took it, along with his glass."

Milo said, "No blood trail or drag marks so he was shot near where he fell."

Petra nodded.

Milo said, "So what, he kicks off his shoes, toasts himself near the table, then gets up to stretch or goes to the head, comes back and gets nailed?"

"That's exactly how I see it." Her eyes swiveled to the neighboring building. Separated from O'Brien's by a driveway leading to its sub-garage and a chain-link fence laced with struggling clematis.

Newer than O'Brien's sixties-era structure. Probably from the nineties when faith in large-scale Hollywood renewal hadn't yet ceded to reality. The charmless block-like design that goes with exploiting every inch of land. Someone paying off a city council member or a municipal pencil pusher in order to violate setbacks.

No balconies, just windows. Row after row of identically sized squares.

Milo said, "Who's the warden?"

Petra said, "Exactly. Hopefully we can narrow down the origin of the shot. One of the techies went to get one of those laser dealies.

Knowing O'Brien's height should help us get a trajectory. Meanwhile, I'll be trying to get hold of the owners and convince them to give us entry. Raul's on his way. When he gets here, we'll assemble a battalion of uniforms and start door-knocking."

"Did you have time to check if anyone 911'd a gunshot?"

"I did and they didn't," she said. "I'm figuring a single pop wouldn't have made an impression, especially from up here. Ready to see *your* crime scene?"

CHAPTER

7

The apartment's single bedroom was twelve square feet carpeted in frayed navy blue and set up with a king-sized bed. Dull black sheets, glossy black duvet. The semicircular headboard, nightstand, and six-drawer dresser were imitation black lacquer chipped white.

Three posters hung on facing walls. Pink Floyd's *The Wall* adorned by a hideous screaming face, a full-on shot of a scarlet Lamborghini Countach looking ready to loft airborne, and a promo for a film called *Blood Warrior.*

Petra said, "Reminds me of my brothers' rooms."

Milo said, "Living in the past. Maybe he was once a contender."

"Or had delusions."

I said, "Have you found his car?"

"Parked around the corner. Ten-year-old black Accord. Another fit to your video."

Milo looked at the Countach. "Definitely delusions."

Petra said, "Where's Marissa's car?"

"Don't know yet. Hopefully near the party where she hung with O'Brien and the BOLO will snag it."

I took a closer look at the movie poster, searching for O'Brien's name in the small print and not finding it.

Milo had already shifted to the blue carpet. Near the edge of the bed was a jumbled pile. Red dress, panties, shoes, a black clutch purse.

Petra said, "Kate Spade. I've got the same one, how's that for creepy? I was ready to send all of it along with the bullet, then I found out about Marissa and wanted to check with you first. Do you want your case number on it or mine?"

He said, "Hmm," and took out a pair of gloves. "May I?"

"Be my guest."

Kneeling, he examined the contents of the purse, removing a wallet holding a driver's license, five $20 bills that he fanned, and a pair of credit cards. Then: a vial of Princess Night perfume, a compact, an eyebrow pencil, and a tube of lipstick.

Putting everything back, he stood. "You have a preference on case numbers?"

Petra said, "Her stuff seems a whole lot more directly evidentiary for you. But I can't ignore what happened to her, because it could end up relating to a motive on O'Brien."

"A vigilante thing?"

"Probably a stretch but this early I hate ruling anything out."

I said, "It could be a vigilante thing not related to Marissa."

Petra said, "O'Brien's done it before and made someone mad?"

"You don't start hunting in middle age." I took in the room. "Also, it's not a décor that would impress a fully conscious woman."

"Putting it mildly," she said. "And we did find date-dope. You think some avenger's been stalking O'Brien and just happened to nail him the night he O.D.'d Marissa?"

Milo said, "You know what they say about karma."

"Yeah," she said, "but I've been on the job too long to believe it."

"Ditto. Okay, how about this: Tag Marissa's stuff with both our numbers and I'll give the lab prior notice to prevent a filing snafu."

"Perfect. Now the larger question: Where do we take it all work-wise?"

He grinned. "You missed me that much?"

Petra placed her hand on her breast. "How could I not, be still my heart. Hey, if we collab, do I get to tap Alex's brain at will?"

"After filling out the appropriate forms. What kind of dope did you find?"

Petra opened the nightstand drawer. Inside were miniature, fish-shaped plastic squeeze bottles filled with clear liquid and capped in red.

"GHB," she said. "The fact they look cute makes them doubly re-pulsive, no?"

She pushed the vials aside and pointed. "The oblong pills are diazepam—generic Valium—and the weed speaks for itself. There's also plenty of booze in a kitchen cabinet."

I said, "Smorgasbord of depressants."

Milo said, "Predator's apothecary."

"A couple of great band names," said Petra. "Okay, I'll get a techie up here and make sure everything is double-tagged."

A voice from the doorway said, "Hi, guys."

D II Raul Biro, typically resplendent in a gray silk blazer, razor-creased black slacks, tab-collared white shirt, yellow-and-black paisley tie, and paper booties over his shoes, gave a thumbs-up and stepped in. His thick black hair was brushed back and furrowed by comb tracks. His eyes were acute and searching.

"Loo, Doc. Petra filled me in. Bizarre."

Petra said, "Yup, once again, it's Hollyweird." To us: "If there's nothing more, I'd like to start trying to get in next door." Back to her partner: "I'll try the owners of this palace again, they're based in Vegas. How about you see how many uniforms we can mobilize for the can-vass."

"Sounds good."

"Sorry for breaking up your day."

"Ha." Raul saluted and left.

Petra said, "Technically it's his day off. He was watching his kids so his wife could go out with her pals. Took a while to get his mom over to sub. Anything else you can think of?"

"Nope, thanks for saving her stuff for me to see."

"Of course. I'll bug my boss to authorize the collab."

Milo said, "Same here."

"Rank doesn't have its privilege?"

"Depends on what you're asking for."

"Don't see that working with us aces should be a problem."

"Nothing should ever be a problem," said Milo.

They both laughed as Petra walked us out of the apartment and over to the stairwell. She held the fire door open and remained on the landing.

Milo said, "See you, kid. Hopefully soon."

Petra said, "I have to say, I'm kind of looking forward to it. The dream team and all that."

8

As we headed back to West L.A., I searched for *blood warriors movie,* found it readily on a film-archive database. Released nineteen years ago, low-budget production, one-star rating.

The archive was more inclusive than the poster. Paul O'Brien was listed on the stunt crew. I told Milo.

He said, "Hired to fall down, probably thought he was gonna be an action star. Anything more recent?"

I ran O'Brien's name through the site, came up with two additional mentions for stunt work. Similar stinkers, one a year prior to *Blood Warriors,* the other two years after.

Milo said, "Three gigs in three years. Mega-delusions."

I said, "He needed to make a living another way."

"To me he looks like an obvious sleaze but it didn't stop Marissa from falling for his I'm-a-producer line. What you said about that dump makes sense. No way she'd fall for his bullshit if she was fully conscious so he had to start dosing her at the party. Easy enough to do it, those weird little fishies. Pop the cap, squeeze it into a Sea Breeze, and you've got your unwilling partner."

I said, "Then you supplement the dose to make sure she's totally out by the time you get her home. O'Brien thought he knew how to calibrate and time because he'd had experience. But something went really wrong."

"Vice doesn't know him but let's see what Petra turns up. Meanwhile, I'll get a victim's warrant on Marissa's place and try to find out where her last party was. Then I work on locating her aunt and do what needs to be done."

"Anything you want from me?"

"Just keep thinking."

We were nearly at the station when Detective Sean Binchy called.

"What's up, kid?"

"Loot, you got a call a few minutes ago, desk sent it to me. Woman named Tori Burkholder, I told her I'd pass anything along but she only wanted to talk to you."

"The perks of personal charm."

Sean laughed. "Got to be, sir. She for real?"

"Friend of my new victim."

"Who's that?"

"Woman O.D.'d and dumped dead near a hospital. It just got complicated but no time to get into it right now, Sean. What's your caseload?"

"Just closed a strong-arm robbery in Pico-Robertson so I'm open, so far."

"Congrats. Any chance of drafting you?"

"Hope so," said Sean. "I'll try to make it happen."

"If you pull it off, let me know and I'll fill you in tomorrow. Moses and Alicia, too. If you don't mind, give 'em a heads-up."

"Will do, Loot. Here's the number."

We got held up under a freeway pass at Santa Monica and Sepulveda. Simmering cars and tempers, a homeless guy panhandling to no avail.

Milo used the time to punch in Tori Burkholder's number.

One ring was followed by "This is Tori, Officer," in a voice that broke twice.

"Thanks for calling."

"Beth and Yoli told me and Bethany about Marissa. They work weekends, we don't, and we were in Camarillo doing some shopping. We're still freaked out."

Milo said, "Terrible thing."

"It's *horrible*," said Tori Burkholder. "I live right near Marissa and Bethany isn't that far. Is there some serial killer looking for girls?"

"Nothing like that, Tori. Beth and Yoli didn't tell you what happened?"

"They said some guy drugged, raped, and killed her. Which is crazy 'cause Marissa didn't use drugs."

"Could we talk face-to-face?" he said.

"Yes, sir."

"When and where?"

"Now and wherever," said Tori Burkholder. "We're on the freeway and right now, I don't even want to go home."

"Would you mind coming to the station?"

"Sure," she said. "Guess that's one safe place."

He gave her the address.

She said, "I can probably do it in half an hour because traffic's going the other way. Beth, you okay with it? She is, hopefully half an hour."

"I'll be here whenever you arrive."

"You sound nice," she said. "This is crazy."

Forty-eight minutes later, standing under a night sky pinholed by starlight, Milo and I were ready when a red Kia headed south on Butler and sped toward us.

I'd just finished telling Robin I'd be late. She said, "No prob, I'll keep working."

Milo had just finished texting Petra to work on scheduling a meeting.

The Kia pulled to the curb and stopped. The passenger window
lowered on Tori Burkholder's lovely, tense face.

Milo said, "Here's a parking pass, ladies. Pull in right over there,
we'll wait."

"Yes, sir."

A few moments later, two identically sized women dressed in snug
black tops, black tights, and black flats crossed the street and came
toward us. Tori Burkholder's hair was still long and blond, Bethany
McGonigal's long and black. They walked in step with each other,
precise as drum majorettes.

Milo muttered, "Is there a machine somewhere that turns them
out?"

He met them halfway, guided them over, said, "I'm Milo Sturgis,
this is Alex Delaware."

Nods, downcast eyes, barely audible *hi*'s.

"Thanks for coming, ladies."

More nods.

Inside, he said, "Elevator or stairs?"

Bethany McGonigal, red-eyed and tear-streaked, touched her
Apple Watch and studied the mini-screen. "I've done my steps."

"Me, too."

CHAPTER

9

The elevator ride was silent, both women pressed together in a corner, still avoiding eye contact.

Milo led the way to the medium-sized interview room he'd set up twenty minutes ago. Small table in the middle, two chairs facing two others. Bottled water and napkins on the tabletop.

Fifteen minutes ago, he'd sniffed the air, left, and returned with a can of citrus air freshener that he used liberally.

Stress-sweat had given way to orange blossoms. For the most part.

"Smell okay to you?"

I said, "Put it down to atmosphere."

He laughed. "Any psych data on that? Which smells get people to tell the truth?"

"Forget it."

He laughed again and looked at the water bottles. "I could get snacks from one of the machines but probably not, huh? The body-conscious generation and all that."

Gazing up at the ceiling, he frowned. Acoustical tiles alternated with fluorescent panels. "Wish it was softer."

"Why the special treatment?" I said.

"Because . . . hell, I don't know why . . . been thinking of Marissa. Barely making it but trying so hard, she gets snuffed out and dumped like garbage. For all I know, these two are gonna be prone to the same mistakes . . . or maybe I'm just getting protective in my old age."

I thought: *You were born protective.*

Now, settled at the table, Tori and Bethany opened their water bottles, drank, kept their heads down.

Milo said, "Again, thanks for coming. First off, I want to reassure you that there's no serial killer lurking in your neighborhoods. I can't give you too many details but Marissa's death was likely an overdose."

"Of what?" said Tori Burkholder.

"We don't know yet."

"That makes no sense, sir. Like I told you, she didn't use anything."

Generally Milo's stingy about giving out details. This time, he said, "Someone may have overdosed her without her knowing."

"Who?"

"Our most likely suspect is a man named Paul O'Brien."

No response.

Milo said, "Never heard of him?"

"Never."

"Never."

"In any event, he's been taken care of and is no threat to anyone else. So the name doesn't ring a bell? Maybe someone Marissa mentioned casually?"

Tori and Bethany looked at each other. Shook their heads.

He showed them the photo of O'Brien and Marissa.

Bethany gaped and stuck out her tongue. "Why would she do that? He looks gross."

Tori said, "Where was this taken?"

"We're still trying to figure that out. Any ideas?"

"No, sir."

Bethany said, "*Not* Marissa's type."

I said, "What type was that?"

"Actually," said Tori, "Marissa didn't have a type. She swore off."

"Swore off guys."

"Guys, relationships."

"No boyfriends at all?"

"Not for years." She studied the photo. "He's like . . . hanging over her. Like he thinks he owns her."

"Maybe he's the producer," said Bethany.

"You think? We told her it was probably bogus."

"You know Marissa. When she gets an idea."

Milo said, "Beth and Yoli told us she'd talked about meeting a producer."

"Yes, sir," said Tori. "Like . . . a few weeks ago. Said he was straight up with her, admitted it wouldn't be big-budget or union-scale but he might be able to use her."

Milo said, "What kind of movie?"

"She didn't say."

Bethany drew the photo nearer and studied it. "Maybe he slipped something into her Sea Breeze. She looks kind of out of it."

Tori studied the image. "Definitely. *Bastard.*"

Milo said, "What else did Marissa say about this producer?"

"Just that she'd met him and that they were going to talk again."

"Where'd she meet him?"

"No idea."

"When?"

"Maybe a few weeks ago?"

Bethany said, "Like three? Four? We didn't take it seriously."

Tori said, "We asked her, 'Don't you think it could be bogus?' She said she had a good feeling about it so we didn't bug her. We didn't want to make her feel bad."

"Wouldn't have made a difference, anyway," said Bethany. "She'd just be mad at us and still do her thing."

"Strong-willed," said Milo.

"That sounds too—like she was pushy but she wasn't."

Tori said, "She just had her own ideas."

She took another glance at the photo. "Gross. Got to be the Sea Breeze because that's all she drank unless they didn't have cranberry juice and then she'd just do the grapefruit part. And only one per, that was her rule."

I said, "One drink per party."

"They weren't parties," said Tori. "They were openings."

"Of . . ."

"Boutiques, clubs, restaurants, whatever. Marissa was on a list. She got us on it, too, but we never went without her."

I said, "What kind of list?"

"You get an email from a company called BeThere.com," said Tori.

Bethany said, "Marissa called it the hot girls list. People wanting faces at their events."

Milo said, "For atmosphere."

"Exactly," said Bethany. "We didn't like it much. Felt like props."

Tori said, "We didn't feel it, you know? It got boring real fast so we stopped and put it on spam."

I said, "Marissa kept going."

"She liked it." Deep sigh.

I said, "You never saw this guy at any of the openings?"

"No way," said Bethany. "He's not what they want. For girls they want you with a face, for guys it's famous or super-rich."

"Situation like that," I said, "you could get hassled."

"Oh sure, we got hit on all the time," said Tori, "but that's guy-nature, you have to know how to smile them away."

"It never got messy," said Bethany. "We know our thing."

Tori said, "Talk to the hand, walk to nowhere land. Also there was always plenty of security and to be honest, the old rich guys were kind of cute. Winking and making jokes. Not taking it seriously, know what I mean?"

Bethany said, "Like it was a game. Some old rich guy would be like 'Hey, gorgeous,' and maybe you'd listen to him for a minute. Then you'd like give him a nice smile and move on."

Milo said, "How'd Marissa get on the list?"

Dual shrugs.

Tori said, "Maybe something she saw online or in *Variety*? I really don't know."

Bethany said, "Could be *Variety*, it's stupid but she'd buy it because she wanted to act and sometimes they'd have cattle calls. I looked at one of her copies once, this Mr. Hollywood column, really dumb."

Milo said, "The acting scene."

"She was always into it. In high school she tried out for plays but she never got parts because she had learning problems—had trouble memorizing lines. So they put her on the stage crew."

Tori said, "She cried *so* much about that."

Bethany said, "She really, really did. But then she got over it. And into it. Being in the crew. She did lighting and was pretty good at it."

I said, "That didn't stop her acting ambitions."

Bethany said, "That's *exactly* what it was. *Ambitions*. This . . . wanting . . . trying . . . putting out so much energy even though you're not getting anywhere. One time she told me, 'I'm on a treadmill, Nee, but treadmills can be good exercise for you.'"

She began to cry.

Tori hugged her. Bethany's head lowered to Tori's shoulder.

Milo held up a napkin. Tori took it and dabbed her friend's eyes.

"Marissa was so sweet," she said. "She liked taking care of the old people, it really made her feel good. We'd say why don't you do more of that, like become a nurse or something, you're great at it. But she was like I'm not ready to give up my passion. I need flexibility for cattle calls."

Bethany said, "I'm like why would you want to think of yourself as a cow? But I didn't say it, I just thought it."

I said, "She get any parts?"

Tori said, "Nothing with lines, just a few crowd scenes. She'd get like a hundred bucks and the on-lot catering, which she said was incredible. But she wouldn't eat the catering because she didn't want to look bloated just in case someone noticed her."

"Like a producer."

"Anyone who could help her. Hey, maybe that's where she met him, a cattle call."

Bethany said, "Maybe. He's nothing but a lot of bull."

Weak smile from her friend.

Milo said, "Those openings. How often did she attend them?"

Tori said, "When we were still going it was like . . . every month and a half, two months."

"When did you guys stop?"

"After like three times," said Bethany. "We all have full-time jobs, need to chill at the end of the day, and that was *not* chilling."

I said, "Hard work."

Tori said, "You come home after a full day's work and *then* you have to get dressed up, put on full makeup, drive over there, stand in line, and give them your name to prove you're on the list. Then once you're inside you can't eat because you could get a stain on your dress. You could drink but not too much because you're there to look hot and not lose control."

"Props," said Bethany, shaking her head. "First time it was kind of fun. Chanel on Rodeo. We saw George Clooney and his wife. Then it got boring and took up too much chill-time."

I said, "Marissa kept enjoying it."

"Not the thing itself," said Tori. "She enjoyed thinking she might meet someone who could help her."

More tears.

When they subsided, I said, "What else can you tell us about Marissa?"

"She grew up pretty religious. Was pretty but her mother dressed her really plain. When her mother was living, they went to church."

I said, "When did her mother pass?"

"Like . . . five years ago. Right after graduation. She was a nice lady, Mrs. French. Audra. She worked as a hostess at a restaurant, that's what Marissa grew up eating. What her mother brought home."

"Her dad—"

"He died when she was a baby, she said she had no memory of him."

Milo said, "We need to contact her family. We've been told about an aunt."

Tori said, "That's the only person we know. She's in . . . I think Stockton. Wherever that is. Don't know her name, just that she's one of you."

"A police officer?"

"Uh-huh."

"Anyone else?"

"Uh-uh."

I said, "Marissa didn't know her dad."

"Nope," said Bethany. "Maybe that's why she really didn't like guys. Said she didn't trust them. That's why it's crazy. Trusting *him*."

"Bet you she was shining him on," said Tori. "Wanting to see if he could help her and if she found out he couldn't, she would've walked. If he hadn't O.D.'d her, she could've totally controlled the situation. So what's going to happen to him?"

Milo said, "It won't be a happy ending."

"Well, that's good," said Bethany McGonigal. "Bad things *should* happen to bad people."

We walked them down the stairs and out to the street, watched as they hurried to the visitors lot.

"Nice kids," he said. "Too bad I didn't learn anything from them."

I said, "The part about an absent father could've made her vulnerable to O'Brien. Same for what they told us about Marissa distancing herself from real relationships."

"How so?"

"Dealing with people takes practice."

"She got rusty."

"That plus ambition could've clouded her judgment. And her going it alone, without her friends, meant there was no one to look for danger signs. And there was plenty to worry about. This wasn't an impulsive thing on O'Brien's part. Her clothes and purse were at his place but her phone wasn't. Maybe he confiscated it early on and wanted to cut off any escape route. Or he tossed it after she passed out to avoid being connected with her. Either way, she was way in over her head."

"Evil," he said. "Even without her phone, I can get her call history. Problem is, with O'Brien dead, none of it really matters. I'll write him up as the likely suspect but it'll just be notes in a file."

"O'Brien, on the other hand, remains a whodunit and Petra wants you involved."

"She was being nice," he said. "No way the boss is gonna allow me to get involved with a Hollywood case."

At the station door, I said, "One question. Why'd you give the girls O'Brien's name?"

"I figured maybe they'd go all social with it and it'd bring in a tip about the last party and that might clarify both cases. That's what I texted Petra about. She said sure, go for it."

He rubbed his face. "Okay, thanks as always, sorry it hasn't been profound. Go and enjoy hearth and home while I search for a cop in Stockton I can make sad."

Quick pat on the back. He's turned dismissing me into an art form.

I smiled and walked away.

———

Robin had waited up for me and ordered take-out sushi.

Slow, quiet dinner on the front terrace, Blanche stretched on the floor to my right, waiting patiently for bits of culinary goodwill.

The air smelled of pine and jasmine. The same stars that had pocked the sky near the station were larger and brighter, freed from the harassment of city lights.

"Pretty night," I said.

"I was going to suggest we eat by the fishpond but given the menu it seemed in poor taste."

I laughed and kissed her.

She said, "Wasabi snog. So what have you been doing all day?"

I told her.

She said, "Poor girl, that is incredibly sad and disgusting. I get Milo's frustration about no final justice. Though when you get down to it, I guess justice is an abstraction."

I said, "Abstractions keep us civilized."

She looked at me. "You say much with few words. Yet another reason."

"For what?"

"Some serious horseradish romance." She demonstrated.

I said, "That wasn't in the least bit abstract."

10

I heard nothing from Milo on Sunday or Monday. Which was fine because Robin and I had planned to make a day of it at Huntington Gardens before returning home with some barbecue we'd picked up at a place in Pasadena.

Dinner was near the pond this time, the fish unthreatened by proximity to red meat and enjoying the occasional toss of koi pellets.

Blanche ecstatic, as always, about proximity to any type of food.

Tuesday morning, Milo phoned at eleven a.m. "Bad time for me to come by?"

I'd just handed a court courier a packet of documents, was planning to check my messages. "Not at all."

"See you soon."

That meant he'd phoned from the road. I was waiting on the terrace when he drove up three minutes later.

Unlike at O'Brien's place, he vaulted up the stairs to the terrace two at a time. When he reached the top, panting and a bit flushed, he said, "My powers of prediction have failed big-time."

I followed him into the kitchen, where he detected among the shelves of the fridge. Pulling out a half-full quart container of milk, he sniffed, then downed. Next came a chunk of rye bread. He knew where to find the right knife and plate, sliced himself a couple of slabs, retrieved marmalade from the pantry, sat down at the table and began slathering.

I said, "What didn't you predict?"

"Bureaucratic stupidity."

"Guess even safe bets don't always pay off."

He smiled but not durably. "Everything started off routine, no problem finding Marissa's aunt in Stockton, she's a civilian dispatcher not a cop. I did the notification over the phone, learned squat. She barely knew Marissa, said her sister—Marissa's mom—was a loner who'd cut herself off from the family."

"Sounds familiar," I said.

"What—oh yeah, guess so. Anyway, then Basia calls and confirms that Marissa died of a GHB overdose augmented by Valium. The only surprise was she hadn't had sex recently."

"She passed out and died before O'Brien had his chance."

"The guy was a scumbag control freak," he said. "I'm surprised it made a difference to him. I told Basia what we found at his place and she's gonna list Manner as Homicide. Which is obviously the right call but still sucks because it means I get an open murder on my record. But what can I do? So I go to work on my notes, am about to leave when Captain Shubb calls me in and when I get there she's got the look—bureaucratic blankness. I'm figuring, great, now I'm gonna get chewed out because Petra requested a collab. Instead, Shubb *informs* me I'll be working with Petra because new data has come up."

"What kind of data?"

"The rifle that killed O'Brien was used in another Hollywood murder and supposedly someone atop Olympus thinks that means time for a team. *Two* Hollywood cases and I'm on it. Make any sense to you?"

"Not on the surface."

"That's 'cause the surface has nothing to do with it. I talk to Petra and turns out the *real* reason is that Shubb is dating Petra's captain, Art DiMeo, hot and heavy. So when Petra tossed the idea out to DiMeo, he figured it would be a great excuse to get together with Shubb and do some ahem strategic planning at the executive level. Starting with yesterday when they were both out all day and didn't return to their offices."

"Motel research."

"Their pay grades, probably a nice *ho*-tel."

"Why didn't Petra know about another Hollywood case?"

"It happened almost two years ago and she was on vacation with Eric, walking part of the Appalachian Trail."

"The victim—"

"Has nothing obvious in common with O'Brien other than he wasn't a model citizen. Aspiring rapper, former Crip, and convicted felon named Jamarcus Parmenter. Parmenter's home base was Compton but he was in Hollywood for some sort of pop-up record-business thing. What they call a showcase."

"New band showing their stuff in order to get a contract."

"You know about it."

"Robin's done plenty of last-minute repairs for guitarists about to showcase."

"Well, this wasn't for a guitarist, it was for a deejay. Parmenter stepped outside to have a smoke and got nailed through the neck just like O'Brien. You know the obvious assumption on something like that."

"A gang thing. What were Parmenter's felonies?"

"Theft, burglary, one carjacking, but all years ago before he discovered his muse. Still, a gang thing was A on the list. But B was a business dispute because Parmenter had been making noise about being ripped off by his producer and manager, the same guy who'd thrown the showcase. And had fired him."

"Parmenter crashed the party."

"Looks like it."

"What was the conflict over?"

"Don't know but Parmenter had thought he was destined to be Jay-Z and bitched about not getting fame and fortune fast enough. The case went nowhere because there was no evidence other than the bullet and no one was willing to talk. The D assigned to it retired shortly afterward and no one picked it up."

"How'd Petra discover the link?"

"She asked around about rifle murders and someone had a vague recollection. She searched, found it, learned ballistics had been done but there'd been no match to any previous shooting. So she rushed through a comparison with O'Brien. Not expecting anything, then boom, same .308 rifle."

I said, "A hunter for hire."

"Looks like it. We're gonna be expanding the search to any similars. How's the rest of your day looking?"

"Open."

"Excellent." He finished the two slices, cut another one, chewed and swallowed, got orange juice out of the fridge, filled a glass and finished it in one long gulp.

"The team's meeting in an hour."

"Hollywood?"

"No, my place because I first-dibbed the big room."

CHAPTER

11

The largest interview room at West L.A. is down the hall
from Milo's office. Not used much; detectives downstairs
have their own spaces, and the cold, lab-like ambience makes it wrong
for meetings with the families of victims. Talking to multiple suspects
is possible, but isolating suspects is the rule and exceptions are rare.

Milo uses the place for group meetings, rolling in a couple of
whiteboards, lugging chairs and long tables from wherever he finds
them, furnishing boxes of pastries he picks up at a bakery in West Hollywood.

Today's group was the two of us, Petra, Raul, the three "baby D's"
he sometimes got to work with him, and an older bald man with a
white brush mustache sprouting under a sunburnt nose.

Milo and Petra stood near the whiteboards, markers in hand. The
rest of us sat facing them.

Petra began by introducing the stranger as Hawes Buxby, the original investigator on the Jamarcus Parmenter murder. The retired D,
eyeglasses hanging from a chain around his neck, had dressed for the
occasion in a wide-lapel gray suit, royal-blue shirt, and tan tie pat-
terned with red fleurs-de-lis.

When he heard who I was he shot me a quizzical look. The type of scrutiny you give a strange animal in a zoo.

Of the young D's, only Sean Binchy matched Buxby's level of formality. His suit was the usual narrow-lapel navy blue, his shirt fresh and white, his tie a Technicolor display of flamingos and palm trees. The tropical touches and Doc Martens harked back to his days as a ska-punk bass player.

Alicia Bogomil, clean-jawed, intense and sharp-eyed, long hair still blue at the tips, wore a fitted brown leather bomber jacket, black turtleneck, and skinny black slacks.

Moe Reed, chronically enlarged by power lifting, had on an unstructured charcoal sport coat sewn from a miracle fabric that stretched past the point of apparent danger, a gray T-shirt, and thigh-accommodating Barbell jeans.

Both boards were nearly filled.

The first held headshots of Marissa French, Paul O'Brien, and Jamarcus Parmenter, each topped by a question mark. A second grouping showed crime scene shots for all three victims. Marissa's revealed where she'd been dumped. An adjacent photo showed her clothes and purse on the floor of Paul O'Brien's bedroom.

Next to that was a blowup of Dr. Basia Lopatinski's Cause of Death summary with *gamma hydroxybutyrate* and *diazepam* ringed in red.

O'Brien was memorialized slumped in the corner of his balcony, Jamarcus Parmenter in gold-embroidered baggy black sweats, sprawled on his back with car bumpers visible on the periphery of the photo.

Night-dimmed parking lot.

Two other images featured Parmenter as a living being: a thirteen-year-old mugshot and a six-year-old DMV portrait. Five-six, a hundred thirty-eight. Had he survived, he'd be twenty-nine.

In the arrest photo, Parmenter wore long dreads and sported flat eyes and a sullen look. In the later image, his hair was neatly clipped, tattoos brocaded his neck, and he offered a crooked, almost boyish smile. But no additional nuance in the eyes.

On the next board was a photo of a red laser beam up-slanting from Paul O'Brien's third-floor balcony to a window on the fourth floor of the prison-like building next door. Slightly rightward of the kill-spot.

That was followed by brightly illuminated views of a white-walled, black-floored room, empty but for a trio of large water heaters, a mass of HVAC equipment, and hefty ductwork, all to the left. To the right was open space, the front wall centered by a high, square window.

Below that, photographs of two double-width gray metal doors, one ajar.

The final illustration returned to the shooter's lair and showed the single window open, a red beam arcing down toward O'Brien's balcony.

Petra pointed to a single yellow marker on the windowsill.

"As you can see, this is all of it forensically and even this is just a little disruption of the dust where the rifle, a bipod, or a stand may have rested. But no prints, hair, skin flakes, zero."

Alicia said, "Too bad the guy isn't a shedder. Would the window be high enough for him to shoot standing?"

"If he was up to five-nine, he could be upright. Taller, there'd likely be some stooping."

"Which could throw off aim," said Sean. "That level of accuracy, some kind of rest was probably used."

"From that distance?" said Moe. "That and a good nightscope."

"Even with all that, it'd take a steady hand," said Sean.

Alicia said, "Sounds pretty professional."

Petra said, "If you're wondering about someone with military experience, so was I. But I checked with a few sources and verified what I already suspected: Serious military snipers prefer hollow points or bullets they customize themselves in order to maximize internal damage. That doesn't rule out a pro who downgraded because basic equipment was all he needed. Including choice of firearm: Winchester 70 Featherweight. But why go easy if you don't have to?"

Hawes Buxby said, "I got one of those. Featherweights. Used it for deer, back when."

"Exactly," said Petra. "You and a gazillion other shooters."

Milo said, "He could've downgraded because he is military and wanted to distract away from it. Not that civilian means unskilled. There's a precise element to both shootings. Leaving nothing behind and hitting the neck off center, which Basia says would've maximized the odds of getting the jugular, the carotid, and the trachea with one shot."

Buxby shook his head. "I was figuring a one-off gang deal on Mr. Parmenter. Now we've got a slick assassin?"

"Open season on sketchy guys," said Alicia.

Silence.

Petra broke it. "Next issue: How'd the shooter get into a full-security building? Anyone want to guess?"

Sean said, "It wasn't that secure."

"Bingo. Despite the locked door up front and a gate across the sub-garage, there are two service entrances."

She tapped the photos of the wide gray doors. "This one, on the southern wall perpendicular to the entrance, was dead-bolted, but *this* one, on the rear wall, wasn't. Both are key-op but the back door isn't a dead bolt, just a latch. Which hadn't been turned. We walked right in and this is what we found."

Her next tap landed on a rising delivery ramp followed by a shot of a dim, cavernous space filled with cartons.

Petra said, "The ramp goes up two full stories, bypassing the garage and ending up in this cheerful place. It's massive and windowless and a mess. Filled with the boxes you see here and here and here, along with tools, stacks of garbage cans and bags, rolls of insulation, replacement AC units."

Raul said, "Lots of rat turds in the corners, meaning no one pays it much attention. Probably because the people using it—delivery drivers, maintenance workers—don't stick around long enough to care."

I said, "Is there any direct route to the main elevators?"

"Nope, Doc. But there is a big key-op freight elevator and an out-of-the-way, unmarked door to stairs that descend to a far corner of the garage. Well away from cars, so no reason for tenants to even be aware of it. But once you're down in the garage, you *can* catch the tenant elevator or use the main stairs. Both of which we examined and found nothing."

Milo said, "Know about the back door and you've got total access."

"Exactly," said Petra.

Hawes Buxby said, "How about cameras?"

Petra said, "Three. Main entrance, first-floor lobby, entrance to the parking garage. None of which would snag someone using the elevator to a floor above the lobby."

Buxby shook his head again. "Another brand of stupid."

Alicia said, "Can we go back to the utility room for a sec? Can it be locked from the inside?"

Petra said, "Yes, by a simple latch. But we found it unlocked and the same was true of the other utility room on the floor."

Sean said, "Assuming the shooter locked it while he was inside, there was still a big risk. Someone tries to get in, it could get nasty."

Petra said, "There are always risks but at that hour the chance of needing maintenance on a water heater would be low."

Hawes Buxby cleared his throat.

Petra said, "Yes, sir."

Buxby's mustache smiled. "Don't make me feel as old as I am, Buck's fine."

"You got it, Buck." She winked. "*Sir.* What's the question?"

"How many units are in the building?"

"Hundred eighty-five."

Buxby whistled.

Petra said, "Exactly. And obviously not every apartment is a single-occupancy so we could easily be talking three, four hundred people. We obtained the names on leases and rental agreements and will try to see if anyone with a violent record pops up, especially firearms violations. Raul and six uniforms and myself did door-knocks. It took all of yesterday to talk to ninety-seven people. No one seemed off and none of the vacant apartments—four to be exact—showed any signs of disruption or someone squatting without authorization. We also talked to the maintenance staff and got the same result but their histories will also be checked out. Even if we do clear everyone, it says nothing about people who'd lived or worked there in the past. Then there's the whole issue of guests. So we're going to lay off that approach for the time being and try to learn more about Mr. O'Brien."

I said, "Makes sense."

Five sets of eyes fixed on me.

I said, "Familiarity with the building is more likely the result of research on O'Brien than the shooter living or working there. Unless it was a bad-neighbor thing—some sort of prior conflict with O'Brien."

Milo said, "O'Brien got stalked for an extended period and whoever was hunting him figured out an optimal kill-spot."

Petra said, "That would mean his death had nothing to do with Marissa and he just happened to O.D. her the night he was targeted."

I said, "That's how I see it but it doesn't rule out someone avenging another of O'Brien's victims. Either as a paid job or getting personal."

"So we need to concentrate on any link between O'Brien and Parmenter. Which is why Buck is here to fill us in."

Buxby said, "And here I was thinking it was my good looks. Okay. The late Mr. Parmenter." Frowning. "He was at a record-industry party dealie—what they call a showcase for new talent. The talent in this case was a deejay, whatever talent that involves. The party was thrown by their producer/manager who also owned the recording company. A

citizen named Gerald Irwin Boykins, aka Jamal B. Another guy with
Crip roots but in Boykins's case a long time ago. He'd signed up Parmenter but not for big bucks, which apparently was his M.O."

"Always has been in the music world," said Sean. His voice, usually
soft and mellow, had taken on an edge.

Alicia said, "Voice of experience?"

Sean blushed. "Yeah, we went through that."

Buxby said, "Who's 'we'?"

"I used to be in a band."

"That so? Which one?"

"You never heard of us—Savage Seashore—anyway, that's the deal
with most indie companies. Pay nothing or close to it and hope for the
best. When there are royalties, the honest ones pay out. If the company loses money, they sometimes try to claw it back from the artists."

"Sounds lovely," said Buxby, fooling with the knot of his tie. "Anyway, that seems to have been the situation between Mr. Boykins and
Mr. Parmenter. But. Parmenter's alleged music never got released.
When I spoke to Boykins he claimed it was because there were quality
issues. Not that I could tell the difference."

Milo smiled. "You actually listened to it."

"Hey, suffering for the job. I was hoping a lyric would tip me off
to something but it was just about having rough sex with women, why
those woke types don't get on the rappers is beyond me."

I said, "Sexual aggression. There's a possible link to O'Brien."

Hurried note-taking.

Buxby said, "Someone avenging women who've been abused?" He
scratched his scalp. "I was concentrating on Boykins, the whole business angle, and there was nothing like that on Parmenter's history. But
who knows?"

Frowning at the possibility of missing something.

Petra said, "We haven't found any sex-crime arrests for O'Brien or
Parmenter but we all know what it's like with sexual assaults."

Alicia said, "Women afraid to report it."

Buxby looked at me. "You're raising an interesting point, Doctor." As if the zoo animal had performed an exquisite trick.

Milo said, "Okay, we'll dig around more on both of 'em. Coupla days ago I took a calculated risk and gave O'Brien's name to Marissa's friends. They had no idea who he was but my bet is it'll be circulating around the sosh platforms and maybe pull in some decent tips. Moe's monitoring."

"Nothing so far?" said Raul.

Reed said, "So far, we're basically getting hearts and flowers and teddy bear messages about Marissa."

Milo said, "Another possible link between O'Brien and Parmenter just occurred to me. Both were entertainment wannabes so a business angle can't be ruled out. Buck, how serious of a suspect was Boykins?"

"He was my only real suspect but I can't say I was sure of anything," said Buxby. "There was definitely conflict the night of the murder. Parmenter made a scene at the showcase and had to be escorted out. Not exiled permanently, they told him to cool out in the alley and they'd give him a second chance. That's what he was doing when he got shot. That and smoking weed."

"Was he by himself?" said Alicia.

"Himself and a big joint. Guess that was his tranquilizer of choice. Not sure how soon after he stepped out it happened. But it was around forty minutes before someone found him."

"Who was that?"

"Bartender, came out for his own smoke break. Hired for the night, like the waitress. Like everyone."

I said, "Where was the showcase held?"

Buxby said, "Big abandoned house on Franklin east of La Brea. One of those old frame Victorians, you still got a few of them on the north side of the street. Place was scheduled for a big remodel to turn it into a B and B but no ground had been broken and the owners were renting it out."

"Not that far from O'Brien's place."

Milo looked at me. "A shooter who lives nearby?"

"Lots of criminals do like to keep it local."

Buxby said, "I was looking at Compton where Boykins lived."

Milo turned and wrote *Geographic Link?* on the board, below the victims' faces. "Where does Boykins live, Buck?"

"Back then he was in Leimert Park."

Upscale district in South L.A. Attractive, low crime, tree-lined, predominantly affluent Black.

Raul worked his phone.

"He's in Beverly Hills now . . ." His eyebrows climbed. "No surprise, sold his music company six months ago to a private equity group. For a"—he made air quotes—"*rumored* thirty mil."

Buxby's whistle was loud and piercing. "Man, we're all in the wrong business."

Alicia said, "With a deal like that pending, there'd be motive for getting rid of a pest. Was Parmenter threatening to sue?"

"All I was told was he was unhappy with his deal and made a scene at the showcase."

Raul typed some more. "Nothing between Parmenter and anyone on the civil docket."

I said, "The threat of litigation could've been enough for Boykins to want to houseclean."

Buxby said, "That's what I figured, Doc. Even as a Crip, Boykins had never gotten busted for anything violent, but years ago he did do some burglaries and larcenies. Before discovering art."

Moe said, "And like Doc said, O'Brien was a Hollywood hanger-on, so he could've also crossed paths with someone like Boykins."

"Not as a musician," said Sean. "But maybe as a bouncer or a bodyguard."

"If that was the case," said Alicia, "O'Brien could've been at the showcase and seen something related to Parmenter's death and became a threat to Boykins."

Milo said, "Twenty-two months lapsed between the murders."

She said, "I don't see a problem with that, L.T. Enough time for Boykins to make a few extortion payments while setting up a permanent solution. If he'd arranged the hit on Parmenter and gotten away with it, why not another one?"

Milo chewed his cheek. "Good point. Okay, Boykins definitely bears looking at."

"Beverly Hills," said Petra. "Closer to you than us."

He laughed. "Happy to do it. Given *my* interest in the arts."

12

The meeting ended with a well-delineated division of labor. Moe would look for prior .308 shootings and field any tips following the postings and if the quantity grew formidable, enlist Sean to help. Until then Sean would work with Alicia researching prior body dumps with any similarities to Marissa's and return to the urgent-care facility to requestion staff.

Petra and Raul would canvass every apartment in Paul O'Brien's building and talk to other neighbors as well as to street people to see if anyone had spotted a person of interest the night of the shooting.

"Which in Hollywood," said Petra, "is a low bar."

That completed, they'd do as deep a dive as possible on both O'Brien and Jamarcus Parmenter.

Buck Buxby would remain "on-call." A euphemism that didn't escape him. He said, "Like the bull with the smaller cojones who waits in the stall in case the real stud gets lazy."

Milo and I would attempt to interview Gerald Irwin Boykins né Jamal B.

"Beverly Hills," said Buxby. "There must be a lesson in there, somewhere."

———

Wednesday at ten a.m. we set out for an address on the six hundred block of North Bedford Drive.

Milo had informed a Beverly Hills lieutenant, who'd said, "Never had any calls there but go for it, we always like to know who we're protecting and serving."

He'd also done background on Gerald Boykins. The former record producer and talent manager, now fifty-one, had been crime-free for sixteen years but before that had amassed a sealed juvenile file followed by a substantial criminal record.

His sheet, as Buck Buxby had said, featured no violent offenses despite Boykins's early involvement as a Compton Crip. Nothing remotely sexual, either, nor was he a party to any lawsuits.

I said, "Same gang as Parmenter."

Milo said, "Good basis for rapport but business trumps all."

The house was a two-story English Tudor replete with half timbering, a slate roof, and enough brickwork to build a bridge. The landscaping was uninspired but impeccable. Like the overall feel of the residence, unobtrusive in this quiet, respectable patch of the Beverly Hills flats. Most of the properties on the block were open to the street. A few, including Boykins's, were fenced and gated.

Through the gate slats, a white Land Rover, a red Bentley, and an orange Camaro were visible on a faux-cobble driveway.

Milo's bell-push was followed by the Camaro's driver's door opening. A man stepped out and looked us over. Fifty-ish, tall, broad, buzz-cut, and sunburnt, he wore a black suit over a red muscle shirt. Small round-lensed eyeglasses shot sunlight back in our faces.

He stepped forward deliberately, never shifting his attention from us. When he got close enough, he removed the glasses and his eyes took on form. Small, pale, scrutinizing.

Milo flashed the badge.

The man smiled. "Figured as much. What station?"

"West L.A."

"Worked Venice for twenty years." Reaching into a trouser pocket, he pulled out a module and opened the gate.

When we were inside he shook our hands, his paw a rough-sanded block of hardwood.

"Walt Swanson. What's going on, guys?"

"We'd like to talk to your boss about a case."

"He's not my boss," said Swanson. "I work for an agency—Pacific Security—and they assigned me."

"Not a fun gig?"

Swanson flashed perfectly configured but yellowed teeth. "Not if you want something to actually do. Which I don't, so yeah, it's okay."

He shifted his jacket, revealing a holstered Glock. "Never used it on the job, don't expect to use it now. He do something?"

Milo said, "Nothing says so."

"But you want to talk to him."

"Exactly."

Swanson ran a finger across his lips and grinned. "We're CIAing, got it."

"Anything interesting about him?"

"Not so far. Maybe you'll make him interesting."

He unlocked the front door with a key and led us into a small, oak-paneled entry hall. Straight ahead was an oak staircase that led to the second floor. To the left was a dining room, to the right a living room.

Your basic center-hall layout. Furnished with your basic respectable, traditional furniture.

A blond-bearded man around thirty sat at the dining room table with a pretty teenage girl. On the table were textbooks, stacks of paper and pencils. No phone or device. *Old-school academics?*

They both looked up. He smiled. She didn't.

Walt Swanson said, "Keep up the studying, Keisha. They're visiting your dad."

The young man said, "Maybe we should go back to the family room."

Keisha bit her lip. Said, "Sure," and collected the study materials.

"Tutoring," said the young man, as he passed us. "Not that she needs it much."

Keisha rolled her eyes. "AP calculus."

The tutor said, "No worries, you'll ace it."

As the two of them walked around the staircase, Swanson pointed left where a heavyset gray-bearded man sat in an electric wheelchair, eyes shut, buds in his ears, iPad in his lap. A café au lait complexion was dotted with freckles. The hands were huge and still, with well-tended nails that glinted.

Listening to something that made his body sway gently.

He wore a starched, blue-striped, button-down shirt, cream silk slacks, and blue velvet bedroom slippers with gold lion's heads embroidered on the toes.

Swanson said, "That's his thing. Music. All day."

Milo motioned Swanson over to the vacated dining room. On a sideboard was a gold-framed photo of Gerald Boykins, a pretty blond woman ten years his junior, and Keisha. From the girl's age, taken five or so years ago.

Milo said, "The wife still around?"

Swanson said, "They're married but I don't see her much. She's off somewhere now, don't ask me where. Nice lady when she's here. I think she was some sort of beauty queen."

"What's with the chair?"

"Some kind of stroke deal, half a year ago. Ask me, he's not that messed up, I've seen him walk when he needs to. But his energy's low so he wheels himself around a lot. Sits around mostly. Like I said, music."

"Anything else you wanna tell us?"

"Nah, like I said, it's super-quiet."

"Why does he need you?"

"They don't tell me that," said Swanson. "I'm assuming something in his past. Or maybe he's just nervous, being Black around here."

Milo looked over at Gerald Boykins. "You wanna wake him up or should we?"

Swanson smiled. "I vote for you. He'll probably get pissed off that I let you in but so be it. If they send me to another job so be that, too. If they hassle or can me, I can always go to another agency."

"Nothing like confidence," said Milo.

"You bet," said Swanson. "Got the pension, anything else is gravy. And compared with the real job, this is babysitting bullshit."

"You mentioned his past."

"What I was told is he made his money in music, that hip-hop crap. You know the type does that. Maybe he pissed someone off. I don't know. Or care."

Anger had crept into his voice. Boredom can only take you so far.

Milo said, "He used to be a Compton Crip."

Swanson's eyes widened. "Huh, go know. He's pretty conservative now. Politically, I mean. Sometimes he says stuff and I can't find anything I disagree with."

I said, "Friendly discussions."

"Nope, no discussions," said Swanson. "He talks, I listen. Perfect, the less anyone knows about me the better. So he was a gangster, huh? And now his kid's getting tutored for Harvard or wherever." He chuckled.

Milo said, "Not sure how he ranked in the gang, just that he belonged. Any pals from back then ever show up?"

"Here? Don't think so, amigo. Only people show up are the maid, the gardener, the kid's violin teacher, and the tutor." Big grin. "Oh yeah, occasionally the wife."

We crossed to the living room, where Milo approached Gerald Boykins and touched a shirtsleeve tentatively.

Boykins's eyes opened slowly, as if operated by motor-driven shutters.

When they cleared, his head jerked back and he raised both fists.

Milo said, "Sorry for waking you, sir," and showed his badge.

Boykins's eyes remained hot but his arms dropped. His lips set grimly as he ripped the buds out of his ears. "Police? What's the problem?"

"No problem, sir. We're looking into a case and wondered—"

"What case? I don't know about any cases? What's going *on?*" Boykins half rose out of the chair, sank back down looking exhausted.

For all his anger, not much volume to his protest. Big, fleshy man with a small, almost boyish voice.

He looked at Walt Swanson. "You just let them in?"

"I didn't think you'd mind—"

Boykins's lips curled in contempt. "You didn't think."

"Due to our prior discussions, sir," said Swanson. "What you always say about being supportive of law enforcement."

Gerald Boykins stared at him. "That doesn't mean anyone's free to just come in here."

"Sorry, sir. Shall I ask them to leave?"

"No, no, just go back outside and do your job."

"Yes, sir."

Swanson turned and left. Shielding the smile on his face from Boykins but making sure we saw it.

The details change but upstairs-downstairs never dies.

When the door had hissed shut, Boykins said, "Let's make this quick. I'm listening to great music. Want to guess what?"

Milo said, "No idea."

"Bullshit," said Boykins. "You're cops so you know about me and even if you didn't you'd see the color of my skin and assume hip-hop. Or some other *jungle* music."

We said nothing.

"Not that it matters," said Boykins, "but it's *Bach*. The Cello Suites. Which you've probably never heard of but there are six and I'm only in the middle of Three."

I said, "Saraband or bourrée?"

Boykins's mouth dropped open. His smile was cold. "Look at this, a cop with culture."

"The suites are among my favorites, too." When I didn't mind feeling clumsy, I tried playing them on the guitar.

"Didn't say they were my *favorites*," Boykins snapped. "Don't try to—don't know why I'm even *tolerating* you."

Milo said, "Again, sir, sorry for the interruption."

Boykins waved dismissively.

Milo pulled out an enlargement of Paul O'Brien's DMV photo.

Gerald Boykins said, "What about him?"

"You know him?"

"I know the face because I'm great with faces. He did some security work for me. Don't remember his name, just his face. Probably never knew his name. Why are you showing that to me?"

He fooled with an earbud.

Milo said, "He got murdered."

No movement from Boykins. "What's that got to do with me?"

"We're collecting data from past employers—"

"How the hell did that lead you to me?"

Milo said, "Sorry, can't get into that."

"Of course you can't," said Boykins, turning to face us. "You march in here and go all gestapo on me while I'm chilling but you can't tell me a fu— a thing about why. Great country we live in."

"Sir, we're just looking for information on Mr. O'Brien."

"O'Brien . . . Irish, huh? No idea about him or his tribe or anything else except he did some door work for me, lots of people work for me. Used to. When I worked. Now can you leave?"

"Just a few more questions, please? When was Mr. O'Brien in your employ?"

"He wasn't in my employ," said Boykins. "We hire freelancers by the job. Hired. Past tense."

"Hire them for—"

"Events."

"So no idea when Mr. O'Brien was hired."

"Now I'm a calendar?"

"When's the last time you ran an event?"

"Not for . . . a year and a half. But if you're asking me when he did door work, no idea. Could be then, two, three. I just remember his face because that's how my mind works. With faces I'm a camera. Faces and numbers, that's my thing. My daughter's gifted with numbers. She loves 'em, going to go places."

Suddenly he winced and shot a hand to his right temple.

"You okay, sir?"

"No, I'm not okay, do I look fu— okay? Got the headache. You gave me the headache. Could be just muscle tension. Or the systolic— the blood pressure's rising. Either way, you're messing me up."

We stood there.

Boykins said, "What are you waiting for? I told you what I know. And I still don't get how some piece-of-shit nothing who worked for me maybe only once—as an independent contractor, like everyone we used for events—how that figures into my life now. I shouldn'ta told you, that's what I get for being up-front. But you caught me off guard."

"What comprises door work?" said Milo.

"Security. Like the fool outside. The Swede. Who obviously isn't worth much, going to call the company, get someone who actually protects me."

"O'Brien was a private guard?" said Milo.

"No, no, no, nothing fancy. Just stand in the door and look big."

"Bouncer."

"Whatever keeps out the riffraff."

"At events," said Milo. "Like showcases."

Boykins's eyes turned hard. "You do some Google shit and think you *know* me?"

Milo said, "Sir. We're trying to solve a homicide. No one's saying you had anything to do with it but we wouldn't be doing our job if we—"

"Didn't barge into my house? What does drinking milk—this O'Brien, anyone—have to do with me?"

Milo showed him Jamarcus Parmenter's DMV shot. "It's possible his case is related to O'Brien's."

Boykins's head shot forward, eyes slitting. "That piece of shit again? I've already been gestapoed on him. Read your own fucking files, it's all in there, not going to add anything to what I already said. Now *go*. Get the hell out. Shut the door behind you and let the stupid Swede open the gate and don't come back without an appointment."

Milo said, "Who do we make an appointment with?"

"Nobody." Boykins jammed the buds back in his ears, shut his eyes, and made a show of settling back. But one hand remained curled in a tight-knuckle fist and his shoulders remained high and stiff.

Just before we reached the door, he said, "Two lowlifes are dead. I don't give a shit and don't pretend you do."

As we closed it, a higher voice: "Everything okay, Daddy?"

"Perfect, baby. Like you. Go study."

13

W alt Swanson was in his Camaro, the seat tilted back to recline. He thrust his arm upward through the lowered driver's window and clicked the gate open.

As we passed through, Milo said, "No collegial bye-bye? I'm feeling unpopular."

I said, "Good for you."

"Meaning?"

"You did your job well."

We traveled a few blocks east to Alpine Drive where he pulled over, put the car in Park, and let the motor idle.

But he didn't idle. His eyes were active, his shoulders humped, his fingers drumming the steering wheel nonstop.

"Touchy fellow, Mr. Boykins," he said "And now we've got him linked to Parmenter *and* O'Brien."

I said, "If he was involved with O'Brien's death why would he tell you he recognized him?"

"Maybe he figured we'd find out eventually and wanted to take some control—make it sound minimal."

"Okay."

"What's the problem?"

"O'Brien's picture didn't set him off, as opposed to when he saw Parmenter's. Did Buxby interview him extensively about Parmenter?"

"Why?"

"Maybe we brought back bad memories."

"Was what we just saw Parmenter-related PTSD? Nope, nothing prolonged. There was one sit-down in Boykins's lawyer's office where they covered the basics, then the lawyer cut the whole thing off and that was it. Basically, the guy was untouchable."

"Drinking milk," I said. "What's that, Crip-talk for murder?"

"You got it. Guy may be working hard at respectable but when he's threatened, he digs back to his roots. And what's more threatening than having a murder you thought you got away with reopened? Meanwhile his kid's being tutored for the Ivy League, lots at stake."

I said, "The Ivy League has always welcomed the offspring of dictators and robber barons."

"Huh . . . anyway, I can't eliminate Boykins for O'Brien just because he stayed cool. O'Brien's a fresh hit, maybe Boykins had mentally prepped for a visit. Parmenter, on the other hand, was ancient history he thought was over. One more thing: Why does he need a rent-a-cop unless he's still got ties to the bad old days?"

"Maybe so," I said, "but when you showed him O'Brien's picture I was looking for the slightest tell and he gave none. Not a blink. And he's not exactly stoic, so hiding a reaction would've been next to impossible. To me that says Parmenter's case may threaten him but O'Brien's doesn't."

"Two victims with links to Boykins just happen to get shot with the same rifle?"

"Can you tolerate an alternative theory?"

He sighed. "What?"

"Suppose Parmenter and O'Brien were at that showcase but it wasn't Boykins they angered, it was someone else."

"Some random partygoer gets dissed by the two of them and takes nearly two years to finish the job?"

The time-lag issue could apply to Gerald Boykins as a dual death contractor. No sense getting into that; Milo's shoulders had bunched higher.

I said, "Okay, alternative two: Parmenter and O'Brien were at separate events, months apart, where they got on the same person's bad side."

"C'mon, Alex."

"It's not as unlikely as it sounds. O'Brien freelanced as a bouncer and Parmenter could've gotten on those invitation lists Marissa's friends talked about."

"BeThere.com," he said. "Tried to reach them, their headquarters are in Thailand. Talk about not keeping it local. Anyway, Parmenter being the gifted vocal artist he was, I went looking for his music like Buxby did, found only one YouTube video. Recorded live in some dive, bad sound and lighting, he's rubbing his crotch and doing unpleasant things with the mic. The song title was 'Fold Over Bitch.'"

"Which could lead us right back to sex crimes by each of them."

"Mr. Sniper's a knight-errant avenging victims of abuse and O'Brien just happens to get nailed the night he O.D.'s his last victim? Talk about poetic justice."

"Sometimes the stars are in alignment."

"Not in my world, for the most part."

I said nothing.

He said, "In the movies, I'd say good riddance to bad rubbish and not bother to work the case."

"In the movies, cheesy music would be playing right around now."

He cracked up. Lowered his shoulders, freed his hands from the wheel, shook himself off like a water dog. Big, heavy dog—a Newfoundland.

"Okay," he said. "So Boykins could theoretically be clean for both shootings. Or dirty for only one of them. Or back to basics and he did pay for both."

He rubbed his face, like washing without water. "*That* clarifies matters."

During the drive to the station something else came to mind. Gerald Boykins's daughter being tutored at eleven a.m.

A homeschooling situation? If so, that could mean heavy-duty parental involvement.

Perfect like you, baby. Go study.

Some of the most engaged parents I'd seen in practice were strivers who'd never experienced the privileged youth they desperately wanted for their kids, and that fit a father who'd transitioned from thug life to a taste for Bach.

Sitting pretty in 90210 only to be felled by his own arteries.

Fearful enough about other threats to hire full-time security.

Maybe Milo was right and Gerald Boykins hadn't managed to break completely clear of his past. Or he had, but remained fiercely protective of the domestic life he'd built.

Pretty house, pretty wife, pretty child with the brains to handle AP calculus.

Had Jamarcus Parmenter's capital offense been coming on too strong with Keisha? Threatening some other aspect of Boykins's carefully curated renaissance?

But even if that had fueled the hit on Parmenter, my instincts told me I was right about Paul O'Brien. Boykins had remained unfazed upon seeing his face. Unlikely to be involved.

Two separate victims, two separate motives?

United in death by one hired killer, equipped with a .308 Winchester, a steady gaze, and an ample supply of full metal jacket ammo.

When I got home I looked up Keisha Boykins's social platforms and learned that until last year she'd attended the Brentwood School but was now being homeschooled due to a bout with what she called "stomach troubles." Despite that, she'd posted only happy photos, her face graced with a wide, warm smile and supplemented by a variety of gleeful emojis.

If her posts were accurate, she'd managed to hold on to a large group of friends even after leaving school.

"Stomach troubles" could mean anything from an eating disorder to bowel disease.

Whatever the diagnosis, in the eyes of her parents, she was now a girl requiring extra care. Which could've heaped an extra helping of stress on Gerald Boykins's plate.

I called Milo and told him what I'd learned.

He said, "There you go. Good-looking rich kid, O'Brien tries to get freaky with her, she tells Daddy, time to drink milk."

"Could be."

He said, "Hey. If you don't want me to grasp, don't keep handing me straws—hold on."

I waited for a couple of minutes before he came back on.

"That was Moe, sounds like there finally might be a decent tip in the junk pile. Guy who knew O'Brien and wants to talk about it. Got an appointment lined up."

"When?"

"Tomorrow morning at nine, if that works for you."

I checked my calendar. "Free until one."

"What happens at one?"

"Work that actually pays."

CHAPTER

14

Thursday at eight fifty a.m., I met Milo on Sunset Boulevard just east of San Vicente in the heart of the Strip.

Like any district that feeds on nightlife, the Strip turns tawdry in daylight. I've always imagined that as the street's empathy with the clubs, bars, and comedy stores that sadden when the sun threatens.

L.A. was streaming another episode of blue skies and crisp air and that helped a bit. But when we entered the Tidy Tavern things got predictably dingy.

The place was narrow, dim, devoid of customers. Tables and chairs were scattered randomly, as if pushed aside in haste. The blue vinyl floor was speckled with trash. A broom and dustpan leaned against a wall painted a repellent, lumpy red-brown.

Before we'd stepped in, Milo had shown me a photo of the man we were meeting. That turned out to be unnecessary. He was the only one in the room, standing behind the bar wiping the cloudy top sluggishly.

He heard us, then saw us. His mouth opened and formed a cartoonish oval. The rag in his hand began making frantic circles.

His name was Martin Kehoe and he'd changed his mind about talking to the police, phoning Milo at six thirty a.m. to say so.

Milo had ignored the message.

"Mr. Kehoe? Lieutenant Sturgis."

Kehoe said, "Oh no."

We took stools at the bar. Mine was rickety. Milo's seemed secure. Or maybe burdened into immobility. He'd bellied up, doing his best to enter Martin Kehoe's personal space.

"Oh no, what, sir?"

"I don't want to do this. I called."

"When was that, sir?"

"Early," said Martin Kehoe. "Like six thirty."

Milo said, "By then I was out in the field. Sorry for the inconvenience but as long as we made the trip, why don't you tell us what's on your mind."

"Nothing," said Kehoe. Even a bass voice can sound small when tremoloed by anxiety.

We gave him time to think. He used the opportunity to grip the rag tighter, creating white knuckles the size of brussels sprouts.

Big, broad man, with the same kind of bulk as Paul O'Brien. Unlike O'Brien he made no effort to show it off. Just the opposite; he wore a baggy white button-down shirt with the sleeves buttoned at the wrists.

The same diffidence applied to his cranium. When men lose their hair young they often shave their heads rather than emphasize pattern baldness. I'd scanned Kehoe's license and knew him to be thirty-eight. His dome was bare except where it was girdled by gray-flecked brown fuzz. What some of my patients call the Dad Look.

Kehoe's rough-hewn face was shelved by a huge chin and fronted by a beak that supported steel-framed eyeglasses. Wrinkles had set long enough ago to deepen.

Not yet forty but aging quickly. Our drop-by wasn't helping matters.

He shrank back as Milo leaned in further. "Really, sir. It's a mistake."

"Hmm. I'm confused, Mr. Kehoe. You phoned and said you had important information about Paul O'Brien."

"That was before."

"Before what?"

Kehoe transferred the bar rag to his other hand, half turned, and pretended to study a mirrored wall full of bottles.

"Before what, sir?" said Milo.

"Before I talked to my girlfriend," said Kehoe, swiveling back but avoiding eye contact.

"She said you shouldn't talk to us."

"She watches all those true-crime shows, reads crap on the internet. She said even when you're trying to be righteous it can come back to bite you in the ass."

"How so, Mr. Kehoe?"

"The person who comes forward. You know."

"Know what, sir?"

Kehoe turned back to us. "They sometimes get suspected."

"Your girlfriend told you that."

"Caitlin's smart."

"I'm sure she is," said Milo. "And what she said has some truth to it. But it doesn't apply to people with the good sense and the moral fiber to phone in tips."

Martin Kehoe took no comfort from the compliment. "Whatever."

"What Caitlin's talking about can happen when someone finds a body in a strange way. Or when a person injects themselves way too much into an investigation."

"Whatever."

"Honestly, Martin—can I call you that?"

"Marty."

"I'm being straight with you, Marty."

"Sure, yeah . . . but . . . I really don't think I have anything. I was just trying to be helpful when I heard."

"About Paul O'Brien."

"Yeah," said Kehoe.

"You were friends with Paul."

"Not really . . . we used to room together. He owes me money. That's how I found out."

"That he'd been murdered."

Kehoe winced. "Caitlin's been telling me I should call him, tell him to finally pay up. I called but he didn't answer so she went online to find out if he'd moved somewhere and it was there. What happened. What he did."

The door to the bar swung open, letting in light and noise before hissing shut. A small, bandy-legged man limped in waving his arms and shouting.

"Life is marvelous, Marty Martian! Here's your chance to make it stu*pen*dous!"

Kehoe reached into his pocket and drew out a ten.

Milo gave me a small nod and I took the bill from between Kehoe's fingers and walked toward the new arrival. As I got near, his aroma took over. Months of unwashed laundry mixed with long-term avoidance of dental care.

I gave him the money.

"Who're you?"

Milo said, "Someone making Marty's life easier."

"Oh. Good for you, man, good for you. He makes *my* life easier. I'm putting him up for saintliness at the Vatican. Even though I'm a Martin Lutheran."

A brief staring contest ensued. Milo won and the man tottered out.

Kehoe said, "Clayton sometimes helps me clean up so I tip him. But the owners don't know. And don't think I do that for everyone."

"If you did, we wouldn't think less of you, Marty."

"Whatever."

"Marty, you're obviously a stand-up guy with a big heart. You roomed with Paul and now he's been murdered. No one suspects you of anything. We need people to give us information. Without that, we're screwed, and so far on Paul's case we're super-screwed."

Kehoe's lips folded inward, emphasizing the size of his chin.

He said, "Whatever, okay. But it's no big deal."

"Thanks, Marty. Now what did you want to tell us?"

"Paul," said Kehoe. "He wasn't a good person."

We coaxed Kehoe from behind the bar and over to one of the tables and sat down facing him.

Milo smiled and said, "Go on, Marty."

"We used to room together," said Kehoe. "At first it was okay, then I learned about him and knew I had to get out of there. Problem was I couldn't afford my own place. But as soon as I could, I was out of there."

Milo said, "How long ago are we talking?"

Kehoe gave the question serious consideration. "I think . . . we started . . . like four years ago? I left like two years ago?"

"And he's owed you money all that time."

"Yes, sir."

"May I ask how much?"

"A lot," said Kehoe. "Like eighteen hundred dollars. Actually, seventeen hundred eighty-five."

"That is a lot," said Milo.

"Not in one bunch, he'd ask for twenty, fifty at a time, then a hundred, then fifty, even ten. That kind of thing. When I'd ask him for it back he'd tell me to keep a record so we'd both know. So I did. That's how I know."

"He pay any of it back?"

Kehoe shook his head.

"So how'd you guys meet?"

"We were both at the Roxy, working the door. Then we found out we had both done stunt work. I stopped because I tore my ACL but

Paul did a little more. He was even in a couple of movies but he didn't get paid much."

"You do any acting?"

"Nah," said Kehoe. "I don't like being looked at. After my ACL surgery, I started doing this and that's what I still do."

"Tending bar."

"And waiting tables. Busing and maintenance when there's nothing else. Here I work the bar and do maintenance. Caitlin says I should go to school and study landscaping."

"You like plants?"

"Those orchids you get at the supermarket?" said Kehoe. "I get a lot of them to rebloom. Caitlin can't do it, she says I've got a knack."

"Sounds like you've got a green thumb, Marty."

Kehoe shrugged.

"So where'd you and Paul live when you were rooming together?"

"Culver City. We got a sublet near Fox Hills, some old guy whose family put him in a home and they wanted rent money. Two bedrooms, two baths."

"Nice."

"Not really," said Kehoe. "Actually it was a dump but we could afford it. I still live there. Not in the apartment, near Culver City. Mar Vista, me and Caitlin have a nice place. She's a massage therapist."

"Sounds great," said Milo. "So what bothered you about Paul?"

"A lot, sir. But not all at once. It was like . . ."

I said, "It took time to get the whole picture."

"Exactly, yes, sir."

"Paul could behave badly."

"Oh yes," said Kehoe. "Real bad . . . okay . . . it was like this . . . We both liked girls. We met them at the Roxy or the Viper Club, any other doors we'd work and sometimes . . . nothing weird, sometimes someone would like you and you got to . . . recreate."

"Sure," I said. "Makes total sense."

"So that was it. For me. A couple of dates, one of them, a nice girl named Jacqui, we dated for like half a year. But Paul . . . how do I say this . . . Paul liked the girls too much."

His eyes dropped to the tabletop. He'd left the rag on the bar, looked at his hand and used it to simulate wiping. Faster and faster.

I said, "Paul came on too strong?"

"Yeah. Yes, sir. You could say that."

Milo pulled out his pad and wrote.

Kehoe said, "You need to do that?"

"I do, Marty, but don't worry, it won't mention you. So how did Paul come on strong?"

"It was . . ." said Kehoe. "Okay. Like, we'd be working a door? And after closing there'd be some girls hanging around? Mostly I'd be tired and want to go home. Not Paul, he was always looking. He'd . . . sometimes bring them home."

His lips folded inward again, pumping the big chin upward. It lowered as he released his lips. Press, release, over and over, like a die-stamping machine.

I said, "Paul would bring them home and . . ."

Final release. Trembling lips.

Marty Kehoe said, "Sometimes they wouldn't be awake."

"When he brought them home?"

"Both times," said Kehoe. "Bringing them in and bringing them out. He'd carry them out. If I saw it, I'd say what's going on, dude, and he'd laugh and say, 'I did her so good she fell asleep.'"

One hand kept frantically wiping. The other covered his eyes.

I said, "They didn't just look asleep."

"They looked . . . okay, yes, sir, they looked out of it. If I saw it I'd say, 'Is she okay?' and Paul would laugh and say, 'She's fine, what're you, a fucking EMT?' Then he'd carry her out."

"Did you ever find out what happened to them?"

Kehoe lowered the shielding hand but avoided eye contact. "I should have. When I read what he did to that girl, it hit me. I was like one of those . . . people who pretend to be moral but they don't go the extra step, you know? Caitlin says it wasn't my fault, what could I do? But maybe I could've. I don't know."

Milo said, "Any idea where Paul would take them?"

"I mean it didn't happen all the time, some of them were okay," said Kehoe. "They'd come out in the morning and he'd give them an energy bar or something and call them an Uber."

"But others got carried out in the middle of the night."

Slow nod. "Yes, sir."

"Those women," said Milo, "where did he take them?"

"I don't know, sir. Honestly. If I asked, he'd laugh. One time, it was bugging me, seeing him carry them and they're looking so out of it, I kind of demanded it. 'Where are you *taking* her, dude?' His face got all red, he put her down on the couch—more like dropped her—and he was in my face and his fists were up. I put mine up and told him, 'Go ahead, dude, that won't change the question.' I knew I could handle him, had taken him down in an arm wrestle plus I knew some mixed martial arts. And he knew it, too. So he laughed—he laughed a lot, he was always laughing but not at things I thought were funny—he laughed and said, 'You worry like an old woman. I'm taking her home, okay? Door-to-door service. Now shut the fuck up and go back to bed.' So I did."

Milo said, "How old were the women he brought home?"

"Young," said Kehoe. "What you get in clubs."

"Did he have any racial preferences?"

"Did he dig Asians or something like that? No, sir, they were all types. He'd laugh—he'd tell me, 'I'm the fucking United Nations. They've got pussies, they get membership.'"

I said, "You suspected he was drugging them."

"Why would they be knocked out like that just from . . . no way. *Doing* it doesn't do *that* to you."

"What drugs did you see in Paul's possession?"

"Just weed. We both smoked. A lot. We drank also. I don't do any of that anymore." He glanced at the bar. "Makes my job easier."

Milo said, "You never saw Paul do anything but weed or booze?"

"At the club," said Kehoe, "he'd sometimes do a little Molly. It was all around the clubs."

"What about at home?"

"Never saw nothing, sir. He kept his bedroom locked."

"When he had women over."

"Uh-uh, always."

I said, "Which made you even more suspicious."

"Yes, sir. Who *does* that?"

"During your time living with Paul, how many women would you say left unconscious?"

"Maybe . . . fifteen? Twelve? I wasn't counting."

"Did any of the women ever show up more than once?"

"Never."

"No girlfriends?"

"No, sir. Paul wasn't into relationships. Said relationships were like cancer, you had to cut them out to be healthy."

"Any reason he'd feel that way?"

Kehoe shrugged. "He was married, maybe he got burned?"

"Married to who?"

"No idea, sir. Way before I met him. He called her The Bitch, that's all I know."

"Did he have any children?"

"Not that he talked about."

I looked at Milo. He paused in his writing and gave me the nod.

I said, "Was Paul from L.A. or somewhere else?"

"He said somewhere in the East, that's all I know."

"He didn't talk much about himself?"

"Just about how good he was . . . with sex. He said he'd worked as a dancer. Doing bachelorette parties. Said he ended up doing a bunch of women at those. That's all I know. We didn't talk much. Just when we were doing doors and it got slow. But not about us. As people, you know? All Paul wanted to talk about was sex."

He squirmed. "He did a couple of pornos. Showed them to me on his phone."

Milo said, "Anything unusual about the films?"

"You mean weird stuff?" said Kehoe. "Nah, what I saw was just the usual. They were old. I could tell 'cause he was younger and they were kind of blurry. He said he could do it again, they were using all types. Said we both could be mature studs and make some buck."

He shook his head.

I said, "He tried to recruit you."

"I told him no way, too many diseases. He laughed and called me a pussy and said he was just kidding anyway."

"Speaking of bucks," said Milo, "what'd he borrow for?"

"Not the rent," said Kehoe. "He always had his half." Another eye shield. Big shoulders quaked.

Milo said, "What's the matter, Marty?"

"I been thinking about that. Did he use my money to dope them? I don't want to be part of that. I hope I wasn't."

He let both arms drop. His face was flushed, his breathing rapid.

Milo said, "Marty—"

"That's the real reason Caitlin didn't want me to talk to you. She says you could try to mess me up for not stopping it."

Milo said, "Tell her don't worry, Marty. All we care about is homicide."

Kehoe's eyes bulged. "Yeah, but what if one of *them* homicided? Look what happened to the one on the internet."

"We've got no evidence of that, Marty. And even if it did happen you've got absolutely no culpability."

Silence.

Milo said, "Okay?"

Kehoe shook his head frantically. "Caitlin says— I hope you're right." He shuddered. Sweat flew. Another Newfoundland lumbering ashore.

"Do *not* worry, Marty. You've done nothing that could be considered criminal and the fact that you came forward to give us information shows you're a good person."

Kehoe looked at him. "Thanks for saying that."

"Anything else you can tell us about Paul?"

"Like what?"

"Like who'd want to kill him."

"Caitlin says a lot of people," said Kehoe. "Because of what I told her about Paul. But I don't know who."

Milo showed him Jamarcus Parmenter's photo.

Kehoe said, "He did it?"

"No, he's a victim of an older homicide. Know him?"

"Never seen him before."

"Could he be a guy Paul mighta known?"

"Sure," said Kehoe. "Yeah, I could see that."

"Why?"

"He could be a club dude and Paul kept doing clubs after I quit."

Milo kept the photo at Kehoe's eye level. "You're sure you've never seen him."

"If I did, I'd tell you. *Believe* me, I'd tell you."

We followed the usual routine, asking the same questions rephrased. Sometimes people get spooked because they realize they're being played. The process calmed Marty Kehoe, loosening his voice, his phrasing, and his posture.

For all that, nothing new to say.

Milo looked at me. I shook my head. We stood.

"Thanks, Marty. If you think of anything else, here's my card."

"Yes, sir." Kehoe retrieved the broom. As we left, he swept. More circles.

———

Out on the sidewalk, I said, "That question about racial preferences. You're wondering about if O'Brien came on to Keisha. Or another woman Boykins cared about."

"You bet. Yeah, it's a racially narrow approach, why would I think Boykins wouldn't care equally about a White woman? But all I give a damn about is doing the damn job." He glanced at his Timex. "Time for your job. The one that pays."

CHAPTER

15

Custody interviews kept me busy until noon on Friday. I drank coffee, had a sandwich, returned to something I'd woken up thinking about, and phoned Milo at his desk.

He said, "Still dealing with the real world?"

"As opposed to?"

"The surreal, reeking underbelly of our city."

"The chamber of commerce should put that on a brochure," I said. "I'm calling because of what Marty Kehoe said about living with O'Brien in Culver City. That could explain why O'Brien chose to drive there to dump Marissa rather than leave her closer to his apartment in Hollywood."

"Sticking with his old comfort zone?" he said. "Sure. So?"

"More than that," I said. "What if he'd had other emergencies with drugged women who'd survived. A woman left impaired could also inspire revenge and a Culver City link could narrow down the search. I looked up hospitals and urgent-care centers and it's a short list. One hospital and four smaller facilities."

"Sean and Alicia already looked for priors, Alex. Zip."

"How'd they go about it?"

"Checked our files for victims left outside hospitals. All they came up with were a couple of male drunks who'd been beaten up and dumped."

I said, "Would a woman found lying outside with no evidence she'd been dumped get into your files? Especially if it was classified as a medical emergency and there was no criminal investigation?"

"In the best of worlds it would," he said. "Could it slide under the radar? Sure. Meaning good luck finding out."

"A malpractice suit would leave a paper trail."

"If it went to trial, it would. If it settled with a non-disclosure agreement, forget it."

"Okay, just thought I'd pass it along."

Silence. "Gimme that short list."

When he'd finished copying, he said, "Long as I have you, might as well give you an update. Such as it is. Marissa's car was found in South L.A., stripped. So someone stole it and had their way with it, which tells us nothing about where her last party was. Petra impounded it and it's being printed. I got Marissa's phone records and there's no activity a couple of hours before she was likely dead. And nothing post-mortem so O'Brien probably did toss it."

I said, "Well before he got her to his place so the towers didn't point there."

"That's what I'm figuring. There's no prior phone contact between the two of them but I did find one number they both called. Another online outfit that runs pop-up PR events. You apply to attend, if they approve you, you get to party. Marissa called it three days before she died, O'Brien, ten days before."

I said, "Another list for her. Maybe a job application for him. Working the door, like Kehoe said, while searching for prey."

"Slimy bastard—it's weird being seconded to Hollywood and focusing on him. That's what Shubb called it. Seconded. Anyway, the number's disconnected, I emailed, am waiting for them to get back to me. Still haven't heard from Thailand so I'm not holding my breath.

What else . . . Petra and Raul's canvass of O'Brien's neighborhood turned up three reports of a guy skulking around the building a few hours before the sniping. Medium size, dark hoodie, one person thought he was Caucasian, the other two said they couldn't tell. All were impaired to some extent and skulking's pretty much routine in that neighborhood. Bottom line: useless."

"Was he carrying anything resembling a rifle case?"

"Wouldn't that have been peachy. Nope, just a guy. The people in O'Brien's building saw nothing weird that night though a few of them described O'Brien as obnoxious and having women come and go frequently. Petra and Raul will be heading back to the building next door to try a second round of door-knocks. Size of the place, they'll probably need to rinse and repeat. I did some phoning around on Boykins and Parmenter. Turns out Crips World is a rapidly changing environment. No one in the gang squad or any of their informants has a clue about either of them."

"Fleeting fame," I said.

"Hey, it's L.A. Any other suggestions?"

"You mind if I ask around at the Culver City facilities?"

"Why would I mind?"

"Don't want to get in Alicia and Sean's way."

"They already did their thing. What do you figure you can accomplish that they couldn't?"

"I might know people."

"Then have them call my people and we'll do lunch," he said. "Sure, why not, it'll free the kids up to keep probing any links between Boykins, Parmenter, and O'Brien. Which I still *think* could be relevant."

I spent the next hour and a half scouring the web for overdose victims, left dead or alive in or near health facilities. Beginning with L.A. County then expanding throughout the state. Nothing but Marissa

French came up, not even the two intoxicated males Alicia and Sean had found in the crime files.

Push the clutch, switch gears.

I phoned Lee Falkenburg, a pediatric neuropsychologist with whom I sometimes cross-referred. I'd worked with Lee years ago at Western Pediatric hospital doing research on the neurological effects of cancer radiation. Smart and industrious, she'd gone on to open up a private office in Beverly Hills and a payment-optional learning disabilities clinic for the working poor in Inglewood near the northern rim of Culver City.

The Bedford Drive office had expanded to a six-psychologist group. I got voicemail offering a numerical menu.

For Dr. Falkenburg, press 1.

Compliance led me to Lee's away-message. She had a beach house in Carpenteria. End of the week, probably off to enjoy the sand. I'd just identified myself when she cut in.

"Hi, Alex. Something interesting?"

"Yes, but not a referral."

"That's okay, we've got more work than we can handle. Is it one of your police-y things?"

I explained.

She said, "Poor girl, that is so sad. I've had a few patients with GHB neurotoxicity, mostly teens with lingering memory issues. But no, I haven't heard about anyone being dumped anywhere and I've got no connections to any of those urgent cares. I am on the staff of Cal Culver so I could ask."

"That would be great."

"No problem, Alex. Except you know what might happen if there was an incident and the patient didn't do well and the lawyers got involved."

"Tight lips," I said.

"I was thinking more in anal terms."

"Official sphincters freeze."

She laughed. "But I'll give it a try."

"Really appreciate it, Lee."

"No prob. Now, can you get my Becka one of those ride-alongs with the cops? She's addicted to gory crime shows."

I remembered a small girl, red-haired, freckled, precocious. "How old is Becka?"

"Twelve."

I laughed. "Don't think that's going to happen."

Lee said, "Yeah, the joys of impending adolescence, those mushy frontal lobes. Of course, it's totally inappropriate. As are her viewing habits, but you choose your battles. When I told someone at the last neuropsych meeting the programs she streamed he looked at me as if I was an abuser. But he's always been an insufferable prig and I know I can tell you stuff because you don't get all judgy."

I said, "How about a visit to the police academy?"

"Where's that?"

"Elysian Park. Jack Webb donated most of it."

"The *Dragnet* guy? Sounds interesting," she said. "Maybe I'll tag along. No, scratch that, if I want to go she'll say that sucks."

I went back online, began looking for hospital-related victim dumps in other states, found plenty.

Seattle, Vegas, Albuquerque, Washington, D.C., St. Louis, Chicago, New York. According to Marty Kehoe, Paul O'Brien had hailed from somewhere in the East. But all the cases on record were gang-related or domestics and each had occurred while O'Brien lived in L.A.

It was nearly four p.m. when I pushed away from my screen. Time to go out to Robin's studio, learn her work plans and her dinner preferences.

I'd just stepped out of the office when the buzz of my phone on the desktop brought me back.

On the screen: *Big Guy.*

I said, "What's up?"

Milo said, "Just learned of another .308 sniping, four months be-fore Parmenter. We've been sticking to L.A. County, this one was in Ventura and it's a definite, the bullet matches. The cop who caught the case heard about O'Brien, brought it down here personally to the lab and pushed to have it tested. They haven't gotten around to telling me but she just did."

"Who got shot?"

"Woman in a rowboat," he said. "Sounds like the beginning of a bad joke, right? You up to view the scene tomorrow? At the least it'll be pretty."

CHAPTER

16

P retty, as promised.

Milo and I set out at eight a.m., hit mild Saturday traffic on the 101 North, made it to the Ventura city limits an hour later. The next twenty minutes were spent coursing along an easterly road called La Calle Vista as it climbed and contorted through foothills shaded by native sycamores and California oaks.

The lowest reaches bordering the drive remained undeveloped. A couple of miles in, modest houses began to appear, followed by ranches on lots that expanded with rising altitude. Horses, goats, duck ponds, chickens pecking with abandon. Citrus groves were supplemented by avocado. The aroma of dung mingled with sage, orange blossoms, and yerba buena.

Our destination was a gated dead end flanked by signs.

Private Road. No Trespassing. Lookout Point, A Private Community.

The gate was an electrically operated rectangle of chicken wire in a wooden frame. Fine for stopping vehicles but a pedestrian intruder could easily pass through the gap between barrier and post. No blockage at all today; the gate had been left wide open.

We continued up a tarred road so dusty it could've been mistaken for dirt. Tall, dense trees curtained both sides. Eucalyptus mixed with Italian cypress, Aleppo, and Canary Island pines, all imports from decades past.

Beyond that was a scatter of houses, single-story and moderately sized with plenty of acreage between them. Tree-shrouded residences arranged in a horseshoe on the north side of blue-green water. Wooden bollards planted in the ground a hundred feet from the shore blocked further car travel but, again, foot entry was easy, the view expansive and welcoming.

A single sign was staked to the left. *Caution: Lookout Lake's Waters Can Rise Above Banks.*

Not this morning; the level was a good yard below shore.

Milo parked in front of the bollards and looked at his Timex. "She should be here soon, let's take a look."

We trod firm, dry ground to the water's edge. The south side of the lake was forest. The houses facing that green-black wall were furnished with canopied docks, some empty, others housing canoes, kayaks, and rowboats.

No motorcraft explained a quiet that went beyond the absence of noise. This was an active aural calm, as if a room had been hushed. Nothing, then a few birdcalls. Then the occasional kiss of breeze on foliage.

As if the air molecules themselves had been altered.

I said, "Not exactly Hollywood grit."

Milo said, "But apparently no safer."

Moments later, engine noise made an entry and the birds went mute.

A red Chevy Tahoe pulled next to Milo's Impala. The woman who got out and waved at us wore an aqua top, jeans, and running shoes. Five-four, square-shouldered, and curvy, with honey-blond hair drawn back in a ponytail.

She walked to us quickly and confidently. Up close her youth was obvious—not yet thirty, with a smooth, almost child-like face and small, well-placed features. Mocha complexion, bright-hazel eyes.

Civilian clothes, but a Sheriff's I.D. badge above her right breast read *S. Flores*.

"Lieutenant? Shari."

"Deputy Flores." Milo shook her hand and introduced me.

She gave my hand a brief pump. "Nice to meet you, Doctor. Shari's fine."

Milo said, "Alex and Milo. Day off or plainclothes?"

Shari Flores smiled and looked out at the lake. "The former. I hope it was worth you coming out here."

"Always good to see the scene. Good job discovering the ballistics match."

"No big deal, I try to keep up with the bulletins," she said. "Yours came through and I said, 'Whoa.' Because you don't see a lot of rifle murders. Hunting accidents, sure, but nothing deliberate. So I got our bullet from the evidence room, drove it down to Hertzberg, and managed to get them to test it quickly."

Milo grinned. "Ever think of moving down to L.A.?"

"Actually," said Shari Flores, "it would be moving back. I grew up in Boyle Heights, got my first assignment working for the L.A. sheriff on my old home turf. Then I met my husband, he was working Westmont and had enough, so when we saw two openings here, we moved."

"Westmont." He shook his head. "Tons of fun."

"Exactly, it was horrible for Miguel. People getting shot walking across the street for no reason. He's in Camarillo now and I got this. I get a lot of animal calls and once in a while a burglary. This"—staring at the lake—"was different."

Milo said, "You're on the case yourself?"

"Except for preserving the scene, I wasn't on it at all," she said. "They called in the heavy-hitter detectives but then they got distracted by a big gang thing near Oxnard so it went cold pretty fast. It bothered me but what could I do? Then I saw your .308 report and figured hmm, that doesn't happen often, can't hurt to find out."

"Great job," said Milo, "but seeing as true love's a factor, I won't repeat my offer for an LAPD gig."

She laughed. "I'll tell Miguel I impressed someone. So what can I tell you?"

"Start at the beginning."

"All right." Flores removed her name tag and slipped it into a pocket. "I responded to a 911 from Dispatch of someone in the middle of the lake, drifting in a boat and not moving with a little kid crying. I figured it was some sort of illness call, asked for the EMTs and a diver. When I got here, it was just like they said, a little rowboat—that one."

She pointed to a pale-green craft in the dock of an A-frame midway along the horseshoe. "And sure enough, this tiny little boy was in there, wailing away, next to an adult just lying there. I called out but she didn't move and my main concern was him falling in. He had a life jacket on but with the cold, it could get bad even if he floated. From this distance there wasn't anything I could do without jumping in so I got my binocs and kept a close eye on him, prayed the diver would show up."

She flinched. "Poor little thing, listening to him was torture."

I said, "How old of a child are we talking about?"

"I figured two and I was close," said Shari Flores. "Twenty-seven months. His name is Jarrod."

"How far was the boat from the shore?"

"Three hundred eighty feet. As you can see, the lake's not that big—more of a big pond, you could say. Later, I looked it up and total area is a little over an acre and a half. If the diver didn't show up soon, I was ready to try out my swimming but luckily he did, was able to attach a rope and get close enough for the EMTs to pull the boat to shore."

She shook her head. "She was dead. Obvious bullet hole."

Milo said, "In the neck, just off center to the right."

Shari Flores stared at him. "That was yours, too? Only thing I got from your report was the likely weapon and the full metal jacket ammo."

"Same deal in both of mine," said Milo. "Happy to get into the details but could you give me yours first?"

"Sure, sure . . . if you want we can go over to the house, sit outside, there's a table with shade. It's not the scene per se, but it's where the scene started."

The three of us walked along the lake, passing through the spacious unfenced backyards of three houses. Tarps cloaked barbecues and watercraft, windows were whitened by curtains. The same open plan applied to every property. No sign of habitation anywhere along the water. The quiet had returned but had taken on another flavor.

Oppressive.

We followed Shari Flores to the rear of the A-frame with the green boat. Small cedar structure, maybe built from a kit, the wood splintering in spots and in need of restaining.

Three railroad-tie steps took us up to a small, flagstone patio. A weathered, bird-specked redwood table was shaded by a tilting yellow umbrella past its prime. Four aluminum-and-plastic chairs offered a full-on view of water, trees, and sky.

I said, "All the houses look unoccupied."

Shari Flores said, "It's mostly second-homers and they don't come here a lot. Some of the properties rent out during the summer. That was her situation. Whitney's. She had a two-month lease, July and August."

I'd read the basics. *Whitney Lara Killeen, thirty-four, five-five, one thirty-two, brown and brown.*

I said, "There's no fencing between the properties. That plus the vacancies says shooting her right here would've been easy."

"The openness was originally the attraction," she said. "Fifties charm, the rental ad called it. And it's always been safe, no one locked their doors until this happened."

"No cameras that I can see."

"There's one at the far end, that house with the blue roof. But it wasn't working and it's aimed down at the lawn, not the lake."

I thought: ideal setup for a casually paced murder.

Milo said, "Any idea where the shot came from?"

"Somewhere across the lake but our C.S.I.'s couldn't be sure exactly because they could never get a fix on the distance and that affects the trajectory."

She pointed across the lake. "Somewhere in those trees."

"Where was the bullet found?"

"In her," said Flores. "Stuck up against her cervical spine."

"Both of ours went clear through," he said. "For yours to lose that much velocity, it was a helluva distance."

"We—the detectives—got estimates based on where the boat was found but there was a wide range—a hundred or so feet. Another problem was that just because she was found in that spot doesn't mean she was shot there."

"The boat could've drifted."

"For sure."

"Who spotted her?"

"A neighbor coming by to check her own place. Lives mostly in Santa Barbara, eighty years old, not exactly a prime suspect and in no shape to try to rescue Jarrod, so she called 911. She was totally freaked out, hadn't seen any strange cars near the entrance."

I said, "A car parked farther down wouldn't have drawn her attention."

"Exactly. The detectives canvassed like half a mile down. They actually did a good job. But you know."

She shrugged.

Milo said, "What time of day was Whitney discovered?"

"Just after noon."

"Any idea how long the boat was out there before it was spotted?"

"Pathologist estimated TOD around an hour prior."

"Morning boat ride with Mom," he said. "The kid was out there all that time."

"Scary, no?" said Flores. "Maybe God was looking out for him. They tried to question him but he didn't talk much and mostly he just cried for his mommy. They also did all sorts of wind analysis to figure out drift but it didn't help 'cause there's no stable air pattern here. It fluctuates between calm and sudden gusts but also sometimes there's a steady breeze. Like today. There's no county or state data, period. It's like its own little microclimate. They searched the southern shore and went back into the trees. No cigarette butts, no bottles or cans, no shoe prints—it's mostly pine needles. That's why distance was impossible to calculate."

I said, "Drive up in the dark, leave your vehicle where it's not going to be conspicuous, walk right in and wait."

"Well planned," said Milo. "Any idea who'd want her dead that badly?"

"Sure," said Shari Flores. "Her baby daddy, there was a custody battle headed for court. But he had a golden alibi. In New York, at a board meeting with a whole bunch of other people."

"Corporate type?"

"Executive at a clothing company based in Japan. That's how they met, Whitney was an accountant assigned to do their internal audits."

Milo pulled out his pad. "Name?"

"Jay Christopher Sterling."

I said, "The relationship went really bad?"

"According to Whitney's mother it did," said Shari Flores. "They had a brief affair, she got pregnant, they broke up soon after the baby. Sterling's much older than her, in his fifties, has kids in college."

"Married?"

"Divorced. According to Whitney's mother, there was no love lost and Sterling didn't want to pay as much child support as Whitney asked for. But the big fight was when he moved to New York and wanted to take Jarrod with him."

I said, "He wouldn't have much of a case unless he could prove her unfit. Did he try that?"

"Not that I know about," said Flores. "Never actually spoke to the mother, what I'm telling you comes from her interview in the murder book. Which I brought you a copy of, it's in my car."

Milo said, "Deeply appreciated. Where's Jarrod now?"

"With his father. Talk about a motive paying off, huh?"

"Your guys had a strong feeling about Sterling."

"He's the only person of interest they developed. I called one of them before I came up here and he verified it. He didn't mind my talking to you, sees the case as an unsolvable loser."

Milo laced his fingers and rocked back a bit. "Obviously, Sterling didn't pull the trigger but a guy like that, plenty of money, easy enough to hire someone."

"You wouldn't even need money," she said. "Miguel told me in Westmont you can find someone to do it for like twenty. Or some dope."

"True," he said, "but money gets you a smarter shooter. I'm assuming your guys checked out Sterling's banking records."

"They had no grounds for a warrant but Sterling let them, he was like, 'Sure, look.' No transfers of cash that looked weird."

"Mr. Cooperative. So maybe he controlled what he showed them."

"Could be," said Shari Flores. Her toe nudged the dirt. "I suppose he could be innocent but no one else ever came up."

We returned to our vehicles, where she retrieved a large box file and handed it over.

"Unbound," she said. "Didn't have time."

Milo said, "Shari, everything you've done is amazing." He winked. "West L.A. has its issues but it's a light-year from Westmont. Just saying."

She smiled. Hazel eyes segued back to the water. "What I did was no big deal. I keep thinking of that little guy. Sitting there, next to her."

CHAPTER

17

Shari Flores's Tahoe backed out, reversed, drove off. Milo stashed the box file in the Impala's trunk and we returned to the water's edge, shielding our eyes from glare.

Milo said, "Weirdly peaceful . . . thoughts?"

I said, "Like you said, smooth and professional. It firms up the hit man scenario, and nothing gets people angrier than child custody battles."

"Accountant in a boat. Can't see Whitney linking to Parmenter or O'Brien so the work we've been doing trying to connect them could be a waste. Then again, wouldn't it be interesting if Whitney had done *his* corporate audits, too? Maybe learned something she shouldn't and it has nothing to do with the ex."

"Easy enough to find out," I said. "Most likely she worked for a firm and CPAs don't have confidentiality."

"There you go with that positive-attitude thing again. Yeah, will do. Anything else?"

"After twenty-six months, Whitney's mother will be frustrated and eager to talk."

He retrieved the box, spent a while thumbing through, said, "Here we go, she lives in West Hills, right on the way back. I'll take that as an omen."

He called the listed number, spoke briefly, listened for a long time, hung up and patted his ear as if cooling it.

"Beyond frustrated. She's waiting."

As we got back in the car, he said, "Here I was, ready for some grub at the Ventura Harbor, there's this great place, fresh catch. Alas, duty calls."

Words of regret but spark in his eyes. It takes a lot to steer him away from lunch.

Thirty-five miles to the Valley Circle exit on the 101 was a forty-one-minute drive. Once we got past the businesses facing the freeway, we were in leafy suburbia.

Milo continued to Roscoe, hooked left for half a mile, then turned right on a gently sloped street lined with ponderosa pines and marked by a *No Outlet* sign. Wide, low-slung houses were arranged around a ladle-shaped cul-de-sac. Basketball hoops were a regular feature and several of them were being put to good use. A few toddlers rode plastic tricycles under the gaze of watchful parental eyes. One man washed a vintage gold Corvette with exquisite care.

Milo said, "No lake. Seems like a good thing today."

Before beginning the drive, he'd done some background on Whitney Killeen's mother, Donna Batchelor. Fifty-four years old, living at the Brunswick Court address for twenty-one years, zero criminality.

Her house was two lots short of the dead end, one-story, teal-sided, with a beige door. The front was a cement parking area divided into diamonds with clover filling the seams. Flowers and shrubs fluffed up every border save the one leading to a double garage. No evident architectural style but a nice-looking, well-tended home.

Milo parked at the curb and we got out. The moment the Impala's doors closed, the beige door opened and a woman marched toward us.

She wore a sleeveless black top and jeans that ended mid-calf. Thin and tan, with ash-colored hair cut short, a pixie face, and wiry arms.

She continued her approach until we met midway, said, "Donna," in a husky voice, shook my hand first, then Milo's, folded her arms across her chest, and examined us.

Milo said, "Lieutenant Sturgis, this is Alex Delaware."

"Glad someone's interested, it's about time. Not that I get what LAPD has to do with Whitney but I'm sure you'll tell me. C'mon in, I made iced tea but if you want coffee, I can fix some."

Without waiting for a response, she turned her back on us and hurried toward her house.

Milo mouthed, "Frustrated."

I thought, *That could be helpful.*

Donna Batchelor's house had white walls and high, angled ceilings. Hand-scored mesquite floors gleamed. Beige couches were spotless; red, orange, and rust accent cushions had been dimpled perfectly. Glass sliders looked out to a meticulous garden centered by an oval pool and let in soft, northern light. The color of the water was a close match to the teal siding. More glossy leaves and pastel petals abounded.

She race-walked us to the living room where a pitcher of iced tea, two highball glasses, and a plate of Oreos sat on an olive-wood tray atop a tufted white leather ottoman. Settling at the short end of a rectangular coffee table, she motioned to a rock-hard sofa.

"Sit. Help yourselves," she said. Generosity via command.

Milo said, "Thanks for meeting with us on short notice."

"Why wouldn't I? This is the first I've heard in a long time about anyone giving a hoot. In the beginning I was hopeful, the Sheriff's detectives actually seemed to know what they were doing. Then they just lost interest. I used to call them every week, Monday at nine, on the dot. For the first month or two, they answered. After that, it was crickets. I went over their heads and complained to some captain. He put on the nice-guy act but said anything that could be done had been.

So I went over *his* head and tried to talk to the main sheriff who never called me back. Instead I got an email from his office bouncing it back to the captain. Obviously, all that *could* be done *wasn't* because you're here."

"We're here, ma'am, because there's some indication Whitney's murder could be related to work we're doing in L.A."

"Work," said Batchelor. "What are you trying to say?"

"A case."

"Hopefully that'll be to my benefit. Who else got killed?"

"Two people." He showed her Jamarcus Parmenter's and Paul O'Brien's headshots.

She said, "Them? Can't see Whitney having anything to do with people like that. Even when she lived in L.A."

"When was that?" said Milo.

"All of her life until she rented that whatever-you-want-to-call-it in Boonesville."

Milo produced his pad.

Her posture relaxed. Someone who appreciated the transfer of facts to paper.

He said, "Where in L.A. did Whitney live?"

"Brentwood, an apartment. To make things easier for him."

"Jay Sterling."

Hearing the name thrust her mandible forward, bulldog-like.

"Bastard. Yes, *him*. He had a big house in Brentwood and she was trying to help out with his seeing Jarrod more easily so she graciously moved from Encino. And let me tell you, it was a come-down, the place in Encino was bigger and nicer and the rent was lower. But that was Whitney. Going along to get along. A lot of good it did her."

"Whitney was a CPA."

"Like me," she said. "We both passed the exam the first time. It's a toughie, believe me, I was proud of her. We were best friends, I had her at eighteen. And no, not as a single mother, Killeen and I were married. I was just starting college but he was already a CPA. He went and died of an aneurysm and I had to pull it together. Years later, I married Batchelor. A CPA *and* a tax lawyer. Then *he* upped and died of prostate cancer."

She bared even white teeth. "I was thinking of myself as a jinx. Then I got actuarial and accepted that twice I'd married older guys. Twenty years in Killeen's case, thirty-five in Batchelor's, so what could I expect?"

She glanced at Parmenter and O'Brien and shook her head. "Definitely *not* her type—you don't want tea?"

"No, thanks."

"Your loss. Okay. My beautiful Whitney. And she was, I'm not just saying it."

She sprang up, walked to an adjoining dining room, and removed several framed photographs from the wall. A bit of effort; something—probably museum putty—had been holding them in place.

She returned. "Here, you'll see what I mean."

She thrust an image at us. Full-faced, brunette teenage girl in a cheerleading uniform, lofting two pom-poms.

Next the same face, leaner, under a tasseled black graduation cap and robe of the same color.

Finally, Whitney Killeen, her hair cut and colored exactly like her mother's, holding a dark-haired, grave-faced boy around two.

Donna Batchelor pointed to the graduation portrait. "That sash she's wearing, they call the color drab but that's not an insult, it's tradition. Signifies business and accounting. This gold braid, here, is because she earned honors."

She re-hung the photos and sat back down. "Honors, dean's list, the works. Getting a great job right out of the gate was a cinch. Deloitte. Know who that is?"

Milo said, "One of the big firms."

"Mega-huge. She made terrific money, took the exam, passed the first time, and got a serious raise. She stayed at Deloitte until she was thirty, then she moved to a smaller firm so she could have more creativity and broaden her opportunities."

Milo said, "Is that where she was when she met Sterling?"

"Unfortunately. Not the job. Meeting him."

"Name of the company, please."

"Lewin, Wolf and Taback. They specialize in the rag trade, have offices in Century City and New York. She met *him* in New York even though he lived here. Was assigned to do internal audits at STL—his company. Which can get tricky, you uncover something and they do a blame-the-messenger thing. But she didn't with STL, everything was kosher, the parent company's Shigihara Limited from Japan, old-school, very big on integrity. *He* was one of their American reps. Whitney's assignment meant spending a lot of time with him and that's how it happened."

"The pregnancy."

"The *relationship*. The pregnancy was . . . let me tell you, that was a shocker, I don't know how it happened, Whitney had always had sound judgment. I couldn't believe it. It was the first time anything came between Whitney and me. I told her to terminate, it could only bring her problems. She got furious and we didn't talk. But we'd started again. After things went bad with him and she needed someone to support her. Emotionally, not financially, Whitney always did great financially."

I said, "Why did things go bad between her and Sterling?"

"Because he was a flat-out bastard. Total commitma-phobe." She reached for an Oreo, broke it in two, and nibbled at one half. "Sure you don't want one?"

Milo smiled and took a cookie.

Donna Batchelor said, "There you go, nutrition, you can always go to the gym . . . what went bad? The whole kit and caboodle. Bastard's living luxe and doesn't want to pay serious child support? Then he started making noises about moving to New York to be with his other kids 'cause they were in college there? Claimed his experience as a parent made him more suitable for full custody. I told Whitney to hire a shark lawyer who out-bastards him but it never got to that point."

Her fingers crushed what remained of the Oreo. Dark dust fell on a white marble tabletop.

"*Damn.*" She sprang up, moistened some paper towels, and returned. Picked up every crumb, then buffed the marble.

I said, "Were Whitney and Sterling communicating through lawyers?"

"No, not yet, they were screaming at each other. That's what Whitney said. Finally she had enough of his crap, took leave from her job and rented *that* place."

"To get away from Sterling."

"To get away from civilization," she said. "Have you been up there? It's Boonesville, half the time you can't even get internet."

"You visited her there."

"Once, that was enough. She wanted me to go out with her on a dinky little boat. Said it was calming for the soul. Maybe hers, not mine. The only water I want are Perrier and my pool."

She glanced at a gold Lady Rolex. "So what're you going to do about him?"

Milo said, "We'll be looking at him seriously. What else can you tell us about him?"

"That's it," she said. "Never met the bastard, don't want to unless it's in court and he's just been found guilty."

"You're certain he's behind Whitney's murder."

"Who else? Everyone loved her. No one had anything against her *except* him."

"He's living in New York now."

"Last time I heard he was but that was when Whitney was still . . . right after she went rural. For all I know now, he's in Singapore or somewhere."

"With Jarrod."

"Yup." No emotion, grandmotherly or otherwise, at the mention of the child's name. "So what are you going to do other than look at the bastard?"

"That's where we're starting, ma'am."

"Fine," she said, jangling her watch. "It's time for my swim."

As we headed for the unmarked, Milo let out a low whistle. "Iron lady. Did you see that cookie abuse?"

I said, "Could be her way of dealing with loss. On the other hand, she did tell Whitney to abort a potential grandchild. So Whitney could've been escaping more than just the conflict with Sterling."

"Getting away from Mom."

"From Mom and everyone else except Jarrod."

"Little green boat, perfect for calming the soul," he said. "Until it wasn't."

As he pulled from the curb, I said, "For all Mom's anger, she could be onto something. If Sterling was out to rid himself of her and get Jarrod, he succeeded in spades. He's an executive so he'd be used to delegating."

"Like Boykins," he said. "Coupla honchos with connections paying to solve their problems. So there doesn't need to be any link between them other than the choice of hit man. And at the risk of being boring, Boykins had dealings with Parmenter *and* O'Brien. First job turns out great, why not hire the same shooter a coupla years later?"

My doubts about Boykins and O'Brien hadn't faded but I said, "Sure. Is there any truth to the dark web being a source?"

"For dope, yes, for hit men not so much. Yeah, that was a big scare a while back but it mostly boiled down to scammers in Montenegro or wherever taking bad people's money and knowing they wouldn't protest. There was actually a case a few years ago, stupid asshole wanted his wife killed, forked out a whole buncha bitcoins to a scary website and of course nothing happened. So he fired off angry emails then shot her himself and left tons of evidence behind."

He got back on the 101 and merged into southbound traffic.

"On the other hand," he said, "there *could* be a link between Boykins and Sterling that led them to the same shooter. Think about it, Alex: the music biz and the rag trade. For all we know Sterling dressed up dancers in Boykins's videos, the two of them became buds, bitched to each other, one of them ends up advising the other about problem solving. I'll check out the dark web, but assuming nothing shows up, where do I take it?"

"No idea."

He put on speed. "Aren't you guys supposed to answer a question with a question rather than admit you're stumped?"

I said, "Would it make you feel better if I did?"

He cracked up. But the mood didn't last.

He dropped me at home and I called in for messages. Light weekend sprinkle: one new referral from a personal injury lawyer, the assistant of an impatient family lawyer wanting to know when my report would arrive.

Last, a call-me-back from Lee Falkenburg, no details.

In the office on Saturday? Knowing Lee, sure.

I called, got the same numerical menu, pressed *1,* and was greeted by her personal recorded message.

I left messages for her and both attorneys and went out to Robin's studio to see if Blanche was in the mood for a sprightly waddle down to the Glen and back.

Her body language said, *Forget that.*

She lay stretched on the floor a few feet from Robin's bench, snoring operatically. My footsteps caused her to raise one eyelid that eventually lost out to gravity. She managed a brief smile and two twitches of a nubby tail before returning to dreamland.

Robin was French-polishing the rosewood back of a hundred-year-old Santos Hernández guitar, her hands gloved in thin plastic as she gently rotated a pad of linen soaked in spirit varnish.

She stopped and smiled and said, "C'mere, it's not toxic."

I went over and kissed her. Sometimes affection between us perks Blanche up and she vamps for attention.

Today: nonstop log-sawing.

I said, "The diva okay? She looks wiped out."

Robin said, "Just took her for a little walk down to the Glen and then she had a couple of treats. Okay, three."

"Sensory overload. I won't interrupt either of you."

"It's never an interruption, darling. Just a momentary shift of focus."

She kissed me again.

Blanche grumbled.

I waited for the little blond sausage body to animate. It didn't.

Robin's fingers flexed. A sprinter stretching before the starter's gun.

I said, "Nice polish."

She picked up the pad. "Helps when you start with lovely wood."

I returned to the house.

During the few minutes I'd been gone, Lee had called back. This time she picked up.

"Hi, Alex. Are you with your police friend?"

"Nope, at home."

"Good. We need to talk in private."

"Sure."

"Not over the phone," she said. "I've got one more patient for another hour, Don's out of town, and Becka's going to a friend's to study. Let's meet somewhere between your place and mine, say ninety minutes."

Lee lived in Little Holmby.

I said, "How about campus."

"Perfect. There's a parking area west of the quad."

"Know it. I'm intrigued."

Lee said, "Not sure I'd use that adjective."

Her call had heightened my senses, which was a good thing. Bad idea to run on the Glen in a distracted state. Too many cars and sharp turns. I began an hour jog with a throbbing but clear head, returned the same way, showered, dressed in fresh clothes, left Robin a note on the kitchen table, and made it to the Seville with time to spare.

19

The spot Lee had picked was a shaded niche on the east side of a quad. Half a dozen metered parking spaces were gratis on weekends and, today, unused. Each corner of the broad, green rectangle was occupied by one of the U.'s four original buildings. Romanesque Revival beauties that evoked a time when art was more than a concept.

I pulled into a slot and had just turned off the Seville's engine when a wine-colored Mercedes convertible glided in next to me.

Lee was at my door before I opened it, looking as she always did. Five-five, minimal body fat, long, dark wavy hair crowning a girlishly open face marked by two of the sharpest eyes I've ever seen. As a postdoc, she'd done brain research with a Nobel laureate, could've easily gone the lab-poobah route but decided to help people directly.

Generally, she smiles a lot. Not today.

We hugged briefly. Between the leanness of Lee's frame and her full-body tension, it was like embracing an iron gate.

She pulled away and looked around. Settled on a couple picnicking in the center of the lawn. "I was thinking we'd walk but let's talk in my car."

We settled in the Mercedes's fragrant beige leather interior.

I looked at Lee. She looked straight ahead.

Finally, she said, "It's complicated. I know that's what people say when they're bullshitting but I'm not."

"Appreciate that."

"Here's the thing, Alex. I'm not sure I can give you any information unless you can assure me that no one will ever find out I was the source. Not for my protection, for . . . doesn't matter. The point is without a source I can't see it being useful for your friend."

"Milo's discreet."

She kept her eyes on the windshield.

"I know *you* respect confidentiality," she said. "For people like us it's a religious observance. But cops are allowed to lie if it gets them what they want. For something to be useful to them, it needs to be recorded in writing. So it can be used in court. Correct?"

"Not necessarily," I said. "Some stuff never makes it into the files."

"Such as?"

"The identities of confidential informants and protected witnesses. Or just content detectives choose to omit because they don't need it."

"But you wouldn't have asked me if you didn't think he'd need it. And if he goes ahead and makes a— okay, I'm going to stop being all spy-novel and give you the gist of what I know but only that. And I'll trust that our relationship will lead you to respect my wishes."

I said, "That I can promise. Something happened at Cal Culver."

She smoothed back her hair. Licked her lips.

"Something did, indeed. However, my source spoke on condition that the information not be made public. The stakes are high, Alex."

"Financially."

"Yes, financially, and yes, a patient was dumped there. Very similar to your case. Weirdly similar."

"When?"

"Several months ago."

"GHB overdose?"

"GHB plus diazepam. The poor woman was left out in the parking lot and lay there for hours before anyone noticed her. The obvious claim was the delay led to significant medical deterioration."

"Claim as in malpractice suit."

"Malpractice plus a request for punitive damages due to institutional negligence," said Lee. "Massive damages demanded. During pre-trial depositions, the hospital's experts tried to claim the victim had arrived extremely impaired and the passage of time wouldn't have made a difference. The plaintiff's experts said that was a lot of bunk. So the hospital legal staff . . ." She paused, blinking hard, and I wondered if her source had been a lawyer. "Their conclusion was that an institution fighting the family of a severely damaged victim would be a loser as well as a public relations disaster. They settled quickly contingent on a total non-disclosure agreement."

I said, "Who found her?"

Another pause, another blink. "A staff person coming on shift who'd parked nearby."

I thought: *Maybe a doctor or a nurse.*

"How was she found?"

"By accident. She'd been left in an out-of-the-way spot, near a hedge behind an outer row of cars, and the person just happened to spot her feet. The lot was patrolled on a regular basis but you'd have to be poking around to find her."

"No cameras?"

"Not right there. What a horrible thing to do to someone, Alex. She's blind, quadriplegic, and cognitively impaired. Twenty-six years old and under full-time care."

"God."

"Apparently God wasn't paying attention that night." Her lips vibrated. "Twenty-six years old, Alex. Whoever did that to her is pure evil. Does it sound like your dead bad guy?"

"It sounds exactly like him. There was no police investigation?"

"Nope, that was part of the deal. There was a lot of pressure to deal with it quickly."

I said, "What can you tell me about her?"

"That's all I'm at liberty to say. The payout was huge and any disruption of the settlement would be disastrous. For the family and for the hospital. The place is already in financial straits, last thing it needs is a scandal."

"The family had no interest in knowing who hurt their daughter?"

"I can't speak for the family and I'm certainly not going to judge. My source wondered if a criminal case would even go anywhere, assuming they could find a suspect. Even if they did, the schmuck could claim she overdosed herself, he tried to take her to the E.R. but she fought him, ran away, and ended up behind the cars. Can you imagine what the media would do with something like that? The hospital gets screwed, the victim gets dragged through the mud, talk about a shitshow."

She turned but looked past me at the passenger door. Wanting me gone but too much of a friend to expel me.

I said, "How about this: Give me her name and I'll do my own research—nothing official, just basic internet stuff. If I learn something relevant, I'll let you know, you can pass it along to your source and see what they think."

"You'd hold back on your cop pal."

"I would."

"You wouldn't go to all this trouble for some scumbag who rapes and dumps women," she said. "So it must be the second murder that's motivating you. Who's that victim?"

"A musician murdered in cold blood," I said. "And a third victim has just surfaced. A mother shot in front of her two-year-old."

Her palms slapped together and remained fused. "Good Lord, Alex, how can you stand to live in that world, even part-time?"

A question I'd long stopped asking myself.

I said, "It can be challenging, Lee. But it's not that different from the other work I do. From what you do."

"Uh-uh, I'm sorry, that makes no sense to me."

"Different tools for trying to fix the world."

"That's a *really* big stretch, Alex— sorry, who am I to judge, your choices are yours."

Neither of us talked for a few moments.

Lee said, "Got a local anesthetic?"

"For what?"

"The acute pain of admitting you could conceivably be right."

I laughed.

She said, "Don's always telling me *my* world's too dark. I deny it and when he picks the wrong time to say it, I tell him writing screenplays is a juvenile attempt to avoid reality. But sometimes . . . like the case I was working on this morning. Fourteen-year-old referred for learning disabilities. I do a full battery and find subtest patterns suggesting a brain anomaly. They do an MRI and it's a glioblastoma. Diffuse, not multiforme, so that's at least a positive."

She let out a soft gust of arid laughter. "The helping professions."

I said, "At least we're doing good deeds."

"If you say so . . . yes, of course we are. But still . . . a two-year-old. *Shit.*"

She inhaled deeply, leaned over and got close enough for a kiss.

"Saucedo," she said. "Victoria Saucedo."

Not an uncommon name in SoCal but it didn't take long to find the likely match.

Victoria "Vicki" Saucedo's presence on social media was one sparse page. The two images posted were eight months old and revealed a smiling, gorgeous twenty-something with sculpted cheekbones, wide black eyes, and thick, straight hair of the same color.

She'd worked as a "fashion consultant" at Chanel on Rodeo Drive and had been photographed in a little black dress and a body-hugging red gown.

Same boutique where Marissa French's friends had attended a party.

I chewed on that for a while, inspected the rest of the page.

Split-second review; no friends, no favorites, no interests.

At the bottom a single italicized line surrounded by rose vines.

Get well, Vicki, everyone's rooting for you!

An image search pulled up a whole lot of other Victoria Saucedos plus the same pair of photos and one other in which Vicki Saucedo wore a white bikini and posed on sand next to a beach chair. The back of the chair read *Regency Cabo.*

Pairing the hotel with her name pulled up nothing. A closer look at the resort produced room rates in the four-hundred-dollar range, a no-kids or time-share policy, and consistently good ratings.

Pairing her name with Paul O'Brien's was a dead end. Same for merges with Gerald Boykins and Jamarcus Parmenter.

I tried matching her with *marissa french* to no avail, had the same luck with each of Marissa's friends.

Broadening to *boyfriend, friend, friends, companion* was fruitless. Then I tried *high school* and found an eight-year-old yearbook page from Torrance High featuring Victoria "Vicks" Saucedo's senior head-shot.

Less-than-ambitious photography couldn't hide the fact that at eighteen she'd been a radiant, beautiful girl. Like Marissa—and Whitney Killeen. Women who'd sidestepped the indignities of adolescence.

At Torrance, she'd been a cheerleader and a member of the Art and Design Club, the Spanish Club, and something called The Fashionistas. That turned out to be a group of students with sewing skills who copied couture.

Three girls and a boy. I copied their names and went on to search *saucedo family torrance*.

Two items in the *Daily Breeze*.

The first was a nine-year-old photo of a middle-aged couple, a girl around twelve, and a boy a few years younger, sitting floor-level at the Forum in Inglewood.

Proud parents Harold and Maria Saucedo, along with sister Susan and brother Michael, watch as eldest daughter Vicki competes in the West Coast Cheer Competition.

Everyone smiling.

The second hit was a two-year-old alphabetized shout-out to local seniors who'd been accepted at selective colleges.

Michael J. Saucedo, Oberlin, full scholarship.

harold saucedo torrance produced the staff list of a local evangelical church. Harold M., the administrator. Nothing on Maria. Maybe a housewife or a stay-at-home mom or whatever they were calling it this week.

Three Susan Saucedos lived in the South Bay city. The one whose age and image matched the *Daily Breeze* photo was a second-grade teacher at a charter school in El Segundo.

Michael J. Saucedo's name appeared in an *Oberlin Review* article. Participant in a student group venturing out at night to feed the local homeless.

Church administrator, grade school teacher, altruistic college student.

No one who seemed likely to hire a hit man.

But maybe someone else in Vicki Saucedo's life had taken action? A friend or a lover who'd suspected Paul O'Brien's involvement in her death?

That depended on O'Brien definitely being the lowlife who'd over-dosed and abased Vicki. A more-than-reasonable assumption, given the similarities between her death and Marissa's.

I phoned the Tidy Tavern, ready to ask for Martin Kehoe.

Not necessary; he answered.

"Mr. Kehoe, this is Alex Delaware."

"Who?"

"Lieutenant Sturgis and I spoke with you the other day."

"Okay," he said.

"I have a question for you. Did Paul ever work on Rodeo Drive?"

"Yeah. At Chanel."

"When?"

"Maybe . . . last year? Half a year? Something like that."

"What did he do at Chanel?"

"The usual," he said. "Security at parties for actors and other rich people. He wanted me to do it with him, said it was easy, we'd mostly hang out. I said I was already busy and also I like to stay home at night."

"How'd he react to that?"

"Called me a fucking wuss," said Kehoe. "I didn't care. I told Caitlin and she's like why *didn't* you go and bring me home some Chanel swag? Then she said she was proud of me."

"For . . ."

"Avoiding *him.*"

I returned to the list I'd compiled of Vicki Saucedo's fellow Fashionistas.

Brianna Dominguez, Brianna Petersen, Sherilyn Dorsey, Matthew Salazar.

The yearbook gave up pictures of three pleasant-looking girls and a small, skinny, pimpled boy who looked closer to thirteen than eighteen.

Time for another dip in the Sea of Cyber.

Unlike Vicki but like most everyone else, her sewing friends had extensive social networks. But none of them cross-referenced her. Or one another.

Going their separate ways after graduation.

Brianna Dominguez was a helicopter pilot stationed at Ramstein Air Base in Germany.

Brianna Petersen repped cancer drugs in Connecticut and New Jersey for a Big Pharma corporation.

No indication where Sherilyn Dorsey called home but she was married to a Redondo Beach firefighter named Bradley Komack and was now Sherilyn Dorsey-Komack. So somewhere in SoCal, maybe the beach town itself, making her a good lead.

Most of her photos featured the couple and their three cute kids. No outside job listed. Sewing was still a hobby, along with surfing and scrapbooking. She'd gone ash blond, put on a bit of weight, grown prettier.

I put all that on hold and looked for Matthew Salazar, now creative director for a high-end bourbon distiller. Production in Bardstown, Kentucky, business office in Lexington where Salazar resided. He'd just married his longtime partner, Ben, a physician. The two of them were currently honeymooning in Aruba.

Back to Sherilyn Dorsey-Komack. I bookmarked her social pages, then switched gears and looked for Chanel celebrity parties.

Six events, but three had taken place recently, so I examined the coverage of the earlier three. Lots of A-list faces and those of the people who worshipped or lived off them. It took a while but I finally spotted an image that included Vicki Saucedo.

Revival celebration of Chanel No. 5 nine months ago. Her lips were cardinal red, her eyes shadowed in smoky tones, the outer lashes upswept like wings. Luxuriant black hair was drawn back as tight as her smile as she stood holding a tray of cocktails.

I kept paging, located another photo of her in an identical pose seven months ago. Fashion consultants drafted for cocktail waitress duty.

A few feet away, dressed in a black suit, shirt, and tie, thick arms folded across a puffed-up chest, was Paul O'Brien.

Narrowed eyes lasered on Vicki Saucedo's back.

At some point, she'd responded to him. And ended up vegetative.

I printed and sat for a long time taking in the image. He, repulsively focused. She, blissfully unaware of what was to come.

In the eyes of the law, every victim deserves full effort. But that's an abstraction, not reality and, besides, I'm not the law. So if a predator's crumpled body on a balcony was the only issue, I'd have left it alone.

But a little green boat . . .

The chance that something in Vicki Saucedo's past would link to a cool, efficient sniper for hire was remote. But at this point, what else was there?

My only possible lead was the high school pal who'd stayed local. But I couldn't see any way to contact Sherilyn Dorsey-Komack and keep my word to Lee Falkenburg.

I took out my guitar and wrestled with Bach, always a humbling experience. He'd never composed for the guitar and attempts to translate him have led to a lot of improbable stretches. I'd thought it a unique situation until a concert pianist friend told me, "J.S. put the notes in place. He didn't give a shit how you got there."

That level of distraction drew me away for a while. But when my fingers began aching and I stopped playing, everything rebounded. I called Lee at home and told her about the Chanel party.

She said, "Used to go to their sales until Rodeo got clogged with gawkers. Never got invited to any of their fancy parties . . . so she definitely worked with your dead guy."

"And he had his eye on her. Want me to send you a photo?"

"Definitely not. Why are you even telling me this?"

"None of Vicki's family looks likely to hire a shooter so I was wondering about an avenging boyfriend. Her Facebook page doesn't list any but there's not much to it, period."

I began describing the rose-wreath.

Lee cut me off. "Too much information. The poor little kid in the boat got lodged in my head until I got home and had two Martinis."

I told her about contacting Sherilyn Dorsey-Komack. "Would that create a problem for your source?"

She said, "Probably. Anything that opens the box would."

"Okay, forget it."

"Shit," she said. "Now I'm feeling like I'm part of some sleazy hush-job—welcome to Murdergate. What the hell, Alex, do your best to be discreet, you know the parameters." Her breath was a whoosh. "Two years *old*."

CHAPTER

21

I searched for Sherilyn Dorsey-Komack's home number and came up predictably empty. But her husband's name led me to Redondo Beach Fire Station 1, one of three in that city. And that linked me to Chairman Of The Boards, a surf shop in nearby Huntington Beach owned by the couple.

Plenty of Facebook, Twitter, Instagram, Yelp, and LinkedIn.

More important, open on Sunday. For another hour.

I spent a portion of that time trying to come up with a believable approach. Came up with nothing and decided to speak in generalities and hope she'd say something that would give me an opening. Not so different from what I did as a therapist. But in therapy, you're out to help the person sitting across from you, and I'd be doing nothing but using Sherilyn Dorsey-Komack.

For a good cause. Theoretically.

At least, I rationalized, I'd be doing her no harm.

I punched numbers.

An adenoidal teenage male voice mumbled, "Chairman."

"Is Sherilyn there?"

"*Sher?* For *you.* Don't *know.* Hold on, dude."

Half a minute later: "This is Sher. What can I do for you."

"My name's Anthony Davenport, ma'am. I work with LAPD and wondered if you could spare a few minutes to talk about a victim named Victoria Saucedo."

"Police? About the hit and run?"

Bingo.

"Yes, ma'am. I'm with Traffic Safety and we're sorting various accidents and doing what's called a victimology. Basically learning as much as we can to see if we can safeguard people better."

"I respect what you do, my husband's an EMT, but what does Vicki's accident have to do with me?"

"We're talking to Vicki's friends to learn more about her. Your name came up."

"From her parents? I knew her real well in high school and for a few years afterward, but not much since," said Sherilyn Dorsey-Komack.

"I see. Well if you feel there's nothing you can say—"

"All I can tell you is Vicki's super nice, really sweet and gorgeous but not full of herself. Just the opposite, super-shy. At least when I knew her."

"Shy with people."

"Yup. Can't see that mattering when a drunk plows into you, huh? Some customers just walked in, sorry, gotta go."

"Thanks."

"Oh sure."

Click.

Thirty-second conversation during which I'd failed to draw out anything related to a vengeful love interest. But I had learned the cover story the family had used to explain her injuries.

And the fact that she was extremely shy to the point of being unaware of her looks. And *that* made me consider the little I did know about her family.

Sister a teacher, brother on full scholarship at a selective college.

Vicki serving drinks to rich people.

Had social anxiety resulted from failure to measure up academi-
cally? Had there been some sort of learning disability?

All that might explain vulnerability to a predator.

So what? These were the kinds of questions and answers that occupied me as a psychologist but not what Milo meant when he asked
for "insight."

Milo had no knowledge, period, of Vicki Saucedo.

With nothing to offer him, best to leave it that way.

I returned to Bach for an hour, was putting my guitar back in its case
when Robin and Blanche came in looking buoyant.

"Good," said Robin. "We're all in fun mode. I'm thinking steaks
and whatever."

Blanche's nubby tail twitched.

I said, "Perfect."

Later, that night, Robin and I lay naked and entwined and kissing
deeply. Her tongue sweet, her compact body smooth and tan and
glossed by sweat sheen.

Guitar-shaped.

22

Monday at ten a.m., Milo called.

"Morning, Doctor Professor. Come up with any overnight insight?"

"Nope."

"Me neither but something different just happened. Remember that party website Marissa and O'Brien both contacted?"

"BeThere.com. They answered your email?"

"They phoned," he said. "Actually, *she* did. Nice lady at a call center in Bangalore, India. She told me they're instructed never to answer unless it's a paying client—as in people throwing fancy parties. Company's business model is they supply bodies for events all over the world and take a per-head cut. She decided to contact me because two of her brothers are Bangalore cops and she wants them to be proud of her. Turns out the last party Marissa and O'Brien attended had nothing to do with music or fashion. Opening at an art gallery on Melrose. I looked it up. Some rich guy's kid who thinks he's an artist."

"Let me guess," I said. "A five-year-old could do better."

"I was thinking Blanche could do better. Anyway, doesn't look like Boykins—or Jay Sterling for that matter—has any connection to that night . . . hold on, someone's beeping in."

He came back moments later. "That was Buck Buxby. Too late to catch him but he left a message to call. Probably wants an update. So that's it, the art gallery, which is basically a dead end."

"Did she tell you who signed in first?"

"She gave me the exact times, hold on . . . O'Brien logged in a little over six hours before Marissa. Why?"

I said, "Trying to get a feel for how it came together. My bet is O'Brien got himself on the list then told Marissa it was exclusive—him being a producer and all that. Then he told her he'd pre-cleared her but she still needed to apply online."

"She's thinking it's hoo-hah, makes it all the more attractive."

"All part of the grooming."

"Asshole. Well, he won't be missed and no one seems to be building a monument to Mr. Parmenter, but poor Whitney Killeen's tugging at my heart. I reached the Sheriff's detective who first worked her case. He's an assistant chief in Goleta now, and just like Flores said, he couldn't care less."

"Any reaction to the bullet match?"

"A grunt," he said. "Then he took another call. Moving on, Petra and Raul got a few more sightings of Mr. Hoodie slouching around O'Brien's neighborhood and one person claims he was carrying a long package. But no leads to his identity."

I said, "Parmenter's shot in Hollywood, Whitney in Ventura County, then back to Hollywood for O'Brien. Our bad guy travels but his home base could still be in that area."

"Petra agrees, she'll check parking tickets in and around that night and Raul will talk to attendants at pay lots. I spoke to Whitney's boss at the accounting firm. Said she was a private person, all business, couldn't imagine anyone wanting to hurt her. The only contact he had with Ventura was a brief phone call."

"Was the boss aware of the conflict with Sterling?"

"Nope, all he knew was Whitney had a kid because she kept a photo on her desk. I also phoned the company Sterling works for in

New York and lucked out with a very helpful executive secretary who informed me Sterling had moved back to L.A. couple of months ago."

I said, "Two years go by, case goes cold, no more need for the golden alibi."

"Interesting, no? According to the secretary they moved Sterling to New York 'cause they wanted him closer to Europe. Now they're back to concentrating on Asia so the West Coast makes more sense."

"Did she sound credible?"

"You never know for sure but my gut says yes. Because when I mentioned Sterling, she said, 'Oh, *him*. He doesn't work here anymore,' as if that was just fine. Clearly not Mr. Popular, so don't think she'd cover for him."

"What did she know about Sterling and Whitney?"

"There was some kind of custody dispute and Sterling bad-mouthed Whitney a coupla times—no details, just an unfit mother. She wasn't even aware Whitney had died, assumed Sterling had won in court and got the kid. She also said Jarrod was cute but extremely quiet. Which would fit going through trauma, right?"

"Definitely," I said. "Sterling brought a two-year-old to work?"

"Sometimes, along with a babysitter. I asked John Nguyen if there was any way to get into Sterling's finances to look for interesting withdrawals. Wanna guess what he told me?"

"Get corollary evidence first."

"That plus why am I messing with a Ventura case. I explained but he wasn't impressed. Same deal with getting a money dig on Boykins. So I'm stuck with two potential conspirators I can't do a damn thing about. As to who contracted the hit on O'Brien, I'm still leaning toward Boykins. Alternatively, if you're right about O'Brien O.D.'ing another woman, someone else coulda hired a caped avenger. But Moe checked again and nothing like that's showed up. Bottom line, I'm nowhere."

My brain churned.

"Alex?"

I said, "There might be something."

"What?"

"It's complicated."

"*Ugly* word. *What?*"

"I found another O'Brien victim." I gave him the basics of Vicki Saucedo's death, citing no names or places.

He said, "How long have you known this?"

"Just found out."

"Who's your source?"

"That's what's complicated."

"Dumped at a hospital," he said. "Some doctor bud of yours who doesn't want to get involved."

Ace detective.

As I considered my answer, he said, "Jesus, Alex. Would it help if I swore on a stack of Bibles not to screw them over?"

"Knowing more isn't going to help you."

"Why not?"

I said, "The info was secondhand and nothing about the case suggests anyone who'd contract a hit."

"Because?"

"The main thing is we know O'Brien was responsible for at least two O.D.'s so there could be more."

He said, "You didn't answer the question. What, this victim's family is a bunch of pacifist vegan saints?"

"Can't say more."

"You can but you won't."

"Trust me on this."

"So far that's worked out," he said. "But."

I laughed.

He said, "I guess that could be construed as humorous. So what do we have here . . . Moe couldn't find anything but you did. Meaning the case never got logged as criminal. Meaning a civil lawsuit. Big bucks, non-disclosure. Gotta be malpractice. What, they didn't treat her fast enough or some other screwup?"

Gold badge earned.

I said, "You're going to nose around."

"Would it help me find who shot O'Brien and, more important, Whitney?"

"Not that I can see."

"If that changes, you'll let me know."

"Of course."

"Even if it causes problems for your doc buddy? . . . Hold on, it's Buxby again."

This time he was off the line for several minutes.

"He didn't want an update, he found something. Now I have to decide if I should tell you about it, seeing as it'll put you way short in the equity department."

"Whatever works for you."

"Oh my," he said. "*Soooo* Zen. Guess that helps with your real job. Okay, I'll blink first. Buck went looking for the lyrics to that rap Parmenter posted online. Here's the interesting part: 'You gotta Keitch? Gonna pick yo peach. Gonna bend her over slip her the snake. Gonna be more than she can take.' Who said romance was dead?"

"Direct threat to Keisha Boykins."

"Damn thing was posted a month before Parmenter got shot, talk about firming up a motive. If this isn't enough for a bank warrant on Boykins, I don't know what is. And if I can figure out who Boykins hired, everything else will fall into place. So tell your doc pal not to worry. At least for the time being."

CHAPTER

23

Three days later, at noon, he was at my kitchen table picking at a monumental DYI sandwich and looking deflated.

"Got the warrant and spent every damn second trying to access Boykins's dough. Problem is, he's got a buncha corporate entities shielding him, could take weeks to peel everything back and even then who knows? I did access a couple of checking accounts. Joint with Mrs. Boykins and relatively small-time. For him. Six grand a month. Probably for household expenses."

I said, "No hit man allowance to go with the grocery budget."

"Nada. Obviously, he's too smart to leave breadcrumbs. I talked to the gang guys again, asked them for a deeper dive into his former life but the same thing came up: youthful affiliation, no violence. Any new thoughts about the kindhearted chia-munching family of O'Brien's other victim?"

I smiled.

He said, "Fine, but keep an open mind."

He lifted the sandwich. Put it down. "With that rap garbage Parmenter put out, I know his death is tied to Boykins but it's outta reach. Like that Greek myth—the guy with the grapes dangling overhead."

"Tantalus."

"Me and the T-man, stymied at every turn."

I said, "Tantalus was punished for trying to serve his own son as a course at a banquet."

"Are you telling me there's a moral there?"

"Just saying that's not you."

"Who am I, then? That idiot with the wax wings who flew too close to the sun?"

"Icarus? Nah, you're a pretty good driver."

He stared at me. "Was that supposed to be emotional support?"

"Nothing but."

Sighing, he gave the sandwich a try. Savored, swallowed, took another bite, then two more before swigging a glass of water and suppressing a belch.

Successful therapy.

"So," he said, "any ideas about anything?"

"I'd stay on Boykins but also look at Jay Sterling."

"I already told you, can't get paper on him, either."

"I meant literally."

"Ah." Three additional bites, a napkin swab of his lips, then out came the file from his green vinyl attaché case. He paged through, jabbed a spot. "He works at home. San Vicente Boulevard, Brentwood, near the border with Santa Monica."

"Nice neighborhood."

"The wages of sin. Okay, let's see if we can *literally* look at this guy."

Jay Christopher Sterling resided and worked in a sizable white two-story Mediterranean on the north side of San Vicente Boulevard. The east–west thoroughfare is divided by a green median loved by joggers and dog-walkers. Lots of fitness on parade. Even the toy canines looked buff.

Most of the properties were fenced and gated and Sterling's was no exception. During the drive, I'd checked and learned the place was a rental.

Milo said, "Wages of sin paid out monthly."

His bell-push was answered by an accented female voice. "Hallo, who?"

"Police. We're here to talk to Mr. Sterling."

"Who?"

"Mr. Sterling," said Milo. "The man who lives here."

"Ohhh."

A minute of dead air was broken by a deep male voice.

"Police? Really? What's going on?"

"Sorry to bother you, sir, but we're working a case and your name came up."

"What case?"

"Whitney Killeen."

"Oh man! You finally found him?"

"Could we talk, sir?"

"You didn't. *Shit.* So what do you want?"

"A few minutes of your time, Mr. Sterling."

"Fine, fine, fine, hold on."

The gate slid to the right with a slight clatter and we stepped into a small courtyard set up with struggling palms.

An oak door studded with oversized nail-heads swung open. Jay Sterling was in the doorway before we reached it, hands on hips, glaring.

He was tall and husky, in his mid-fifties, with silver hair faded at the sides and clipped short on top. Eyeglasses dangled from a chain. He wore a charcoal sweatsuit that draped beautifully and might've been cashmere. Pale feet were bare, ending in manicured toenails. Same for his fingernails. A ruddy face featuring high-wattage true-blue eyes was shaved glossy. As we got closer, the aroma of a citrus-based cologne asserted itself.

"Total letdown," he said. "I was hoping you finally found him."

Milo said, "Him."

"The fucking asshole who killed her. What's your name by the way? And how about some I.D."

Milo flashed the badge. "I'm Lieutenant Sturgis, this is Alex Delaware."

"Lieutenant?" said Jay Sterling. "That mean Whitney's finally being taken seriously after two fucking years?"

"You feel she wasn't?"

"I don't feel, I know—you're Ventura County, right?"

"LAPD."

Sterling squinted. "Well that's good, I guess. The Ventura guys were clowns. But why LAPD? I don't get it."

"Could we come in?"

"Place is a mess but sure. Been here nine weeks, finally scored a cleaner but she's no great shakes."

Inside, the house was spacious with whitewashed walls, Mexican tile flooring, and high vaulted ceilings crossed by hand-hewn oak beams. The only visible furniture was a pair of brown Ultrasuede couches facing each other at a careless angle. Cardboard shipping crates stacked four-high filled an entire wall. Across the room, brightly colored plastic kids' vehicles took up a generous chunk of floor space.

Said cleaner was young and skittish as a colt, avoiding eye contact as she repetitively swept an empty corner.

Jay Sterling frowned. "There's nothing there, go upstairs and vacuum both bedrooms. Especially Jarrod's, he's allergic to dust mites."

Biting her lip, the woman hurried up a curving staircase.

Sterling said, "You let her, she does the same thing over and over, total OCD. Finding competent help's the bane of my existence. This one won't last, you blink the wrong way she gets all teary. Got her from my mom, her maid is this one's aunt. Great lady but this one's a ninny. C'mon, sit." He took the left-hand couch and we faced him.

Milo said, "Nine weeks."

"I know what it looks like, it should be set up by now. But most of my shit didn't arrive until two weeks ago and I've concentrated on getting set up for my kid and my office. The whole move took me by surprise, first they ship me to the Big Apple, then sorry, Jay, back to La La Land."

"What business are you in?"

"*Shmaates*," said Sterling. "That's Yiddish for the rag trade. I'm not. Of the Semitic persuasion. But that's what we call it. My bosses are Taiwanese and the company's Japanese." He rolled his eyes. "That's a whole different story."

I said, "The company moved you back suddenly."

"Yup," he said. "Big Apple's a mess but the vibe can be good if you know where to find it. I had a nice place on the Upper West Side and the bonus was my two older kids are in college there, NYU and the New School. Not that I saw them much, but still."

He threw up his hands and dropped them to his lap. "Got to admit, I have a bad feeling about the whole deal. The move. Supposedly they want me closer to Asia again but I'm pretty sure they're going to dump me. Fine with me, plenty of other fish in the sea, I might quit first."

He waved a hand. "You don't give a shit about any of this. You're here about Whitney. That's good. I hope."

His voice faltered. Water had collected around bright-blue irises. He swiped quickly.

I said, "You feel Ventura Sheriff's didn't take her case seriously?"

"I don't feel, I know. C'mon, a woman's murdered, who're you going to talk to? The love interest. Aka me. Yeah, I was in New York but you'd think they'd do more than a five-minute phone conversation."

"That was it?" said Milo.

"That was it," said Sterling. "No follow-up, either, and when I called them for updates they had nothing to say."

He crossed and uncrossed his legs. "In the beginning, I was totally freaked out. Whitney dying was bad enough but what's to say some fucking head-case isn't going to come after me? Plus I was *totally* freaked out about what my little guy went through. I assume you know about that."

"Jarrod left in the boat."

"Miracle he didn't drown or freeze to death." Sterling shivered. "I had nightmares, thinking about what could've been. Moment I was notified, I took the first red-eye out to L.A., drove straight to Camarillo, and liberated him from this Kiddie Jail where they put him. Took him to the pediatrician Whitney used, got the okay, and flew straight back to the B.A."

Milo said, "Kiddie Jail?"

"County facility," said Sterling. "Alleged safekeeping for toddlers. Jarr-o looked okay physically but he was totally blitzed emotionally and when he saw me he latched onto me like one of those monkeys you see in those nature shows my twins used to watch. For a long time he was quiet, spaced out, waking up in the middle of the night. Couple of years later, he's okay. I got him into a Montessori preschool not far from here, very highly rated. I had my mom check, she used to be a teacher and she gave the thumbs-up. So he seems okay. For the most part. But sitting in that fucking boat for what, an hour?"

He rolled his hands into fists. "If I knew who was behind it, I'd . . . not going to say what I'd do."

Milo said, "Horrible situation."

"Beyond horrible," said Sterling. "So why's LAPD all of a sudden involved?"

"Whitney's murder may be related to one of ours."

"How so?"

"Sorry, sir, can't get into that."

"Yeah, yeah, got it. But the truth is, I don't have any more to tell you than I would've with those clowns if they *had* talked to me. So sorry if you wasted your time."

I said, "Could you tell us about the relationship between Whitney and yourself?"

"Not relevant, but sure, why not?" said Sterling. Another attempt at a leg-cross. Another reversal. Finding it difficult to get comfortable. He swung his legs up and lay across the couch.

"Like at the shrink's office," he said. "Our *relationship*, such as it was, started when Whitney came to do the books at the company. They tell me a CPA's coming, I'm expecting some mumbly bald dude and *she* walks in. I assume you've seen pictures of her."

"We have."

"So you know. Gorgeous. Hotter than hot. But different from your typical L.A. woman. Like she didn't care about being hot. Later I found, she just didn't care what you thought of her, period. She was different from the get-go. All business, no flirty-flirt. But man, I was smitten. I'd been divorced for twelve years, first wife's the typical L.A. woman, probably running up a major-league Botox bill on the sucker she snagged. Not that Whitney needed Botox. She was young. Fresh. I just fell, man. I was hers, whatever she wanted."

He sniffed. Dried his eyes again. "First CPA thing visit, I held back. Second, I asked her out and she said yes. Like she'd been expecting it. I'm planning to take it slow, be a gentleman, she's clearly one of those who needs time. But she didn't. That night was . . . her idea, she ran the whole show. I assumed she was taking birth control, why wouldn't I? Turns out Jarrod was conceived that night. She didn't tell me for a couple of months. When she did obviously I was freaked out but happy. 'Cause I was really into her. And she seemed into me. Then she wasn't. Why? She wouldn't say. It was like a switch got flipped. You're on, Jay, now you're off. By then I realized how different she really was. Personality-wise. Not into expressing her feelings. Icy calm. If she wasn't so hot she'd be tagged as a nerd. Even with that, basically a loner."

"When you broke up," I said, "was she still pregnant?"

"Yup, seven months," said Sterling. "And we didn't break up. She dumped me. Just stopped taking my calls. I thought it might be hormones, once she had the kid it would change. But it didn't. She never wavered. That was Whitney, once she made up her mind, don't waste your breath."

"Was child support—"

"Not an issue, my friend. I'd been paying for the twins for twelve years, never missed a month, am still footing their tuition. So what was another kid? Problem was, Whitney started out letting me see Jarr-o, then she flipped another switch. Canceling appointments, changing her number and not giving it to me. I go by her apartment, no answer. I'm like what the fuck's going on? Is she isolating him or something? Then I started to think, she's different, maybe she wants Jarrod to be different in the same way."

"Not social."

"Totally asocial. I'm telling you, she had no friends, not a one. Said she hated her mother. Which I couldn't relate to, I love my mother. I've got tons of friends. I didn't want my son brought up to be a loner weirdo, so I called my attorney and he got me a good family lawyer and I sued to get joint custody, physical and legal—there's a difference. Then when I found out I was moving to the Big Apple, I amended it to full custody. Lawyer said I didn't have much chance but I could probably get joint and because Jarrod was so young, there could be mandated transportation."

He swung back to a sitting position. "It went on for nearly two years. And that's where it stood when it happened. See what I mean about sending in the clowns?"

Milo said, "Not exactly."

"C'mon," said Jay Sterling. "Custody battle, one party gets mysteriously killed and the other ends up with the kid? You wouldn't suspect me? You'd be happy with a five-minute phone call and no follow-up?" He shook his head. "You say yes, please leave."

"You wanted to be investigated thoroughly."

"It's not a matter of that. Lieutenant." As if unsure the title was merited. "I had nothing to do with it but at least try, okay? Then I know you're going to be trying every other thing."

"Makes sense," said Milo. "So you're okay with letting us examine your financial records."

"Don't you need a court order or something for that?"

"Not if you voluntarily grant permission." Milo tapped his attaché case. "We could write up a release, here and now."

"Financial records," said Sterling, shifting his body back and forth. "What exactly are we talking about?"

"Bank and brokerage accounts, anything else that might produce interesting withdrawals."

"To pay someone to shoot my girlfriend? I'm that kind of murderous fuckhead, I'm going to leave a trail?"

Milo smiled. "How would you go about it, then? Speaking theoretically."

"I don't know," said Sterling. "Because I've never hired anyone to shoot anyone, including Whitney. But sure, you want to look at my finances, go right ahead. Give me your form and I'll sign it right now."

Snapping open the case, Milo drew out a sheet of paper and used the hard top as a writing surface. A few minutes later, he was up on his feet and handing the sheet to Sterling.

Sterling lifted his glasses, perched them on his nose, and read. "This is it? No official form?"

"No need to get complicated, sir."

"You're right about that, Lieutenant." No doubt about the title now. Jay Sterling was grinning. "I think I could possibly like you. I think if anyone can figure out who the fuck shot Whitney it could possibly be you."

He scrawled, held out the paper. "Signed and dated, do your thing."

Milo said, "Please list all your accounts at the bottom."

"It's not like there's a collection of them," said Sterling. "Got a checking at Chase and a brokerage dealie at Morgan Stanley."

"Please supply the account numbers."

"You think I know those by heart? Hold on." He stood, grimaced in pain, muttered, "Bursitis," and went up the stairs, gripping the banister. Several minutes passed, during which the sound of Sterling's deep voice filtered down. Lecturing about the fine points of vacuuming.

He returned with a pale-blue Post-it that he handed to Milo along with the impromptu release.

"Ms. OCD, found her doing the same thing up there. Dusting one spot over and over."

Milo said, "Thanks, sir," and placed the papers back in the attaché case.

"That briefcase thingie of yours," said Sterling. "Haven't seen one of those since I was in junior high. You're old-school, huh?"

"Whatever works, sir."

"Sir. *That's* old-school. I called my friends' dads 'sir.' My kids' friends call me Jay."

I said, "Who do you think might've murdered Whitney?"

Sterling's head drew back. "Back to business? Good idea, I'm running my mouth. No idea. Not a clue."

"Was there a love interest before you? Someone who could've been jealous?"

"Same answer," said Sterling.

"No knowledge at all."

"None. Like I said, Whitney never talked about her past. About herself, period. Maybe I'm not getting it across: She was *different.* Okay, weird. Gorgeous and hot but icy when she wasn't having sex. Most girls after they do it, they want some affection, right? Whitney? She'd go pee and not want to talk. When I was mad at her I'd think, 'You are strangely wired, girl.' But I never said it." He sighed. "Now I'm glad I didn't."

I said, "You can't think of anyone who might've resented her."

"Not saying there wasn't anyone," said Jay Sterling. "Just that I don't know about them. That's your job. Finding out. Hope you do. Want to one day be able to tell my little man Jarr-o a story with some kind of ending."

24

We walked away from Sterling's house with Milo shaking his head and studying the sidewalk.

I said, "Not what we expected."

"He's either a total psychopath daring me to investigate him or a sincere loudmouth. I'll get on those accounts but you know what it's gonna accomplish."

"Nothing to hide, nothing to learn."

In the unmarked, he said, "What's your take on him?"

"My guess would be sincere."

He started up the engine, looked back, pulled onto San Vicente, and U-turned around the median after a woman walking two Frenchies had passed.

"Not as cute as Blanche. Not even close."

"When I see her, I'll pass that along."

A couple of miles later, he said: "Yeah, I'd also guess Sterling was being righteous. Open-book kinda guy, loves to hear himself talk. Guess that wouldn't go over well with Whitney."

"Despite that," I said, "she had a child with him."

"And according to Sterling, she planned it. What, she saw him as good breeding stock?"

"Maybe she'd observed him with his other kids and thought he was good dad material in the short run."

"Not a candidate for romance, just good sperm? If so, she was pretty calculating. Interesting woman, our Whitney. In any event, if Sterling's clean, who the hell killed her? Or paid to have it done?"

I said, "She embraced secrecy. That could've simply been her temperament. But she might have closed up because something in her past was too dark to share. Abuse, a stalker."

"Problem is how do I find out? Most cases I hear plenty from friends and family but Donna Batchelor's all the family Whitney had and we saw how little she knows. And what she told us syncs with what Sterling and Whitney's boss said: no pals."

I said, "You could try looking into conflict at any previous jobs. A relationship that went bad. Call her boss and find out where she came to them from. Also, the one personal thing Whitney did divulge to Sterling was that she hated her mother. That could've been because Donna was hard to get along with. But Donna was married twice so Whitney's resentment could've been due to some issue with her stepfather."

"Mr. Batchelor," he said. "The old blended-family thing. Donna's not gonna admit any problems and he's dead."

"There could be stepsibs. Another potential powder keg."

"True," he said. "Why the hell didn't I think of that? You don't mind if I use your computer."

Not a question, a statement. I chose to take it as a compliment.

I sat on my battered leather couch while he hunched at my desk and typed hard enough to make the keyboard rattle.

Step one was learning the full name of Donna Batchelor's second husband. Easily accessed by scanning marriage records.

Donna Killeen had been wed fourteen years ago to Rolf Edward Batchelor Jr. Civil ceremony in the chambers of a Superior Court justice named Leon McCarry.

Milo said, "I knew McCarry. All business, not the type to get cel-
ebratory. Someone had an in."

He ran a search on Batchelor. Thirty-five years older than his bride;
well into old age but still working. Attorney and certified public accountant, office address on Wilshire and Rimpau in Hancock Park.
Home address not far from there, on Las Palmas Avenue.

He said, "I had McCarry sign a warrant at home once. He lived
the next block over, on June. There's the in."

Step two was a dive into county property tax rolls. The newlyweds
had lived at the groom's place for eight years, after which Donna
Batchelor was assessed at the West Hills address.

Milo said, "Downsizing."

The chronology narrowed the time frame for step three, and within
seconds, he'd pulled up a coroner's summary listing the manner of Rolf
Edward Batchelor Jr.'s death as natural causes (*adenocarcinoma of the
prostate*).

Time for the inevitable shift to the public arena. Keywording *rolf
edward batchelor obituary* yielded a tribute published by Legacy.com, a
subsidiary of Forest Lawn Memorial Park.

First came the deceased's educational achievements. Cum laude
graduation from UC Berkeley, law degree from UC Hastings, MBA
from USC business school, CPA certification a year later. Next came a
brief list of Rolf Batchelor Jr.'s predictably respectable civic activities.

At the bottom: the crux.

*Predeceased by loving wife Helen, survived by loving wife,
Donna, and son Rolf III.*

"Not an everyday moniker," said Milo, assaulting the keys. "Okay,
here we go, Portland, Oregon . . . oral surgeon . . . here's his picture."

The faculty headshot of Rolf Batchelor, D.D.S., M.D., supplied
by Oregon Health and Science University, featured a full-faced, ruddy,
apple-cheeked man in his forties with a bushy rust-and-silver beard

and sparse gray hair drawn back into a ponytail that dangled over his shoulder. Black T-shirt under a white coat. Broad smile.

Associate professor, specialty: maxillofacial reconstruction with a focus on accident and burn victims. Multiple side trips to Colombia where he'd worked on the shattered visages of cartel victims.

Milo called the listed number. A receptionist said, "I think he's in, one moment, please."

Twenty seconds later a soft, slightly nasal voice said, "This is Rolf Batchelor. Police? Something came up with my sister?"

Milo introduced himself and gave a capsule explanation.

Batchelor said, "Wow, after all this time. I kept waiting for someone to call me and when they didn't, figured it wasn't going to happen. I thought of contacting the police but didn't have anything to offer. The whole thing was so incredibly shocking. Not only poor Whitney but Jarrod floating around in a boat."

"How'd you learn about it?"

"From Donna. Whitney's mom. She was so agitated I could barely make out what she was saying. When I finally understood, I couldn't believe what I was hearing. It took me a long time to wrap my head around it."

"You knew Jarrod."

"No, never met him, but any child going through something like that? Horrible. So why are you calling now, Lieutenant—was it Stargill?"

"Sturgis."

"Like the biker thing. I went once. So what's come up with regard to my sister?"

"You viewed her as that."

"You're surprised because we were steps? Well, yeah, I did. I welcomed having a sib, being an only for so long."

"You were close."

A beat. "We got along really well but when our parents married I was already in med school up here and Whitney was like . . . eight, nine? So with my being away, we didn't see each other very often. But the times I was home, we had fun. Whitney was a super-bright kid, we used to play two-handed bridge, chess, do puzzles, math games."

I'd been scrawling notes, showed one to Milo.

He said, "What was Whitney like as a person?"

"Like I said, super-smart, but also super-shy. I used to feel protective of her. Because of her being so quiet and to herself. Donna seemed to think there was something wrong with that, she kept prodding Whitney to quote 'come out of your shell, you're not a hermit crab.' I assume you've met Donna."

"We have."

"Not the most . . . pliable person. How's she doing? Has she remarried?"

"No."

"That surprises me," said Batchelor. "She seemed to need having someone to talk to. My dad was perfect for her, a great listener."

Another note.

Milo said, "Good marriage?"

"Oh yes," said Batchelor. "Dad had been torn up by my mom's death and Donna brought him out socially. She was also much younger and I guess today you'd call her arm candy."

He chuckled. "Dad liked making an appearance."

"Sounds like you haven't had much contact with Donna."

"Not since my dad's funeral. She was invited to our wedding but didn't make it. So yeah, it had been a while when she called to tell me about Whitney. Then she emailed me about Whitney's funeral and I attended."

"You were close to Whitney," said Milo. "Donna, not so much?"

"Well," said Rolf Batchelor, "to be honest, Donna and I didn't mesh super-easily. It's not that we had conflict but some people you just don't . . . the main thing is Donna was good to Dad. Nor did she ever try to put a wedge between Dad and myself, nothing like that. She and I just didn't . . . mesh is the best term for it. But Whitney, she always seemed so vulnerable. Being shy and to herself."

"Can you think of anyone who'd want to hurt her?"

"From what Donna told me Jarrod's father sounds like a pretty good bet. I assume you know about the custody battle."

"We do, Doctor."

"I mean that would seem to be a logical point of departure, no?" said Batchelor. "As far as anyone else, I have no idea."

"What about Whitney's former boyfriends."

"Hmm," said Rolf Batchelor. "Can't say I'm aware of any. Then again, when Whitney was of dating age, I was here working and doing a lot of travel."

"When's the last time you and Whitney spoke?"

"Probably . . . a couple of years before she died? She emailed me Jarrod's birth announcement, I emailed her back and sent her a baby gift. Monogrammed blanket, my wife picked it out. Whitney called to thank me and we chatted but not for very long. Whitney wasn't one for small talk."

"We've heard she wasn't one for talk, period."

"I suppose you could say that, Lieutenant. But it really does take all types."

"Agreed, sir. We're just trying to find out who might've resented her."

"So you've cleared Jarrod's father."

"It's an ongoing investigation. What did Whitney tell you about Jarrod's father?"

"Nothing," said Rolf Batchelor. "The only reason I know about him is through Donna. I know this probably sounds strange, my considering Whitney my sister but having so little contact with her. Part of that was me. Living my own life, working. But part of it was Whitney's choice."

"She refused contact?"

"Like you said, she wasn't one for conversation. I don't want to stigmatize her and I'm sure not qualified to get psychological, but you do take some psychiatry in med school and I remember coming across this term and thinking that sounds like Whitney."

"What term was that, Doctor?"

"Schizoid personality type," said Batchelor. "It sounds worse than it is. Not schizophrenic or anything like that. And maybe it's just some jargon label the shrinks thought up for really shy people. Like I said, it takes all types. Silicon Valley's full of people like Whitney and they're changing the world."

His voice had risen. Armor-plated by defensiveness.

Milo said nothing.

Batchelor said, "Do I wish we could've stayed in touch more? Very much so. I'm not blaming it on Whitney, I had my own life. . . . Things get away from you."

Lowered volume. Faltering. Cracks in the armor.

"They sure do, Doctor. So no one you can think of who'd resent Whitney?"

"I'm afraid not."

"Okay, thanks. If you don't mind, I'd like to run some names by you. Please tell me if they mean anything to you."

"Sure."

"Gerald Boykins."

"Nope."

"Jamarcus Parmenter."

"Nope."

"Paul O'Brien."

"I've got a colleague by that name. Emeritus professor of endodontics. He's like eighty-eight years old so I'm assuming he's not who you're referring to."

"No, sir. One more: Marissa French."

"Nope, never heard of her. Who are all these people?"

"Their names have come up, sir."

"Not Whitney's friends?"

"No, sir."

"Too bad," said Rolf Batchelor. "I was hoping she'd finally found some."

25

Milo pushed away from my desk.

"Dr. Compassionate. Think he's too good to be true?"

"You do?"

"Nothing he said twanged my antenna but his dad's estate had to be substantial so one less heir would be nice."

"His dad died years ago."

"Maybe there's been a money battle making its way through the system. What if it dragged on and Rolf Three lost patience."

"Donna didn't mention anything like that and she's not the type to gloss over a fight with anyone, let alone a stepson. More than that, if eliminating heirs was the goal, she'd be in jeopardy herself and once Whitney was murdered, I can't see her overlooking the threat."

"Unless she fixated on Sterling—please don't say it."

"What?"

"Anything's possible. My job, that's terrifying."

He wheeled around in my chair for a few semicircles. Came to a quick stop, looked up his call history, and punched buttons.

Three rings later, Donna Batchelor said, "What now, Lieutenant?"

"We just spoke to Dr. Batchelor."

"R-Three? How's he doing?"

"He seems well, ma'am. He told us he thought of himself as Whitney's brother—"

"Why wouldn't he? Blood doesn't matter, relationships do, and theirs was great. Three wasn't around much but when he visited he was great with Whitney and she adored him."

"That's consistent with his description."

"Why wouldn't it be?" she said. "And why are you wasting your time with Three or anyone else when I told you where to look. That *bastard*."

"We're taking that seriously, ma'am, but we wouldn't be doing our job if we didn't explore all possibilities."

"Oh boy," said Donna Batchelor. "Can't stop you from meandering but in the end you'll see I'm right. Besides that, what could you expect to get from talking to Three?"

"You may find the question ridiculous, ma'am, but I need to ask: Was there any sort of conflict related to Mr. Batchelor's estate?"

Donna Batchelor's laughter had the soothing effect of ball bearings in a metal bowl.

"No-o," she said. "And there wasn't much of an estate. R-Two was a lovely man who'd inherited money and despite being a great CPA for other people, he didn't care much for his own finances. With both of us working, we always had what we needed and never tapped into a blind trust set up by his grandfather. When Rolf passed we found out the trust had been funded with stupid stuff that didn't appreciate much and that taxes had sapped most of that. So the *estate* amounted to a house in Hancock Park that was falling down and sold for a couple of mil, plus a few hundred thousand in miscellaneous assets. I split the proceeds down the middle with Three per the terms of the will. He's like his dad, couldn't give a rap about money, so it wasn't life changing for either of us. I had my own investments for the long term and used my half to get the hell out of L.A. and buy my current place. Got it?"

"You've been extremely specific, ma'am."

"Why wouldn't I be?" said Donna Batchelor. "And *specifically*, you should be looking at that bastard. Even if it means flying back to New York. But don't imagine the bureaucracy you work for would ever think of funding that."

Click.

Milo shook his head. "Why squabble over a measly two mil? Okay, looks like Dr. Rolf's off the table. And despite what La Donna thinks about Sterling, I'm not feeling him, either."

He yanked open the top drawer of my desk, drew out a pad of Post-its, peeled one and waved it.

"Know what this is?"

"Square One."

He sighed. "Why do I bother?"

He'd been gone for ten minutes when I thought of something. But it didn't solve any of his immediate problems so I put it aside.

Time to put all of it aside. I made coffee and brought it out to Robin.

Milo called just after seven p.m.

"Moe came up with a coupla unsolved .308 shootings but nothing that sounds similar— probably hunting accidents and none are within a thousand miles of here. Adding to that joy, no more sightings of creepy Mr. Hoodie skulking around Hollywood but Petra pulled up thirty-nine parking tickets from that night. Eight of the drivers have serious criminal records—how does that make you feel about tooling around our city? She'll follow up on all of them. Raul got no sightings from any parking lot attendant, but the morning guy at a place on the east end of Hollywood that closes at ten came to work the following morning and found the chain cut."

I said, "Our boy carries wire cutters along with his rifle?"

"Yeah, at first glance it does feel professional. Especially because that lot has no cameras and is out of the way. But on second thought, maybe not so much because it was needlessly risky. What if someone came by and found the damage and a car parked illegally? He gets towed and I.D.'d."

"Maybe whoever did it knew it was safe because he's familiar with that lot."

"Back to the local thing."

"If the chain-cutter's our shooter, it raises the probability of him being from that area. Where's the lot?"

"East Hollywood."

"Makes sense," I said. "Walking from the east end to O'Brien's place would be tough if you're toting tools. Alternatively, he used to live there but no longer does."

"Or the chain-cutter's just a low-impulse scrote wanting free parking. Next item: Boykins's finances. Slooow ride, only thing I've accessed so far is a seven-figure brokerage account with no withdrawals at all. Looks like he's one of those buy-and-hold guys. Whatever he's doing, it's working, kiddo. If moolah's the goal, gangsta to promoter's the way to go and we are both in the wrong businesses. What else . . . oh yeah, on the off chance, I got one of our technically gifted officers to check out the dark web for supposed contract killers. No word back, so far. And that's the day's wrap-up, sports fans."

His bringing up Boykins's accounts reminded me of what I'd put aside.

I said, "Don't want to complicate your life but if we're right about Parmenter threatening Keisha as the motive, she's got two parents."

"Mrs. B's involved?"

"Affluent people often have individual accounts."

"Hmm, sure why not, let's see if we can take a look at Mrs. B. Don't even know her name. Have a nice evening."

"You, too."

"Rick's on-call so I'm staying at the office to eat cold pizza and think. For what that's worth."

26

Anice evening sounded like a great idea. I focused on that, placing the rifle murders in one mental box and everything else in another.

I've always been pretty good at compartmentalizing. A useful strategy when you're the object of child abuse, live by the fruits of your own labor, spend years treating pediatric cancer patients, and want to segregate the horror you see at crime scenes from the rest of your life. And your lover. And your dog.

Robin, Blanche, and I enjoyed dinner and a few mindless streamed TV shows before Blanche was escorted to her crate and rewarded with a treat and we returned to the bedroom making the night even more pleasant.

I slept well initially. I usually do. But this time it only lasted until three a.m., an hour hospitable to insomnia and random thoughts. But struggling to fall back asleep wasn't my problem. I had *intentions*.

Throwing on a robe, I padded out of the bedroom and walked up the hall to my office.

I use a filter to screen blue light from my computer monitor but whatever illumination remained kicked me fully alert.

Tap, tap, tap as I began the search for *gerald boykins wife*.

Not an elusive goal. Kiki Boykins wasn't shy.

Blond, hazel-eyed, with Marilyn Monroe lips and hips. Ten years younger than her husband, she'd been born KarenAnne Amundsen in Palo Alto, the only child of a custodian at Stanford and a convenience store manager.

Early years as a tomboy shifted radically in the face of puberty. A few local beauty contest wins followed by a move to L.A. where she'd modeled swimsuits, lingerie, and yoga wear, then danced in music videos, attracting the attention of Jamal B.

The couple had been wed two decades ago in Las Vegas, a bond that had apparently endured free of rumor or other social blemish.

One child, Keisha, born seventeen years ago.

The devoted care Kiki Boykins gave her husband following his stroke was noted on several entertainment sites. It's easy to be cynical when you're dealing with that world, and money can affect coverage. But those posing as entertainment journalists mainline dirt and the Boykinses' avoidance of even a hint of tarnish suggested earned respectability.

Kiki's other love, after her family, was travel.

So grateful and excited to see the world God has created for all of us!!!

Pages of photographic gratitude filled her platform.

In a gondola on the Grand Canal in Venice; sitting atop an elaborately saddled elephant in Sri Lanka; pointing to the entrance of the Louvre in Paris; at the Western Wall in Jerusalem inserting a prayer message (*praying for healing for G, MSD, and everyone else*) between the crevices of ancient stones.

Who was MSD? Nothing came to mind and I plowed on.

What wasn't given over to geography was devoted to Keisha. And that answered the question.

My sparkling diamond!

Straight A's again!!!!! She didn't get it from me. LOL.

I didn't recall any mutual admiration on the girl's pages but checked.

No mention of Kiki or Gerald.

Mom worshipping daughter, daughter totally ignoring her parents.

Adolescence 101.

I sat back and thought about Kiki's devotion. Worship can lead to more than prayer. A mama lion springing when her cub was threatened.

Logging off, I returned to the bedroom and managed to get back in bed without evoking more than a sweet purr from Robin.

I kissed her hair and fell back asleep quickly.

The following morning was taken up by patients. It was twelve thirty when I checked for messages. Milo had called me at eleven.

He answered his office phone. "Nothing iffy in Mrs. Boykins's past."

I said, "On the surface."

"What does that mean?"

I described Kiki Boykins's posts.

He said, "She loves her kid. So what?"

"Her only child with a high IQ, suffering from some sort of illness that keeps her home? It was serious enough for her to offer a prayer note when she was in Israel. Maybe that's why she went in the first place. We're talking a vulnerable young girl who Parmenter threatened not very subtly. The other thing is, Kiki travels a lot, which could expand her opportunity to find a skilled shooter."

Silence.

I said, "You think I'm making too much of it."

"I'm thinking what Nguyen would say if I asked for a warrant based on someone being a good parent. Where else does Kiki do all this travel?"

I recited a few locales.

He said, "Globe-trotting like a proper rich woman. Nice spas and boutiques and she works in a meeting with some International Man of Intrigue? Forget the local hypothesis?"

"Fine," I said, "forget double-oh seven but the threat posed by Parmenter to Keisha was still real."

"Only child . . . so maybe Mama—or she *and* Daddy—are into crime prevention. Which is what I've been saying from the beginning. Have to tell you, can't say I'd blame them, those lyrics were *ugly.* But it still doesn't change the warrant situation, Alex. It was all I could do to get an okay on Boykins's money paper and that was mostly based on his criminal record. And it's still not yielding anything. So where the hell do I take it?"

I had no answer for that and kept silent.

He said, "I was afraid you'd say that."

CHAPTER

27

Robin was busy in her shop but my workday had ended. Nothing like free time to make you antsy.

I tried to tolerate the quiet, failed, left the house and got into the Seville.

The drive from the Glen into the flats of Beverly Hills was smooth and pretty. At North Bedford Drive, I hooked a right off Sunset and cruised two and a half blocks to Gerald and Kiki Boykins's impeccable Tudor.

As before, the gates were closed. Unlike before, Walt Swanson's orange Camaro was gone, replaced by a black Mustang GT. And a different guard.

Swanson had preferred sitting in his car. This guy had positioned himself in front of the house's main door, face impassive, arms folded across his chest. Pink face but everything else black. Black suit, black shirt, black shoes, black crew cut, clipped black beard, black sunglasses.

Bigger than Swanson. Arms as thick as thighs. A defensive-tackle-sized column of muscle, bone, and hard suet. If he cared about my slow drive-by, he didn't show it.

Our easy entry to the house the first time had angered Boykins. Time for an upgrade.

The Swede's useless, give me someone scary.

I continued a block, reversed, and returned, wondering if that would capture the new guard's attention. Thought I caught the merest movement of a face, florid and compressed as a canned ham.

By the time I risked a third pass, the guard had moved and stood facing the house's open door talking to someone.

Voluptuous, good-looking blond woman in black velvet sweats, standing just outside the doorway.

As Kiki Boykins spoke, Ham listened attentively. Short conversation, business-like, no evidence of emotion or urgency. Neither of them noticed me and as she walked back inside, he began to turn back to the gate and I drove off.

I kept going to Lomitas Avenue, drove to Whittier Drive, the westernmost street in the flats, and hooked north. Caught a red light at Sunset and used the time to wonder.

Had there been a reason other than a client complaint for Walt Swanson's departure?

What if Swanson had taken on an after-hours assignment and once Milo and I showed up asking questions, needed to disconnect from his client?

No need to travel to find help for a certain type of problem. Not with an ex-cop attached to your household.

Back to keeping it local.

The longer I contemplated, the more what-ifs piled up.

Kiki Boykins—or her husband, or the two of them in concert—paying Walt Swanson to deal with the problem Jamarcus Parmenter had become.

That job accomplished cleanly, no problems for nearly two years, use the same guy for Paul O'Brien.

For the same reason as Parmenter: protecting Keisha.

I'd resisted Milo's assumption that Boykins had contracted O'Brien's death but now I wondered. There was no indication O'Brien had ever gotten on Gerald Boykins's bad side. Yet. But O'Brien had worked for Boykins and he had a penchant for poor impulse control when it came to women. Meaning ample opportunity for Boykins to bristle at something O'Brien had done. After that, sniffing out O'Brien's predatory nature and realizing he'd hired the wrong guy to guard the door—especially with Keisha around—he'd taken action.

My original thoughts about the girl returned: a bright only child with some sort of health issue could easily kick up the protectiveness level, meaning no need for O'Brien to have actually made a move on the teenager. An errant glance, a smart remark, the wrong kind of wink might've been enough.

Or just Keisha complaining about the creepy security dude.

Time to take action: *Got a second, Walt?*

The light turned green, I turned left on Sunset and thought about the scenario most of the way home. Nothing illogical about it and an ex-cop hit man could explain the professionalism of the kills. But there wasn't a single fact to back any of it up and I needed to be careful not to jump on it out of self-interest.

And maybe I was over-eager because the Boykinses contracting a hit on O'Brien eliminated a link to Vicki Saucedo and conveniently got me off the hook for holding back info.

Then my thoughts shifted to a young woman and a toddler in a boat. To Jay Sterling somehow linking up with Walt Swanson and hiring him to clean up his custody mess so he could take Jarrod to New York.

Sterling had come across likable and horrified by Whitney's death, but he was a salesman, expert at promoting himself. So maybe I'd been snowed.

But there was a problem with that. A possessive father allowing his son to witness the murder of his mother then drift in a rowboat seemed unlikely.

A whole different level of cold than the elimination of Parmenter and O'Brien. Was Walter Swanson cruel enough to pick off a mother in front of her child?

Time to learn more about the man in the orange Camaro.

Back at my desk I drank coffee and ran a search. Futile; Swanson had no online presence.

That could be explained by a middle-aged guy not enamored of the cyber-world. Or did Swanson have a good reason to maintain a non-profile?

Over the years, I'd learned about several sites on the alleged dark web and tried them.

Lots of ominous logos and sinister allusions but a big zero. Everything boiled down to blather and cons and piling up clicks.

The amateur route wouldn't work. I called the pro.

Milo listened and said, "Him. Why?"

"Cops have been known to use .308s."

"On the other hand, he could just have been fired."

"Absolutely."

"Hmm. Lemme see what I can find out."

Forty minutes later, he was back in touch.

"Guy worked Venice for twenty years, just like he told us. Twenty-one, to be exact. Started out on patrol then, ten years in, earned himself a motorcycle gig working Traffic near the beach. Did that until six years ago when he had an accident and hurt his back. Instead of quitting, he got himself transferred to a desk. Maybe because he liked being on the job. Or he wanted to stretch it out to get max pension plus disability."

I said, "Add private security to all that and he's got a good thing going money-wise. Where does he live?"

"Not some pricey place if that's what you're getting at. Cop Central, Simi Valley. Ran a Google Maps on his address and if he's raking it in, he's not spending it conspicuously. Your basic box. Camera even caught the Camaro in the driveway. Next to a minivan, so maybe he's a family guy trying to pay bills."

"Any excessive force complaints?"

"Nope, spotless record. Including a couple of commendations for helping accident victims. I called the private outfit—Pacific Security—and asked for him, got told he no longer worked there, they had no idea where he'd gone. So the firing thing is feeling likely. Can't rule anything out but I don't see a way—or a reason—to do a deep dig on him. But thanks and keep thinking."

"Even if it hurts?"

He laughed. "Long as I have you, here's the current situation. Or lack thereof. Petra checked out the eight serious criminals who got parking tickets and they're all alibied, no other sightings of Hoodie Man have surfaced, and Raul's visits to every damn pay lot fizzled to nada. Given all the less-than-zero, I'm gonna opt for the classic coping mechanism."

"Meditation?"

"A meeting. Can you make it tomorrow around noon?"

CHAPTER

28

The following morning I was up early enough to have breakfast with Robin, walk Blanche, feed the fish, take a run,
shower and dress, and be out of the house by ten after nine. That hour
meant likely commuter traffic on the 405 North, but Waze and its
cousins all agreed that the freeways remained the best way to get to
Simi Valley.

Turned out pessimism wasn't justified. The alleged fifty-minute
ride boiled down to forty-two as I zipped north, switched to the 118
West, and drove the longer arm of the trip toward Walt Swanson's address.

The sun was avid, evoking patches of glare where tree-shade failed
to intervene. Leading to a curious mottling that gave the road an odd
piebald look.

No street trees, these were well-established sycamore, eucalyptus,
and liquidambar trees planted by homeowners on their own sod, trying to soften the character of tracts jerry-built after World War II.

I'd pulled up a photo of Swanson's property last night but that
didn't help much because most of the houses were aspiring ranchitos
like his.

Much of the northern valley shared by L.A. and Ventura counties is like that, mile after mile of hasty construction undertaken in the fifties to accommodate the flood of aerospace workers migrating to SoCal. Back when the region had been about more than movies.

Later decades witnessed an influx of retired military plus cops and firefighters lured by the low-cost, open-space atmosphere and the distance, actual and emotional, from the mean streets they worked every day.

Back when I was in grad school, one of my classmates had rotated through a Simi clinic and returned sneering.

"Cops. Slimy Valley."

I'd looked at her in surprise.

"What?" she said.

"Nothing."

"Figures," she said, with the kind of florid confidence that results when it's based on nothing.

"What does?"

"You're from the boonies? Indiana or something."

"Missouri."

"Same difference. All those places are fucking intolerant."

No need to search for the address, the orange Camaro was a beacon. I continued past it, covered the rest of the block, reversed, found a view-spot several properties west, and took in details.

Walter F. Swanson's gravel-roofed and spray-stuccoed pale-pink house sat primly behind a tiny but brilliantly green lawn sharing frontage with a two-vehicle cement pad. Multicolored impatiens and thriving sago palms nudged the façade. No sign of the minivan.

Milo was right: If Walt Swanson was raking in illicit cash, he wasn't spending it for all to see.

On the other hand, the web had estimated the current value of the twelve-hundred-sixty-seven-square-foot "ranchito" at nearly nine hundred thousand.

Ah, Southern California.

Toss in a full pension, disability payments, and some private free-lancing and Swanson would be primed for a move to a normal real estate market—Idaho, the dry side of Washington—where he could live like a land baron.

I chewed on that for a few seconds, knew I was filling mental space with empty conjecture.

Time to get out of here. Just as I reached for the ignition key, a vehicle approached from the east, driving slowly.

Narrow and tall, small tires, silver paint, Ford logo on a black grille.

The minivan turned into Walt Swanson's driveway and parked next to the Camaro.

Swanson exited. No black suit or muscle shirt or trendy eyewear. Gone also was the swagger the ex-cop had shown at the Boykinses' residence. Today's baggy brown T-shirt, wrinkled khaki shorts, and sandals made him look smaller.

Today he trudged and had conceded to a slight hunch.

He walked to the passenger side of the van, took several minutes to emerge.

Guiding a woman. Not chivalry, she needed it.

Smallish, wearing a beret from which ginger curls escaped, border-line emaciated, with that unmistakable pallor. Every step she took was labored but she smiled at Swanson as they proceeded slowly and he smiled back.

When the two of them finally made it to the front door, he kissed her cheek then patted it gently.

Holding on to her, he unlocked the door and helped her in.

She'd never stopped smiling.

I was just about to leave when Swanson reappeared and returned to the rear of the van, this time exiting with three supermarket shopping bags that he brought into the house.

Then nothing. For five minutes, ten, fifteen.

I escaped.

Seeing people in new contexts can be educational and what I'd seen moved me in that direction. But I resisted total conversion to the innocence of Walt Swanson despite his loving care of the woman I assumed to be his wife.

Easy enough to be charitable, peg him as a devoted husband and leave it at that.

But entering Milo's world had long disrupted conventional thinking and I found myself wondering about the financial and emotional cost of caring for a loved one with health issues. The possibility that had led to criminal freelancing.

On the other hand: *Slimy Valley.*

An acrid, vicious appraisal, tossed out by someone training to be a therapist. Last I'd heard the appraiser was treating movie stars and trying to write a book.

None of which was relevant to the guilt or innocence of Walt Swanson.

I reached Milo while waiting to get on the 118 on-ramp and told him about my drive-by.

He said, "Talk about beyond the call of duty. Gracias. Yeah, a sick wife could exert financial pressure. Or like you said, he's just a devoted husband. See any connection to Boykins being in a wheelchair? And, now that I think about it, to Keisha being sick. Maybe some kind of rapport between them?"

"Interesting question," I said.

"You come up with an answer, let me know. Bottom line: Any gut feeling either way about Swanson?"

"Nope."

"Honesty," he said. "Don't get to deal with that often. Okay, see you soon."

29

I walked into the meeting a few minutes late.

Same room, same whiteboards, different atmosphere.

The first time the aura had been anxiety tempered by the excitement of taking on a new case. Today the room felt deprived of air and the detectives looked dejected.

That included Buck Buxby, who looked surprised to be there. Probably invited as a courtesy. Or Milo hoping some old memory from the Parmenter case might surface.

Two long tables were occupied by him, Alicia, Moe, Petra, and Raul. Two empty seats: mine and Sean Binchy's.

Milo looked at his Timex. Made a call. "Voicemail. Anyone seen Sean?"

Alicia said, "Not since yesterday."

Moe Reed nodded assent.

Buck Buxby said, "Hey, maybe he solved the whole darn thing and is writing his report."

The attempt at humor was met by sad smiles. Buxby flushed and looked down at the table.

Milo said, "Your mouth to God's ears, Buck." Throwing the old D a lifeline. He makes cracks about me never taking off my therapist hat but he sells himself short in that department.

Another glance at his watch. "Okay, let's start. Obviously, I'd love to report progress but we'll have to settle for pooling data. Petra?"

She said, "We pulled thirty-nine traffic tickets—mostly parking— within a mile of O'Brien's murder scene that night. Eight offenders had felony records. I've spent the last few days tracing each of them and conducting face-to-faces. Unfortunately they could all account for their whereabouts during the murder."

Buxby said, "Watching a Disney show at the Pantages?"

Petra said, "Actually one of them was, Buck, with two grandkids. Former armed robber turned gramps. My best candidate, a man-slaughter parolee, was getting soused at Café Berlin and his presence is backed up by CCTV. The same goes for the remaining seven. That leaves me with thirty-one citizens I'll need to talk to. Now that Raul's free, we'll split that lovely task."

Raul said, "I'm free because all the pay parking lot stuff zeroed out, the only exception being one place where the chain was cut. But of course, there's no surveillance there so no idea what that means. I did go back and search for anything that might be evidentiary. Unfortu-nately, the area was cleaned and cleared."

Alicia said, "Sympathies, guys. What about Mr. Hoodie?"

"One additional sighting," said Raul. "The informant would be in a position to actually observe something—he sleeps in several alleys pretty close to the crime scene. But he's also homeless and conspicu-ously psychotic."

I said, "Despite that, did he have any details to add?"

"Sorry, Doc, no. Just a pedestrian in a hoodie, no idea if he was carrying anything."

Petra said, "On the one hand, there's consistency to the sightings. On the other, there's no shortage of guys in hoodies in Hollywood after dark. We also went over O'Brien's apartment for the second time and found a big stash of GHB under his bed that we missed. So doping and exploiting women was a thing for him. Which is backed up by Milo's interview of his former roommate."

Milo summed up the talk with Martin Kehoe.

Moe said, "Other victims, other potential avengers."

Petra said, "Unfortunately. They've got to be out there but we haven't found them and despite Marissa's death being on social media, there's been no tide of me-too."

Alicia frowned. "Same old story, too ashamed to come forward."

Petra nodded. "No doubt. But even if victims do surface, someone who paid to have O'Brien murdered isn't going to be one of them."

Milo had listened to all that without a glance at me.

By the way, Alex knows of another victim.

Friendship.

He returned his attention to the boards. "Which brings us back to the one decent suspect we do have. A gentleman who knew both Parmenter and O'Brien."

He tapped Gerald Boykins's photo. Did the same to an image that had been added next to it. Kiki Boykins in a smiling party shot taken from her Instagram.

"His wife?" said Moe.

"Yup, calls herself Kiki."

"Why're you considering her now, L.T.?"

Milo tapped a third shot. Keisha Boykins, smiling prettily. This time, he looked at me.

I said, "You all know that Parmenter laid down a vulgar rap focused on Keisha. We've since learned she's an only child with some sort of chronic illness that keeps her out of school. That could kick up the parental protectiveness level so we need to look at both parents. Operating individually or in concert. And given the fact that O'Brien worked for Gerald Boykins, we can't eliminate the possibility that he wasn't just fired, he was taken care of permanently because of something to do with Keisha. Real or imagined. The wrong comment, the wrong look."

Petra said, "The serpent can't control its nature plus Mommy and Daddy are already primed after Parmenter, so they're looking for problems."

"Exactly," I said. "And ready to use the same shooter because he'd done a clean job on Parmenter."

Buck Buxby said, "You finally find a good plumber, keep calling him."

Moe said, "On the other hand, like we said, O'Brien could be the result of another pissed-off family."

No tell, from Milo.

Moe said, "Wide, wide world of suspects."

Milo said, "If the Boykinses are behind one or two hits, there's someone we need to look at as the shooter. Private guard who was there the day Alex and I visited them. Guy named Walt Swanson, used to work at Pacific Division."

He looked at Buxby.

The old D said, "Sorry, never get that close to the beach."

Moe said, "Why's he on the radar?"

Milo said, "He really isn't. But turns out he no longer works for the Boykinses or the private security firm they got him from. It's possible Gerald got pissed off because Swanson opened the gate for us easily so he canned him. On the other hand."

Alicia said, "Guy did two freelances for the Boykinses then you show up asking questions and it's time to make himself scarce. Anything scary in his background?"

"Nope, spotless record when he was on the job. Alex did me a favor this morning and took a look at his place of residence. Simi Valley, low-key, but he does have a sick wife so theoretically that could exert financial pressure."

Alicia said, "Are we going to start watching him?"

"Don't see that as high priority unless we get something else on him. First thing is to learn if he was fired or quit, but Pacific Security isn't being helpful."

Buck Buxby cleared his throat.

Milo said, "What is it, Buck?"

"I might have an in, there. Nothing high-level but a—someone— a person I used to know, worked there, maybe still does. Which office did you call?"

"Their main one, North Hollywood."

"Oh," said Buxby. "She—the person—is in the Orange County office, Buena Park. That's how I met her, there was this gang case, Mexican Mafia shooting up the competition across both counties, one of them actually had a job at a warehouse and Pacific had security footage there so I—" Another flush. "Sorry. TMI, like the kids say. Anyway, I could call, see if she can find out."

Milo said, "That would be great."

"Want me to do it right now?"

"Why don't you wait until we've gotten through everything." Another look at the Timex and Binchy's empty seat. "Try Sean, Moses."

Reed made the call, shook his head. "Voicemail."

"Weird," said Alicia. "He's so into punctual."

Milo frowned. "Okay, onward. Buck, thanks for looking into Swanson. If you learn he was fired due to a complaint by the Boykinses, he's probably not involved. If he suddenly quit, it gets more interesting. What's the surveillance situation at his home, Alex?"

I said, "Not ideal. Quiet street in Simi."

Buxby said, "Used to live there. Nice if you want to hang a flag, which I do, but yeah, *too* quiet, couldn't sleep."

Milo smiled, turned serious. "Okay, that's about it. Any questions about anything?"

I turned to Moe. "Milo said you'd found a couple of .308 shootings."

"I did but nothing thrilling, Doc. Both in Ohio, and a long time ago. Also, more like hunting accidents than planned-out homicides. They were filed as undetermined by the coroner but the police report says likely accidental."

"Were they neck shots?"

"Nope," he said. "That would've gotten my attention. One was to the back, pierced the spine, the other was in the brain stem."

"Same rifle for both?"

"That would've also been nice, so I tried to find out but couldn't. We're talking small-town and no one who's still around at local law enforcement remembers anything about either case. I tried their coroner, who turns out to be a mortician who bought the business two years ago from another mortician who'd died. No record of the bullets being preserved."

Buck Buxby muttered, "Welcome to Mayberry."

I said, "Where were the shootings?"

Everyone looked at me. *Why's he so interested.*

Then they smiled knowingly. *That's Doc, being meticulous.*

Moe pulled out his pad and flipped. "One was in a place called Shelter Lake, Ohio, the other in a tinier hamlet called Vantage."

"Morticians," said Alicia.

"Yup, the few times they need a pathologist they bring one in."

I said, "How far apart are the locales?"

Milo had already worked his phone. "Twenty-six miles."

I said, "Don't want to keep anyone here but at some point I wouldn't mind details."

Milo said, "This point, we're not speeding off anywhere. Moses?"

Reed paged some more. "The first place was Vantage, sixteen years ago, victim was a Caucasian male, forty-six years old, named Leonard Wiebelhaus, no criminal connections, worked at a tire shop. He was out shooting ring-necked pheasants in a wooded area when he got nailed. The second occurred six years later, similar terrain, victim was a Rainer Steckel, fifty-six, Caucasian male, school custodian, again no record. He was hunting deer and not wearing a proper orange vest."

Alicia said, "Honestly, Doc, don't see anything in common other than two middle-aged white guys. Which is your basic hunter demographic."

Buxby said, "And six years in between ain't exactly serial killer stuff."

I said, "The cases may not be relevant but I think anything remotely similar needs to be looked at. I'm wondering if our guy convinced himself he's a savior righting wrongs and that delusion began early. I'd especially be interested in the first victim—Wiebelhaus—because if his murder was a maiden voyage, the shooter could've been motivated by personal anger. If we're talking someone who's now in his thirties or forties, he'd started out as a teenager or in his early twenties. Both are peaks for criminality. And the six years between victims could be due to military service, which would fit a marksman."

Alicia said, "Joins the service, works on his shooting, and gets rewarded for it."

I said, "This is purely theoretical but I can see a discharged-with-personality issues deciding to turn his skills into a part-time career. Part-time, at this point, because as far as we know he hasn't shot enough people to make a steady living."

Petra said, "Unless he's pulled off other hits with different weapons."

"That's a possibility."

Milo said, "If not, we're talking a day job that he augments and you know where that leads me."

She said, "Back to Swanson."

Buxby said, "Just what we need, a bad cop."

"When you talk to your source, Buck, try to find out if Swanson has any roots in Ohio."

Milo said, "Moe, try to dig a little deeper into those shootings. Not the locals, but maybe newspaper articles."

"Will do, L.T. Anything else?"

Milo turned to Petra. "You want help on those citizen parking tickets?"

"If you've got the time, that would be great."

"My time is yours, stick around and we'll divide the chores. Meanwhile if there's nothing else—"

The door swung open and Sean Binchy ran in.

None of his usual aw-shucks amiability. Wide-eyed, one hand clutching his phone tight enough to whiten the skin but turn his freckles darker, he raced to the empty chair but remained on his feet.

"We just got another one."

30

M ilo recovered first. "C'mon up here and tell us about it."

Sean stepped up to the boards, looking uneasy. First time as a lecturer.

He said, "It came in at a quarter to, Captain Shubb called me in and ordered me to take it. When she told me it was a .308, I said that sounds like it could be related to what we're already working on, Loot needs to be informed right away. She said, 'Forget that, he's been seconded to Hollywood, has his hands full, we'll see if it turns out to be relevant.'"

Buck Buxby said, "Sheesh."

Everyone else kept quiet and looked at Sean.

He said, "Haven't been there yet, no way I was going before cluing you guys in. Spoke to the uniform managing the scene, everything's in place but I do need to go and I'm assuming someone else will want to."

Milo said, "I'll go with you, the rest of you can take care of the other business."

Nods all around.

He turned to Sean. "Since everyone's here, give us the basics."

Sean studied his notepad, closed it, and began speaking softly. Picking up volume as he gained confidence.

"Victim is a retired schoolteacher named Emmanuel Rosales, fifty-five, lives near the border between West L.A. and Culver. Not far from here, actually. Rough estimate of TOD is twelve to fifteen hours ago but his body wasn't discovered until two hours ago lying near his open rear gate. Gate leads to an alley and a garbage bag on the ground near him says he was taking the trash out when he got hit. Single shot through the neck, full metal jacket bullet lodged in the cushion of an outdoor chair behind him then splintering the wooden seatback and getting stuck."

I said, "A careful shooter but he's lax about discovery of his ammo."

Milo said, "Meaning?"

"He doesn't want to get caught but he does want to be noticed."

Buxby shook his head. "Ex-schoolteacher?"

"At Hamilton High," said Sean.

"Maybe he gave someone a bad grade."

Silence.

Buxby said, "Sorry, it just seems so wrong, we're not talking some scumbag sexual predator."

Moe said, "Whitney Killeen was a solid citizen."

"Yeah, true . . . I need to go and call Pacific, okay?"

"Sure, thanks, Buck."

The old detective left muttering, "Thanks for what?"

When he was gone, Alicia said, "Does Rosales live with anyone?"

"Don't know," said Sean. "Don't know anything except what I just told you."

He shut his pad, pumped a Doc Marten boot up and down.

Milo said, "Let's learn more." He and Sean moved to the door.

I stayed in place. He stopped and looked at me. "You don't have time?"

I said, "Didn't know—"

"Now you do." Wolf-grin. "Let's get educated."

31

"Close to here" translated to a twelve-minute drive that began by traveling south of the station then switching to a westward swoop that led us just below the Santa Monica Freeway.

The neighborhood was the usual mix of original bungalows, many of them embraced by old, lush landscaping, and boxy, newer two-story houses bullying the lots they sat on and deprived of vegetation.

Milo's unmarked arrived the same time as Sean's.

As we walked to him, he said, "See? Hop, skip. Maybe that's part of it, too. What you just said about craving attention. Shoot someone this close to the station, it's an F-U to the cops."

I said, "Could be."

"Or . . ."

"He was hired to get rid of another victim who just happens to live here."

Emmanuel Rosales's house was one of the older ones, not dissimilar from Walt Swanson's residence in Simi Valley but painted walrus gray with white trim. Ornate New Orleans–style ironwork graced a two-post outdoor frame that announced a front door set several feet back. The door was shut and sealed, the property taped off. A brown Honda Civic sat in the driveway.

Four black-and-whites and one crime lab van but no one from the Coroner's. Come and gone or hadn't arrived. A few neighbors stared from behind the tape.

Four uniforms stood around. Milo beckoned one over. *A. J. Beam.* "Where's your sergeant?"

"In back."

"Have you canvassed?"

"Waiting for you, sir."

"I'm here, so let's do it." Milo eyed the neighbors. "Start with the gawkers. Curious people are a treasured resource."

Beam said, "I'm doing it by myself, sir?"

Milo took in the scene. Four black-and-whites had transported eight officers, meaning four in front, four in back.

"Three of you," he said, "leave one officer to guard the tape."

"Yes, sir." Beam jogged off and began conferencing.

Milo turned to Sean. "Anything out here look interesting?"

"Not to me."

"That makes two of us. Alex?"

I held up three fingers.

Milo loped up the gray house's driveway and we followed, heading for sadness.

The late Emmanuel Rosales's backyard was tidy but modest, not much more than precisely clipped grass running to redwood fencing that had grayed and some outdoor furniture with floral plastic cushions and redwood frames. The chair that had absorbed the bullet was I.D.'d by a yellow plastic evidence marker. Not necessary; it stood ten or so feet behind the humped-up tarp lying on the grass. The house's rear door was open but taped.

The three of us booted and gloved and walked past four uniforms. A sergeant joined us. *S. Lincoln.*

She said, "Hi, Milo, what do you need?"

Milo said, "Glad it's you, Shirl. Be great if you mobilized to the max for the canvass. I got three in front to start, could use three more. Leave one officer to keep watch over this. Could be you, or you can door-knock, your choice."

"Sure," she said. "We were waiting for you in order to mobilize. We after the basics? See, hear, smell anything?"

"Exactly."

"What are the canvass parameters?"

"See what you can cover in a couple of hours and let me know." He pointed to the open rear door. "You gained entry?"

Shirl Lincoln said, "With a DB in plain sight, we felt we had to clear it. Easy access, the door was unlocked, makes sense when you're taking out the garbage."

"Anything interesting?"

"Once we cleared it, we didn't stick around, figured the techies needed to do their thing first."

"Okay, thanks."

She left.

Milo turned to Sean. "Given all that, not sure we need a victim's warrant but let's be careful and get one."

Sean moved a few feet away and talked to his phone.

He came back, nodding, and we headed toward the tarp. Positioned just inside an open redwood rear gate. Surrounded by its own rectangle of crime scene tape. One tech standing by waiting. *G. E. Soames.*

He said, "Hey, Lieutenant."

Milo saluted. "Grant. Can we get closer?"

"Sure, this was just to keep it pristine until we photo'd and took samples of the blood." Soames twanged the tape like it was a harp string, then produced a pocketknife and cut it.

"Lots of blood," he said, "must've hit a big vessel." He pointed to red-brown splotches on the grass, shifted to pointing out speckles on planks of the gate and a few fence boards. Finally, the chair, pocked by a hole through which tufts of stuffing protruded.

Milo said, "Where's the bullet?"

"My partner took it, along with scrapings, et cetera. I'm here in case you or the C.I. need anything else."

Milo said, "Where's the C.I.?"

"On the way," said Grant Soames. Drawing back the tarp, he receded several steps.

Emmanuel Rosales lay on his back in blood dried to tackiness. Open eyes, open mouth with a clear view of gold on molars. The neck wound was discreetly vicious. Identical to what I'd seen on Paul O'Brien's corpse.

Rosales was midsized, with thick gray hair cut short and an equally bushy mustache. He'd fallen on his back, but his eyeglasses had remained in place. Round, gold-framed glasses that looped around the ears and fit tight. I imagined them lending him a scholarly mien as he tried to influence adolescents.

His barley-colored sweatshirt read *Berkeley* in maroon letters arranged in an arc. Below that, *1868,* set in a horizontal oval. Below that, *California.*

The lettering was a creepy color match to the blood that stained the fabric then trailed down to generic black sweatpants where it had settled as chocolate glaze.

The glasses hadn't budged but the shirt had ridden up on impact, exposing a band of abdomen fuzzed with white hair. Purpled by blood. White New Balance walking shoes on Rosales's feet were similarly stained.

Sean said, "Poor guy. You go to take out the garbage."

The three of us got down and examined the neck wound.

Sean said, "Right of center, just like the others."

Milo said, "Calculating bastard, we need to stop this."

He stood, rubbed his face, like washing without water. "Okay, time to learn more about him. Sean, how 'bout you run him through the usual while I go inside. Your eyes are better with the small print."

Sean smiled. "So far."

"I used to say that."

Emmanuel Rosales had been a good housekeeper but his house gave off an apathetic bachelor vibe. Brown leather furniture was oriented toward a sixty-five-inch flat-screen. An undersized fridge in an undersized kitchen with bare counters hosted soda, beer, ketchup, mustard, mayo, hot sauce. The freezer was stacked with TV dinners, pre-cooked sausage, and a single barbecued chicken.

Perpendicular to the screen, a bookcase pretending to be wood was stacked with one shelf of spy thrillers, the rest given over to textbooks on math, physics, and chemistry. College and high school levels.

A single bathroom was situated midway between two bedrooms. In the medicine cabinet were OTC cold remedies, decongestants, antacids. In the cabinet below, a twelve-pack of toilet paper shared space with two large bottles of mint-flavored mouthwash. The same green liquid had been poured into a small apothecary jar that sat atop the counter. A drinking glass held toothpaste and floss.

The smaller bedroom didn't take long to search. Nothing but a recumbent bike and a treadmill, both facing another big screen. In the closet, an old, deflated soccer ball, a portable rotary fan, and VHS tapes neatly stacked.

Nothing with which to play the tapes. Milo examined them. More spy stuff, action blockbusters, comedies.

Milo said, "Probably lives by himself but so far, no porn. Maybe he keeps it where he sleeps."

The larger bedroom—generous relatively but not actually—was set up with a single closet and king-sized bed that left scant passage on one side, barely enough room for a pecan-finish rococo nightstand on the other. On the stand was a plaster-based lamp—off-white, corrugated, resembling an oversized larva—sunglasses, reading glasses, a set of keys, and a tissue box.

In a top drawer a laptop and a cellphone. Milo removed them and set them on the bed.

A six-drawer dresser facing the bed matched the stand in style and color. In the center, an identical lamp. Flanking the lamp on both sides were four photos in standing frames.

Emmanuel Rosales, at least a decade ago, his lush hair black and longer, his mustache a drooping Zapata, standing next to an older couple, each no taller than five-three.

Then Rosales, in his twenties, bearded and grinning, wearing a cap and gown. UC Berkeley insignia on the bottom of the frame.

The third shot featured a broadly smiling Rosales already graying, with a slightly younger couple and five children. Two boys, three girls, my guess, eight to fourteen.

Clear resemblance between Rosales and the man. The woman was petite and blond.

I said, "Bachelor uncle."

Milo said, "I know the drill."

Photo four was a full-color shot of gorgeous mountains and sky. Probably the Grand Tetons in Wyoming. Likely clipped from a calendar.

Milo went through the dresser drawers. Boxer shorts folded neatly, socks rolled meticulously, T-shirts, sweats, and polo shirts arrayed precisely.

Under the shirts, a framed Cal diploma proclaimed that Emmanuel Garcia Rosales had graduated thirty-three years ago cum laude with a bachelor's degree in physics. Below that, in a legal-sized manila envelope, was a California state teacher's certificate issued two years after the diploma.

The closet was small, with a single aluminum rack from which hung a blue suit and a gray suit, both from Men's Wearhouse, a couple of pairs of slacks, and three pairs of jeans pressed with precise creases.

A folding ironing board was propped against a wall; a steam iron sat on the floor, its cord coiled into a meticulous circle.

On a shelf above the hanging garments were two boxes. Milo opened them eagerly.

Unused pairs of white New Balance walking shoes.

He felt around the shelf, said, "Not even dust," and turned to me. "What are we talking about, Nowhere Man?"

We left and just reached the back door as Sean approached.

"He doesn't seem to ever have been married, Loot, and he's got no record, not even a parking ticket. I was able to access the basics of his employment records. He began teaching in some tough schools— Dorsey, Fremont, Jefferson—transferred to Hamilton three years ago, retired last year. On his pension docs, he lists a contact number in North Hollywood. Francisco and Laura Rosales."

Milo said, "Brother and sister-in-law, there's a photo of them inside."

Sean said, "Anything interesting inside?"

"Feel free to check it out yourself, kid, but unless he's got something stashed under the floorboards, *nadissimo.* We're talking someone who lived a *very* spare life. I left his phone and his laptop on the bed for you to take."

I said, "Maybe an outwardly spare life. But an honors degree in physics plus science and math books on the shelf say he could've been someone whose headspace was taken up by abstractions. Which wouldn't necessarily go over with a class full of teens."

Milo said, "Mr. Brain trying to convince the savages the beauty of ergs and joules? Yeah, I can see that leading to problems. So maybe ol' Buck was actually onto something and he gave the wrong kid an F."

Sean said, "He hasn't worked for a year, Loot. Don't see someone waiting around that long."

Milo said, "Someone sure didn't like him. Let's see if any teacher ratings are still online—you know the web, infinite dirt."

The three of us worked our phones. We each came up with the same thing. Half a dozen ratings, between five and seven years ago, all by students in magnet programs. Mostly five stars, a few fours.

Sean said, "Looks like he taught the smart ones."

Milo said, "Maybe one's too smart for his own good."

He clapped Sean on the shoulder. "Here's proof I'm benevolent, kid. Besides the phone and the computer, you get to go to Hamilton and see what you can learn from the administration. I'll do the fun job."

"Notification."

Milo exhaled. "Nothing like it. Though if Dr. D. doesn't mind, I'll have some sensitive psychological backup."

I said, "I'm relegated to third person?"

"Hey, that's how royalty's addressed. Is Your Highness up for a drive to North Hollywood?"

CHAPTER

32

Just as we were about to leave, a new person entered the crime scene. C.I. named Gloria Mendez, whom we both knew well.

Milo told her who the victim was and the highly probable cause of death.

She said, "How much commission do I owe you?," kneeled, went through the pockets of the black sweatpants and came up empty. Then she removed the white sneakers and examined them. Same result.

"Nothing, Milo, sorry. The shoes don't even smell."

Milo said, "Clean living. A lotta good it did him."

It was close to four p.m. when we set out for the home of Francisco and Laura Rosales. Nice part of North Hollywood bordering Toluca Lake where movie stars avoiding the Westside used to live.

Trying to avoid commuter clog, Milo took Benedict Canyon and fared reasonably well.

"Don't even know if they're home," he said. "But calling and then having to explain . . ." He shook his head, took a curve fast, and said, "God, I'll never stop hating this."

———

Google's spy camera said the residence was a two-story brick-faced Colonial and Google hadn't lied.

Generously proportioned, green-shuttered house, skillfully land-scaped, on a quiet, pretty, magnolia-shaded street. High-end vehicles predominated up and down the block. Perched in this driveway was a silver-gray Land Rover.

Milo said, "Not exactly Emmanuel's setup. Wonder if there was tension."

"Not according to the photo he kept."

"Hmmph. Okay, here goes."

The front door was deep green, paneled, and set up with a peephole and a shiny bronze lion's-head knocker. He lifted the ring and let it collide with the strike plate.

Seconds later, a child's voice said, "Mo-om, the door."

"Who?"

"I dunno."

"Hold on."

Movement behind the hole. Maybe one of those peephole cameras. Milo showed the little glass sphere his badge, then stepped back so his face was visible.

The door opened on the blond woman from the family photo, now brunette streaked with ginger.

Milo gave her his name, then mine.

"Police? Is Frank—"

"Frank's fine, ma'am. It's about your brother-in-law."

"Manny? What happened to him?"

"Could we come in?"

Laura Rosales's hand clawed her cheek. "That sounds bad. Is it—*is* it?"

"Unfortunately—"

"Omigod omigod. I have to call *Frank*!"

———

She seated us in a spotless, out-of-a-magazine living room and rushed off to get her phone. A couple of kids appeared, staring from the neighboring dining room. Familiar faces from the photo in Manny Rosales's bedroom, a few years of maturity tacked on.

Milo said, "Hey guys."

They scampered off.

He said, "Did I just do something scary?"

Before I could reply, Laura Rosales returned, hands shaking, and lowered herself to the edge of an overstuffed chair. Her skin was a shade paler, her eyes wide.

"You're going to tell me Manny's dead."

"Sadly, we are, ma'am. So sorry for your loss."

"My loss, the kids' loss, and most of all *Frank's* loss." Hunching, she buried her face in her hands and cried, shoulders rising and falling.

Milo did what he always does. Waited out every painful second then produced a tissue.

Laura Rosales took thirty or so seconds before dabbing and hazarding eye contact. "Frank's on his way, his office isn't far from here. He's a dentist. Periodontist . . . what happened?"

"At this point we don't know much, ma'am, but it looks as if Mr. Rosales was shot leaving his backyard to take out the garbage."

"Shot? Murdered? Oh, that's hideous, it's absolutely *hideous!* What, a gang thing? I know they're crawling all over Venice like vermin but Manny assured us his neighborhood was safe. What did they steal?"

"Apparently nothing, Ms. Rosales."

"Then *what?* You just shoot someone in cold blood who's taking out his *garbage?* What's the *point?* Who *does* that?"

"As I said, ma'am, we don't know much."

"Oh God, this is like a bad dream . . . how did you locate us?"

"Manny kept a photo in his bedroom—"

"That one," she said. "We'd gone out to dinner and Frank said, 'Let's memorialize this.' Because it was so rare."

I said, "Manny going out with you."

"Not for lack of trying. Of course he was with us on holidays—Christmas, Thanksgiving, and birthdays. The kids loved it, he was great with the kids. But after a while he'd want to leave. Said it exhausted him. That was Manny. Sweet, generous, but he had his own way of doing things."

I thought: *Fatigued by social contact: introvert.* Said, "But that time you got him to agree to stay."

"It was the tenth anniversary of his and Frank's dad's death, we all went to the cemetery and paid our respects and I guess Manny was feeling emotional. Not that you could really tell. He was such an *even* guy."

Milo said, "Not the type to make enemies."

"Of course not! Everyone *loved* Manny. He was *sweet!* When he did come over, he'd let the kids crawl over him. When they got older, he'd give them math puzzles, physics stuff. That was his thing. Math. He was brilliant, could've gotten a Ph.D. and gone on to be a professor anywhere. He was certainly smart enough."

I said, "Not interested in that."

"Nope and don't ask me why. His professors encouraged him but he turned them down. We have no idea why."

Milo said, "I'm going to read you a list of names and if any of them ring a bell, please tell me. Whitney Killeen, Jamarcus Parmenter, Paul O'Brien."

"No, no bells," she said. "Who are they?"

"Sorry, can't get into that."

"They're suspects?"

"No, ma'am."

"Then—oh forget it, none of my business and I don't care anyway."

The door opened and Dr. Frank Rosales hurried in wearing scrubs. Slim, graying and balding, younger than his brother with a fuller face, but the resemblance was strong. He walked past us, headed straight for his wife, and embraced her.

When he let go, his face was tight with fury.

"Someone hurt my brother." Statement, not a question.

Milo said, "Unfortunately—"

"They killed him."

"Sorry to say, Doctor—"

"A gang thing."

Laura said, "That's what I thought but—"

Frank Rosales said, "Of course you did. It's logical."

Milo said, "Did your brother have any problems with gangs?"

"No, not yet. But it was only a matter of time, they multiply like maggots. Not that your district attorney cares about that."

He closed his eyes, clenched his fists, and held them tight against his flanks. Breathing in and out deeply, he opened them and sat down. His wife followed suit, laid one slender arm over his shoulder.

"Thanks, honey—I'm sorry," said Frank Rosales. "Don't mean to do a kill-the-messenger thing, it's just the shock, I mean there was no warning, no indication . . . Manny was the last person you'd think would be . . . in this situation."

I said, "Peaceable."

"Peaceable, kept to himself. Had nothing of any value to steal. Stuff wasn't his thing, whatever money he had, he kept in the— Have you checked his bank accounts?"

"Not yet, Doctor, but it doesn't appear to have been a robbery."

"How do you know?" said Frank Rosales.

"No one entered his house."

"Really? I assumed some sort of home invasion. Then what? This just doesn't make sense."

Milo said, "I'll give you the few basics we have. Your brother was shot as he walked out to the alley behind his property to take out the garbage. As far as we can tell, the killer didn't even enter the backyard, just fired once and fled."

"That sounds," said Frank Rosales, "like an assassination. I don't understand."

He stifled a sob, produced a gulping sound then several coughs. "'Scuse me."

Milo said, "We know this is a terrible, terrible time for you, Doctor, but solving cases depends on information. So anything you—or Mrs. Rosales—can tell us about Manny would be helpful."

Frank said, "Like what? He never had conflict with anyone."

I said, "He was a teacher. Sometimes students can be problematic."

"Not Manny's students. If he'd taught regular classes, I'd say sure, the public school system's a joke. But he was in the magnet program, taught math and science to the smart kids. College-bound, motivated. Manny loved it. And they loved him. He'd never brag but I got curious and looked up his online ratings. Basically all five stars, a couple of fours because the subject matter was too hard. But no one complained about Manny."

Laura said, "He really did love teaching."

Frank said, "He could've earned a doctorate. Or gone to med school, dental school, anything. But after he graduated Cal, he pursued a high school teaching credential and that's been it for thirty-plus years."

Milo said, "Got it. Let's move on to his personal relationships. Other than you."

Frank and Laura looked at each other. She sighed. He turned to the side.

We waited.

Laura said, "There really were none. Relationships."

Frank said, "And in answer to your next question, no, he wasn't gay."

Laura said, "That's the assumption, right? A bachelor has to be gay. When our kids got old enough they asked. Is Uncle Manny gay? Because it is a normal question."

"But he's not," said Frank. "He dated girls in high school and college. Then . . . it stopped. I didn't understand it but obviously I wouldn't ask. Because it was none of my business. Then one day, out of the clear blue, he was over for . . . probably Thanksgiving, this was a few years ago, and he drew me away and said, 'If you're curious, Little Bro, I'm not gay.' Not that it would be a problem for me if he was but I was pretty shocked. That he brought it up. Manny never got personal. Even when we were kids he preferred to talk about ideas, not people."

I said, "The definition of high intelligence."

"To a T. Manny was all *about* ideas. Formulas, theorems. I was decent in math, he was a total whiz. Like our dad. He was uneducated, never made it past ninth grade but he could memorize columns of numbers . . . anyway, that's what Manny told me. About his sexuality."

"Any idea why he stopped dating?"

"The way he put it," said Frank Rosales, "he didn't want to spend energy on it. Maybe he'd been hurt by a girl, I don't know. There's eight years between us. When he started Cal, I was in fifth grade."

Laura said, "Some people just aren't interested. So what? It takes all types."

Her husband looked at her then back at us. "Not going to lie, it was a little tough on our parents. They wanted what everyone wants for their kids. Settle down, raise a family. But they never bugged Manny, that wasn't our family, we're live and let live."

"We have five kids," said Laura. "You learn to respect their individuality."

Frank didn't respond. A moment later: "So no, there'd be no one who'd want to assassinate him. Unless it was one of those crazy things."

Milo said, "What kind of crazy thing?"

"You know," said Frank. "Some maniac on the street, you look at them the wrong way and voices tell them to get you. There's homeless all over. Not in Manny's neighborhood but Culver City? It's a sty. Do you know how they're going to deal with those people who camp out on the sidewalk? Spend taxpayer money to widen the sidewalk. You believe that? Lunatics running the asylum."

"That makes sense," said Laura. "A lunatic who for some lunatic reason targeted Manny."

"I mean you just shoot and you don't even bother to try to steal anything?" said her husband. "That's totally irrational. But that's the age we're living in."

Milo said, "Things have gotten complicated."

"Not complicated," said Frank Rosales. "Simple and crazy."

Milo handed out his cards and we left them standing in their doorway, wet-eyed and clutching each other. A black Porsche Panamera sat next to the Range Rover. *GUM DDS* on the plates.

"American success story," he said as he drove away. "Doesn't insulate you—so what do you think?"

I said, "Frank was right, Manny was assassinated. Targeted just like the others. So it had to be personal and despite what they think they know, he may have had a relationship that went bad. I know there wasn't any evidence of that in his house but that could just mean it was long over. And that can mean lingering anger. It'll be particularly interesting to see what's on his computer and his financials."

"Not gay." He smiled. "If they're right and we don't find any women in his life, where does that lead? He lied about it? Or he was some kind of voluntary celibate?"

I said, "Like the sister-in-law said, all types."

"Except all types don't get murdered just for fun. There's got to be something in this guy's past."

He phoned Sean.

"Hey, Loot. Just got out of Hamilton High. Principal says Mr. Rosales was one of their best teachers, dedicated, high standards, taught the smart kids, everyone loved him."

"That's the picture we just got from his brother and sister-in-law. No issues at all?"

"Not that the principal would cop to. Only thing I did notice—

and it might turn out to be nothing—is when we were walking out and he was assuring me of all that, his secretary gave me a look."

"What kind of look?"

"That's the thing, Loot, can't really decode what it meant and it was just for a second. Basically, I'd call bothered. Almost like she was annoyed with him. But maybe I'm looking for something that isn't there. I circled back and gave her my card. She said, 'Why would I need this?' so maybe she ended up tossing it in the circular file. But who knows?"

"Good thinking, kid."

"Grasping at straws, Loot."

"Aren't we all," said Milo. "Let's get to work on Rosales's phone and his financials."

"The phone and the computer are both password-protected so I dropped them off with Layton—that new tech whiz D I—and told him I'd initiate the affidavits. Soon as I get back, I'll go to work on them."

Milo hung up. "So nice when the kids turn out right."

33

I heard nothing from Milo for the next two days, which worked out perfectly; I was swamped with consults and report-writing.

During spare moments, I'd found myself drifting back to Paul O'Brien's murder. If the Boykinses had hired a killer twice, no problem. But Vicki Saucedo's family as contractors raised a question: With no criminal case filed, how had they known O'Brien was the one who'd O.D.'d and dumped their daughter?

The only answer I could come up with was that a witness had come forward but had been ignored in favor of a financial settlement. On the face of it, that seemed mercenary, but who was I to judge the monumental grief of a family left with a grievously damaged daughter?

Either way, I had nowhere to go with it.

At ten a.m. on the third day, Milo called.

"You have time for a summary?"

"Absolutely."

"First item: Walt Swanson. Buxby learned he had indeed been dismissed from the Boykins job due to a complaint. The company offered to put him on another gig but he told them he was packing it in to care for a sick wife. Apparently she's got some sort of cancer. Top of that,

Swanson has no Ohio connections, California born and bred. So looks like ol' Walt's off the radar. Next: Ballistics tech identified the probable spot in the alley where the shooter stood but nothing forensic showed up there. In fact, there was evidence of some surface dirt being swept away in order to obscure shoe prints."

"Our boy brings a whisk broom along with his rifle."

"Huh. Some image. No one in Rosales's neighborhood heard any gunshots, though a couple of people thought they heard a car backfiring. The canvass pulled up one witness, a woman walking her dog, who saw a guy in a hoodie going into the alley about ninety minutes before the body was discovered. She didn't think much of it because he was carrying what looked like a garbage bag. She assumed he was headed for the trash. Which he was, but for a whole other reason."

I said, "Big bag's a good way to pack gear without attracting attention. Maybe that's why no one in Hollywood saw a rifle case. Any other details?"

"Not overly short or tall, just a guy taking out the trash. Video surveillance turned out to be a bust. Most of the homes don't have systems, though a surprising number have dummy cameras and warning signs. The few that are operative are narrowly focused on front porches with no view of the sidewalk. Top of that, there are no overnight parking restrictions so we can't cross-check violations with the ones Petra found. Speaking of which, she's checked out twelve of the remaining thirty-one solid citizens and none of them are viable suspects. Now the possibly interesting stuff. Possibly with a small p."

He paused for breath. "Mr. Rosales's use of the internet was pretty much limited to online chess, word games, math games, and puzzles. He spent hours a day on brainy stuff. There were also some searches of local restaurant menus but no sign he followed through on actually ordering. The only other sites that came up were for porn. Hetero, conventional, and not frequently used, we found ten searches over six months."

I said, "Life of the mind. What about his phone?"

"Also barely used," he said. "Zero texts and there were days at a time with no calls, in or out. The few personals he did make were to his brother's house and a number in Culver City that we traced to a woman named Hannah Gardener. I've left her three messages but she hasn't responded. I looked her up and found out she's also a teacher, but not at Hamilton, at Fairfax High. Forty-nine years old, clean record, big shock."

"How often did Rosales contact her?"

"Last time was two months ago, the previous four months he reached her eleven times and she initiated six times. Relatively long calls—five, ten minutes."

"Despite what Laura and Frank said, maybe a relationship."

"I just phoned Fairfax and found out she called in sick. Figured I'd drop by her place, maybe get lucky. You up for it?"

"A teacher?" I said. "Always happy to be educated."

I drove to the station and we continued in his Impala to Hannah Gardener's address. Four-unit mocha-colored box west of Overland and south of Washington. Twenty-minute ride from Butler. Less from Manny Rosales's house.

Entry was blocked by a glass security door. Four buttons, *Gardener* in Apartment 2.

Milo said, "Here goes nothing."

We got something.

A woman said, "Yes?"

Milo identified himself.

She said, "About Manny."

"Yes, ma'am."

Buzz.

Unit 2 was on the right side of a minimal lobby. By the time we got to the door it was open.

The woman who watched us, nodding, was short, plump, with a pretty, round face under henna-red curls. She wore a pink *Scripps College* sweatshirt over brown leggings and bare feet. Red toenail polish, pearlescent white for her fingers. Hoop earrings the size of drink coasters dangled from her ears. Dusting of freckles on a pixie nose.

Like Laura Rosales, her eyes were weary and raw, pink sclera rimming bright-blue irises.

She said, "Please come in," in a barely audible voice. As we followed her inside, the nods turned to head shakes.

Hannah Gardener's apartment was compact, made cozier by oversized, overstuffed seating. A coffee table with barely enough room to avoid feet was topped by glass that shielded a dense array of seashells. Copies of antique maps took up most of the wall space. Images conjured centuries ago from fancy, not fact.

That and a carved floor-to-ceiling bookcase crammed with hardcovers, some of them leather-bound, and lilac fragrance in the air, evoked a library in an esoteric club.

"Something to drink?" she said, without enthusiasm.

"No, thanks, Ms. Gardener."

"Hannah's fine. I just found out about Manny and I'm having trouble processing it." She bit her lip, kept gnawing it, worried one hand with the other. "Please. Sit."

We faced her across the seashells. Scores of them, jumbled, as if deposited by a giant wave.

Milo said, "How'd you find out?"

"They called me from Hammie. I used to work there before I transferred to Fairfax in order to teach AP history and geography."

She touched her breast. "I threw up then I called in sick."

I said, "You worked with Mr. Rosales at the Hamilton magnet."

Hannah Gardener grimaced. "I wish. No, I worked at the regular school, which was not very stimulating and sometimes downright unpleasant. Magnet jobs are impossible to get, once people score, they stick around. I'd given up and was just about to go private at Buckley, despite having to drive into the Valley plus losing some of my pension. Then the position at Fairfax came up. Did you find me on Manny's phone?"

Milo said, "Good guess."

"Well, there'd be no other way, Lieutenant—this must be an important case for a lieutenant to be involved. That's good, Manny deserves it. Manny and I didn't talk often but we did chat so I figured I'd be on his call log and it was just a matter of time. Not that I have anything to offer."

Milo said, "Anything you can tell us about Manny will be helpful. Starting with your relationship."

Hannah Gardener's chest heaved. She crossed her legs, then thought better of it and placed her feet on the floor.

"Relationship." Her mouth twisted. As if trying out a new word in a foreign language. "Primarily, we were friends. I was widowed three years ago, shortly before Manny transferred to Hammie. We met in the teachers' lounge and ended up talking. He saw how low I was and was extremely supportive. I really needed that. David had been ill for years but still, when it happened."

I said, "Primarily but not exclusively friends."

She shot me a sharp look. "My, you're a precise one, linguistically. If you're asking did it ever extend to something beyond friendship, I'm not sure I want to get into that level of detail about my personal life. It certainly can't be relevant."

I said, "No offense."

"None taken." Spots of color on her cheeks said otherwise. "Look, guys, I understand, you've got to delve. But nothing that transpired between Manny and myself will help you solve this."

We remained silent.

Hannah Gardener fooled with her hair. "Let's just say that there was a brief time—months ago—that we did attempt to . . . stretch the friendship. But we ended up mutually deciding pure friendship would be preferable. Then I began dating and though I assured Manny that it wouldn't affect our friendship, he apparently thought differently and reduced our contacts. I tried calling him but he never responded. That would have to be a couple of months ago."

She gulped. "I didn't want to hurt him but he . . . it just wasn't in the cards, Manny was all about ideas, not the physical world."

The blush had spread down to her neck. "This is so embarrassing."

I said, "Sorry, but thanks for the information. What was it like when you were friends?"

"Like? I don't get the question."

"Did you socialize in person—"

"Of course we did," she said. "We're not automatons or online freaks. We'd go out to dinner or brunch on Saturday. He'd come here and we'd do Saturday crosswords together in ink, they're the hardest. Manny was great company. Which, from a woman's perspective, means he knew how to listen."

She crossed her legs again, this time maintaining the position. "Now may I ask some questions? What exactly happened? All Jeanine—the secretary at Hammie—told me was a cop showed up and said he'd been murdered. Was it a home invasion? A burglar who went nuts?"

Milo said, "Neither, ma'am."

"Then *what*?"

He gave her the bare minimum.

She grimaced. "Someone shooting him and running off and not taking anything? That's nuts. That sounds like what I guess you people would call a hit."

The flush had spread to her entire face. Her hands clasped and her eyes rounded, widening the pink halo.

Milo said, "Can you think of anyone who'd target him?"

"Of course not— oh, crap. No, couldn't be."

She sprang up, ran to the kitchen, uncapped a pale-green glass bottle and brought it back.

Topo Chico mineral water from Mexico.

"Manny introduced me to it. Great bubbles. You sure you don't want some?"

Milo said, "No, thanks. What couldn't be, Ms. Gardener?"

"That there was someone actually out to get Manny."

"If something has come to mind, please tell us."

"Oh my," she said. "Here I was thinking I had nothing to offer and I still probably don't. But I suppose there could be one thing. Not that it's factual, it's not even close to factual, just— and I can't even give you details."

She gulped water. Put the bottle down, picked it up and drank some more.

Breathing hard, looking away.

We waited.

Hannah Gardener said, "You won't quote me on this, okay? I don't want to get myself into something."

Milo said, "We deal with facts, Hannah, not theory. There'd be no reason to get you involved. But a lead, even one that doesn't pan out, would sure be helpful."

"You can't even call it a lead," she said. "It's just a possibility. Theoretical . . . oh, crap . . . fine. Let me preface this by saying that Manny was a great teacher, devoted, fair, but he had standards and he *could* be firm. You need to be firm with kids, especially the smart ones. They must understand that the real world isn't perpetual daycare where everyone coddles— oh, crap, I'm blathering."

She picked up the bottle, drank long enough to empty it. Let loose a soft burp and said, "Great, like you needed to hear *that*."

Scooting forward, she said, "Okay, let me get this out. Around a year ago, right before Manny retired—I'm sure it played a role in his retiring—a terrible thing happened. Not Manny's fault, not remotely his fault, but I suppose if someone thought so . . . it's far-fetched, but with what you've told me about how someone was out for him specifically . . . okay. Here's what happened. One of his students committed suicide. Manny was devastated, he had no idea it would get that far."

Milo said, "There was a problem with that student?"

"Nothing earth-shattering," said Hannah Gardener. "Not in a normal world but nowadays . . . the kid was a great student except for physics. He got consistently bad grades on the AP physics tests and Manny wasn't one to grade-inflate. He was compassionate, he was understanding, but in the end you got what you earned."

I said, "He failed the student?"

"No, no, nothing like that, he gave him a B minus, which according to Manny was more than what was merited, it should've been a C. But the kid went ballistic. Until then, he'd had straight A's and was convinced it would ruin his future forever. He begged Manny to change it. Manny tried to explain that he'd already been generous and couldn't go further. The kid went home and hung himself. Disgusting. Tragic." She shuddered. "Over a stupid *grade*!"

I said, "Did the family blame Manny?"

"They blamed everyone. The school, the entire magnet program, and yes, Manny. He told me they even made noises about suing but of course that went nowhere, what would be the grounds? In any event, Manny retired. Refused to talk about it but it's pretty obvious why."

She pointed a finger. "I'm sure the family is devastated forever so I certainly don't want to get anyone in trouble. But if anyone had a bone to pick with Manny, it would be them. And let's face it, they probably created the situation in the first place."

I said, "Putting pressure on the boy."

"That's what Manny said. It's like that with most of the smart kids. Crazy parents giving them an either/or view of the world: get into the Ivy League or end up homeless. That's where the problem lies, not with teachers doing our job. We are *not* paid to delude."

Milo said, "What was the student's name?"

"All I know is his first name. Errol. That's all Manny told me and I resisted the temptation to find out more. Because frankly, I was horrified, and after what I'd gone through with my husband I'd developed a severe allergy to horror."

She played with an earring. "Not going to get into detail but David had some sort of neuromuscular disease. Not ALS, nothing they could even put a name on."

"So sorry you had to go through that."

"So am I," said Hannah Gardener. "That's why I've changed my life. I'm also allergic to bullshit and so I concentrate on what's important. That's why I really don't want to talk about this anymore. Now or in the future."

She got up, walked to the door and opened it. "Sorry if this seems rude, but end of discussion. I appreciate what you're doing and hope you succeed but I want nothing to do with it and I trust you'll respect my wishes."

Milo said, "We appreciate your talking to us."

"Sure," said Hannah Gardener. "But I hope it turns out to be useless and you solve it some other way."

Walking through the lobby, Milo said, "A kid gets a bad grade. Go Buck, out of the mouths of babes and old cops."

In the car, he said, "Errol. That shouldn't be hard to find."

It wasn't.

A call to the Coroner's pulled up the death certificate, filed fourteen months ago.

Errol Morgan Moffett, seventeen. Cause of death: asphyxiation due to hanging. Manner of death: suicide.

Home address in Woodland Hills.

Milo said, "That's an hour's drive from Hamilton each way, minimum."

I said, "It was probably the only magnet he got into."

"Dedicated parents."

"Like she said, devastated parents. It's easy to see them blaming Rosales. The question is, how far did they take it."

"Let's try to find out. Starting with who are these people."

"Facts, not theory," I said. "Unlike the maps on her walls."

"Huh?"

"She collects antique reproductions from when cartographers just made stuff up. The largest one had the world shaped like a cloverleaf. Another had an octopus—"

"You notice stuff like that? And could still concentrate on the main topic?"

"It's not that hard."

"Yeah, yeah, don't tell me about *your* physics tests."

34

Back in his office, he printed Errol Moffett's death certificate, studied it in detail, and passed it to me.

Found hanging in the family garage by his parents, Scott and Lindsay Moffett.

Both had sparse Facebook pages, Scott a computer engineer, bald with a bristly gray beard, Lindsay a dance instructor with a lean face and spiky black hair.

Minimal self-promotion because their online attention had been concentrated on a memorial site for their son?

Those pages were heralded by a photo of a nice-looking, tentatively smiling boy with long brown hair and a fledgling mustache. Strong resemblance to Mom. The portrait was bordered by black roses. From the looks of it, taken not long before his death.

Both parents offered heart-wrenching memories of their son. Next came tributes from Errol's older sister, Brynne, and his younger brother, Shelton. Then more of the same from friends and acquaintances, many of whom added their headshots to mini-essays, doggerel, and lyrics from popular songs.

Errol had been "brilliant," "intense," "passionate about science," "a great human being," and a "mind warrior," whatever that meant.

No hobbies or outside interests cited. As far as I could see, Errol
Moffett's priority had been limited to "wanting to be a great neurosur-
geon."

I scrolled a bit more. Sad stuff, well meaning, repetitive. I stopped
reading and returned the printout to Milo.

He rubbed his face. "A seventeen-year-old feeling the need to do
that over a B minus."

I said, "Probably not that simple."

"What do you mean?"

"Cases like his typically get blamed on situational factors—
bullying, video games, some sort of failure, including grades. Those
can be triggers but there's usually a serious underlying depression."

"Start off in a gray world, doesn't take much to turn it black?"

"Well put."

He returned to Scott's and Lindsay's pages. "Not much here about
them. Maybe 'cause they lived for their kids."

I said, "Two hours of commuting a day says they were highly invested."

I used my phone to look up Brynne's and Shelton Moffett's social
platforms. She was a freshman at Pierce junior college, he a sophomore
at Woodland Hills High School. Both into sports, music, friends. Perfectly normal, conventional kids, but no evidence of exceptional aca-
demic achievement.

I pointed it out to Milo. "Looks like Errol was tagged as the gifted
one."

He said, "Star of the family show, then he stops living. That defines
devastation, no? Maybe leads them to looking for a scapegoat. We
know they blamed Rosales initially."

"If so," I said, "they stewed on it for a year. Or they're just poor,
grieving parents who've done nothing wrong."

"We've found no one else so far who had anything against Rosales.
Which leads me to a big problem, Alex. How the hell do I approach

them? *Hey, folks, not only did you lose your golden boy, now we want to find out if you conspired to commit murder.*"

I said, "You're right, wish I had an easy answer. If they're not involved, you'll be compounding their grief. And if they are guilty, all they have to do is refuse to talk to you. I guess a look at their phone records and their financials might tell you something but I don't see how you'd ever get subpoenas based on what you have."

He swiveled and stared at me. "That was therapy?"

I got up. "If I come up with something, you'll be the first to know."

As I left, he said, "All I can ask for, amigo. Keep thinking."

35

I thought plenty but it led to desolate dead ends. I kept that to myself over dinner, figured I'd done a good job of pigeonholing so I could be good company for Robin and Blanche.

The dishes washed and dried, Robin and I settled on the terrace nursing bourbon Manhattans, Blanche curled up between us. Enveloped by the night. Nice. I concentrated on that.

A couple of sips in, Robin said, "What's wrong, honey?"

"It's that obvious."

"No, actually it isn't. You're great at keeping things buttoned up, I'm sure that's good for your patients. And I'm also sure a casual observer wouldn't notice but casual ain't us."

She rubbed the back of my neck. "I have developed Alex ESP. No big whoop, you'd do the same for me. That said, if you don't want to talk about it."

I did.

She said, "Poor, poor kid. Destroying yourself over a grade."

"Likely more than a grade." I told her what I'd said to Milo about depression.

"Even worse," she said. "There he was dealing with that and no one noticed because it was all about achievement."

I said, "Teens are great at hiding stuff. Serious depression can be mistaken for adolescent moodiness."

"We had something like that when I was in high school. Brilliant girl, long-distance runner and student council vice president on top of straight A's. Allison something. One day they found her in the girls' locker room, laid out on the floor with an empty bottle of her mother's antidepressants next to her. They rushed her to the hospital but couldn't revive her. That was a message, no? Using Mom's pills? And Mom also being depressed. Is it genetic?"

"It can be."

She smiled. "Spoken like a guy who testifies in court. Let me ask you this: Are bright kids more susceptible?"

"Actually, their suicide rate is lower," I said. "It's the struggling kids who are at higher risk because having fewer resources leads to a tougher life. But there's plenty of room for exceptions. Especially when high expectations fall short."

"One B minus," she said. "I'll remind myself of that next time I'm sweating over a millimeter of veneer. So how'd *you* survive, being all precocious?"

"No problem, I was anything but a golden boy."

"Oh sure."

"Really, babe. No one expected anything from me. Including me."

"Even though you were always straight A's. Right?"

"In my family, it didn't matter."

"What did?"

"Nothing."

"Well," she said, "you sure got past that."

"Gradual process."

"College at sixteen is gradual?"

"I didn't think about it, was just happy to get away. And I had bills to pay."

"Guess we share that," she said. "Low expectations. I was no star student, no one thought I'd amount to anything except Dad. And then he upped and died and Mom didn't exactly build me up."

Her voice faltered. She drew herself up. Grinned. "Pain followed by gain. Guess we're the lucky ones."

We drank in silence, her head on my shoulder.

A few minutes later, she said, "In a way isn't this case kind of like the other one you told me about? The hip-hop producer with the smart fragile kid? Both murders could be about family rage, no? Parents avenging their kids, only the producer didn't wait for it to get tragic."

My gut tightened.

She felt it. "What?"

"Now that you mention it, it could also fit the woman in the boat. She was embroiled in a custody dispute. Faced claims she was an unfit mother. Getting killed by someone protecting her child is twisted but maybe you've hit on something."

Which led me to the case I hadn't talked about. Couldn't. The grieving family of a young woman brutalized and left as a shell of herself.

No police report filed not because the Saucedos had been content to be compensated with money? Because they'd decided to take matters into their own hands?

I took Robin's face in both my hands and kissed her.

She said, "Whew. All that for letting my mind wander?"

"All that for a whole bunch of brilliant."

We sat out there for a while, drifted into the bedroom and made unusually silent, easy love, then showered, streamed a few minutes of a Nordic-noir movie that turned out to be turgid, and switched off the lights just after ten p.m.

Robin slept peacefully. My slumber came to a halt just after four a.m. when I woke wide-eyed in the midst of a dream I couldn't remember. Something that had set my heart pounding.

Muddled thoughts began coming at me like cards from the trick deck of a sleight-of-hand magician. Vanishing before contact, only to be followed by another bizarre onslaught of what-ifs that finally took shape as I flashed back, lucidly, to where Robin had led me.

People hiring a ruthlessly accurate killer for the sake of their kids.

In the cases of Keisha Boykins and Errol Moffett, gifted kids. Two sets of parents, unknown to each other, putting aside reason and morality in favor of crazily focused protectiveness?

Golden kids. Both high school juniors. I'd treated enough eleventh-graders to know that year was often the peak of anxiety about college acceptance.

Parents of high school juniors had been known to bribe, con, and swindle in order to get their offspring into top universities. If you bought into the fantasy that enrollment at a selective institution guaranteed lifelong ecstasy, why not take it further?

On the other hand, college issues had nothing to do with the death of Whitney Killeen, mother of a toddler. And Vicki Saucedo was a woman in her twenties.

So forget the narrow focus and concentrate on the process.

Children of any age as objects of selfish love.

Jarrod, the prize in a custody battle.

Vicki, the physically beautiful but vulnerable sib. That was harder to fit. So maybe a simple revenge plot.

The more I thought about it, the more consistently it came down to families and offspring. I chewed on that for a while but it didn't take long for early-morning inspiration to pale.

All I'd created was another theory, useless for moving the case forward.

I got up and began trudging back to bed when it hit me.

Jarrod had two half sibs in college, Vicki Saucedo, a brother in college. Brilliant, on scholarship at an exclusive college, what was his name . . . ?

CHAPTER

36

Michael Saucedo.

I returned to my keyboard and began typing. It didn't take long to locate a sophomore named Michael J. Saucedo who'd achieved high distinction in mathematics during his freshman year at Oberlin College.

Oberlin, Ohio.

The state where Moe Reed had unearthed two old, cold .308 shootings.

A couple of small-town incidents, assumed to be unsolved hunting accidents. I'd forgotten the names of the towns. Online payment to a nationwide newspaper site pulled up citations in a couple of local weeklies.

Leonard Wiebelhaus, forty-six, a semi-truck tire installer, shot sixteen years ago in Vantage, Ohio.

Rainer Steckel, fifty-six, slain six years later, in Shelter Lake, Ohio.

Moe had described Steckel as a school custodian. The bottom of the page in the *Shelter Lake Clarion* described him as *a caretaker at Oberlin College.*

Michael J. Saucedo.

I looked up the distance from both hamlets to the college. Shelter Lake was eighteen miles away, Vantage, twenty-four.

Vicki's gifted brother had been a toddler during the first shooting, a preteen during the second. So nothing to do with him directly.

But maybe he knew someone else with ties to Oberlin?

Someone with an easy trigger finger in whom Michael had confided about his sister's brutalization?

A local who'd learned the joys of picking off human targets a long time ago and decided to bring his skills to L.A. to pursue it professionally?

I went back to Michael Saucedo's Facebook page. No photos, nothing recreational beyond trying to solve some famous math problems. Unsuccessfully so far, *but you have to keep trying, it's all about perseverance.*

That was followed by a paragraph in the school paper, *The Oberlin Review,* that listed him as one of twelve high-honors freshmen.

Below which he'd written: *No big deal and can't take full credit. Professor Thalberg was a six-star teacher and the foundation I got from the inimitable Cameron Flick has proved to be invaluable.*

Click, click, click.

Sidney G. Thalberg, an endowed professor of mathematics at Oberlin, was white-haired and emaciated and looked to be in his eighties.

Well past retirement age, he admitted in his faculty bio, *but Oberlin has indulged me.*

All of which added up to an unlikely sharpshooter.

Cameron Flick, on the other hand, was a young man, blond and bearded, whose website proclaimed him to be a *world class math tutor,* with a host of first-name testimonials to back that up.

Cameron made all the difference in my getting into Stanford. Melanie.

Cameron makes numbers come alive. Brian.

Cameron's the bomb with AP calc. Lucas.

He listed his educational credentials as a nine-year-old bachelor's degree from Oberlin, where he'd studied with *the eminent, Weinglass Prize winner, Sidney Thalberg* followed by enrollment in the doctoral program in theoretical mathematics at the U.

More important than any of that, Cameron Flick was a familiar face.

The tutor I'd seen with Keisha Boykins the day Milo and I had paid an unannounced visit.

Soon after our arrival, he'd guided Keisha toward the back of the house. No reason, then, to see it as anything more than wanting peace and quiet for his student.

Not anymore. Escape at the sight of the cops seemed a lot more likely.

I returned to Errol Moffett's memorial page. Yesterday, I'd skimmed the sad repetitive messages, turned away well before reaching the end. This time I gave them a closer look. Found what I was looking for six posts from the bottom.

You were a bright light, E-man. Didn't deserve this. Cam F.

My heart was beating faster than when I'd woken up, but in a different key: less confusion, more like the aerobic boost you get during a great run.

Next step: digging for info on Jarrod Sterling's half sibs. Jay Sterling had described his older children as twins, both studying in New York.

NYU and . . . the New School.

The proud father's pages gave up those details with glee.

Rhiannon Sterling, a bright-eyed, apple-cheeked brunette, was majoring in economics and business at NYU with an emphasis on econometrics.

Rory Sterling, her morose-looking, shaggy-haired brother, was studying art at one of the New School's five colleges, the Parsons School of Design.

The twins' individual pages produced no evidence Rory had enlisted the services of Cameron Flick but Rhiannon cited the math tutor as a *huge influence turning me on totally to the beauty of math and encouraging me to go for double-major gold.*

Typing manically, I searched for anything I could learn about Cameron Flick.

Nothing beyond the self-promotion of his tutoring business, The Numbers Game.

That was enough.

I texted Milo.

When you wake up, call me. Important.

CHAPTER

37

I caught a couple more hours of restless but triumphant sleep, was up by six forty-five. Robin had risen half an hour before, was already in the studio with Blanche. She hadn't left the kitchen long ago; the coffeepot remained hot.

I drank two cups waiting for my phone to ring.

At six fifty-eight, it obliged.

"What?" said Milo.

"I have a likely suspect."

"What?"

"I have a—"

"I heard you. Who?"

I told him.

He said, "Don't go anywhere."

He was in my office half an hour later. Remaining on his feet, no side trip to the fridge, placing the coffee I gave him on my desk and avoiding it as if it was toxic.

"You plucked this out of the air?"

"It was a process."

He pulled out his pad. "Details. If this is going to end up real, I need to understand *everything*."

"Robin helped me zero in on a common theme: protecting kids. The Boykinses, the Moffetts, and Sterling all fit that. So did the case I haven't told you much about."

"Robin," he said. "Did the pooch have anything to offer?"

"She did smile."

"Huh. How about something *on* that other case. It's evidence now, Alex."

I described the similarity between the body dumps of Marissa French and Vicki Saucedo, whom I left anonymous. How wondering about family protectiveness had led me to her college-student brother, also unnamed.

"He turned out to be studying math at Oberlin College in Ohio and that flashed me to the two cases Moe found. Both crime scenes were a short drive from the college so I checked out the brother's social platform and the big surprise was Flick being his tutor in addition to Keisha's. My gut told me it was more than coincidence but I had to be sure, maybe he just was one of L.A.'s hot math teachers. Then I found out he'd also taught Errol Moffett *and* one of Sterling's college-aged twins."

"Math and murder," he said. "The guy has a sideline?"

"On the face of it, bizarre," I said. "And I suppose it's possible Flick worked with someone else who did the actual shootings. But the Ohio connection makes it more likely that it's been his finger on the trigger. More than that, the Oberlin connection. Flick himself graduated from there and was present when the second victim, Steckel, worked as a campus custodian."

"Some sort of run-in with a janitor so he kills him?"

"If I'm right Steckel wasn't his first trophy. He graduated Oberlin nine years ago, making him thirty-one or -two, meaning fifteen or sixteen at the time of the first Ohio shooting—Wiebelhaus. Violent acting out often starts in adolescence. And often a sexual component is there. If we can find a connection between Flick and Wiebelhaus and Steckel, we've got a whole bunch of bricks for the wall."

"Unbelievable," he said, sitting in my desk chair and taking a long time to exhale. "I go to sleep and produce night-music, you reinvent the wheel. Okay, let's learn more about this scholar but I need to do it by the book, don't want to mess up the evidence chain. Ergo we use my computer, not this one. Since you're a wizard, wanna beam me up to the station?"

Without waiting for an answer, he charged past me, through the house and out the door.

I hadn't run this morning, settled for following his long strides.

He drove to Butler Avenue way too fast, had barely shut the Impala's driver's door before he was charging through the staff lot, continuing across the street, and flinging open the station door.

He pressed past the civilian clerk's greetings with a wave. Cursed violently because the elevator was engaged and made rare use of the stairs, then sped toward his office where, flushed and panting, he jammed his key into his lock as if it were a lethal weapon.

Remaining on his feet, he logged in using his police I.D. and got onto NCIC. At first glance, unaware of my presence as he typed viciously.

No hits on Cameron Flick. He sank down hard enough to make his chair squeak and growled like a bear in pain.

Social Security records were more agreeable. Flick had received a card at the age of eighteen, and that led to his birthdate and birthplace.

Thirty-one years ago, Vantage, Ohio.

I said, "The town where Leonard Wiebelhaus was shot. It's a hamlet so there's a good chance Wiebelhaus was known to Flick. Maybe intimately, as in stepfather."

He said, "Blended family gone to hell? Thank God it's an unusual name."

He plugged *Wiebelhaus* into the SSA records, came up with two names.

Crystal Jo Wiebelhaus, thirty-six, Akron, Ohio.

I said, "Right age for a sister."

Felicia Sue Wiebelhaus, sixty-nine, still in Vantage, Ohio, living in a trailer park.

He said, "Right age for a mommy. Let's see if she and Leonard ever made it formal."

The couple *had* obliged, obtaining a marriage license twenty years ago at the Lorain County Probate Court in Elyria, Ohio. Second try for both. Felicia's previously registered surname: Flick.

Milo sat back, breathing hard. "You royal-flushed again. Screw crime control, let's catch a flight to Vegas." He rubbed his face. "Step-daddy, who better to hate."

I said, "When Felicia married Wiebelhaus, Cameron was eleven. My guess is they didn't get along, maybe even to the point of Cameron being abused. Cameron endured it until he was fifteen then made his move. He'd be in a great position to know where and when Leonard would be hunting pheasants."

"If Felicia suspected she never said."

"Maternal protection. Or Wiebelhaus had been rough on her, too. Or she was scared of Cameron. In any case, we're talking a smart kid who planned well and got away with murder at fifteen, which is pretty intoxicating."

"He convinces himself he's an untouchable genius."

"And he is objectively smart," I said. "Great math skills, a low-income townie getting into Oberlin."

He said, "Then he kills the janitor six years later and earns himself another notch? That makes me wonder if all that good self-esteem led him to do others in between or before ours. But let's dial back to the here and now. Assuming Flick is our button man, how would the actual contracting go down? The families know him as a helpful tutor, why would they think he'd be willing to hunt humans?"

"Maybe they didn't until he found a way to let them know."

"How would it work its way into a conversation? Keisha's doing great with equations and by the way I can take care of ol' Jamarcus? Big risk, Alex. All he'd need was one solid citizen ratting him out." He smiled. "Unless getting the prodge into college outweighed all that."

I said, "There is another possibility. There were no conversations between Flick and the parents. No contracting, period. What if Flick took it upon himself to defend his students?"

"Mister Math decides it's kind to be cruel? C'mon, Alex."

"If Flick had been abused by his stepdad and was proud of how he'd set things right, why not? The earliest California murder we know about is Whitney Killeen. It's not unusual for tutoring sessions to venture beyond subject matter. We know that Rhiannon Sterling had high praise for Flick. What if she'd complained to him about all the terrible stress her dad was going through because of a horrible, unfit bitch of a stepmother intent on depriving Daddy of access to his darling two-year-old? If she painted Whitney in a bad enough light, Flick could've been inspired to come to the rescue. Just like he did for himself at age fifteen. I'm not saying a normal person could slide into murder that easily. No doubt Flick enjoys shooting people and I will bet there's a sexual component to it. But he needs some sort of justification. Once he got it from Rhiannon, he stalked Whitney, found the right time and place, did the deed."

"He's a rescuer but leaves a two-year-old in a boat?"

"Maybe he was planning to pluck Jarrod out of there and drop him somewhere safe. Then the neighbor showed up first and made Flick's life easier. In any event, it would've been at least Flick's third successful kill and really fed his ego. And his libido. So when Keisha Boykins—smart, sweet, chronically ill—came to him upset about Jamarcus Parmenter, it would've felt like another golden opportunity to be noble."

"Or Gerald and Kiki somehow connected with Flick to do Parmenter. Ditto O'Brien, who'd worked for Gerald."

"Parmenter's a possibility as a parental contract but so far O'Brien's relationship with Boykins was brief and tangential and we have no evidence there was any conflict with Keisha. I know how you feel about coincidence but this one wasn't necessarily huge, because O'Brien worked security all over town. So I still think his murder was more likely related to the Culver City victim. A case that was never pursued criminally, giving Flick yet another level of self-justification."

"Murder for fun rationalized as a good deed." He shook his head. "If there was no criminal charge, how'd this brother—you know I can find his name—learn O'Brien had attacked and dumped his sister?"

I said, "I've been wondering the same thing and now I'm going to try to find out. Got a spare office?"

38

My workspace: the same large interview room, expanded visually by solitude.

The two whiteboards, wiped clean and free of images, had been pushed against a wall. I sat at the long table and pulled out my phone.

Milo stood in the doorway for a second before closing it.

Lee Falkenburg said, "Hi. What's up?" Tight voice; guarded.

I said, "Things have changed and I really could use more information. I'll do everything I can to protect your source. But without me, the police may get there first."

"Why do you say that?"

"A suspect has been identified and there's a good chance he's got a connection to the Saucedo case. We're talking multiple murders, Lee."

"Oh God. What kind of connection?"

"In confidence?"

"Of course."

"There's a link between the suspect and Vicki's brother. I've told the cops my assumption the brother wasn't criminally involved and I've withheld his name but it's only a matter of time before they identify him."

"If he wasn't involved, what's the connection?"

"He may have complained about his sister's attack and unwittingly given the suspect ideas. For your sake I'm not going to say more."

"Multiple murders," she said. "How many?"

"You don't want to know."

"Oh shit, Alex. What exactly is it you want to know now?"

"There had to be a witness the night Vicki was brutalized and dumped. My money's on your source. Whom I'm assuming is the staffer who found the body."

Silence.

I said, "Lee, I need to know what he or she saw."

"You realize the position you're putting me in?"

"I do and I'm sorry, but one way or the other it'll come out."

"Oh God—next time you call me make sure it's just a mundane referral."

"Promise."

"Multiple murders," she said. "Okay, no promises, give me a few minutes."

"Thanks, Lee."

"Guess I should say, *You're welcome.*"

"A few minutes" turned to five, ten, fifteen. At eighteen I was ready to leave. As I got to my feet, the phone rang.

A woman's voice, tremulous and high-pitched, said, "Dr. Delaware?"

"Yes."

"It's just you there?"

"Absolutely."

"I hope that's true."

"It is."

"I hope . . . okay, this isn't going to take long and don't try to trace this phone, it's not mine. I am the person who saw what happened the night Vicki Saucedo was dumped. And you need to keep me out of it. Swear you will."

"I'll do my best but I can't guarantee anonymity if the cops dig deep."

"I'll take my chances with the cops," she said. "Because frankly they don't seem very competent."

Intake of breath. Long exhalation. "Okay. Here it is: I did not see the poor woman get discarded, just a car speeding through the parking lot, and that led me to look around for a problem. We get homeless and other problems in the lot after dark so I'm security-conscious. Carry pepper spray, try to be aware of my surroundings. The car was really going fast, I figured stupid kids joyriding, next time they could kill someone. So I tried to write down the license plate and managed to get five out of seven numbers. Then I found poor Vicki and dialed 911 and went to get the staff from the hospital. Culver City cops showed up and they had a really bad attitude. I literally had to push myself on them just to get their attention. Finally some guy in a uniform wrote down what I told him and made me feel stupid for not getting the make and model. Then he told me with incomplete plates, there was little they could do. Not exactly digging deep, huh?"

"Shameful," I said. "Did you ever inform the family?"

"A few days later, I felt it was my duty," she said. "Her parents were too upset and so was her sister. Just devastated. But her brother seemed approachable so I gave him the information."

"How'd he take it?"

"What do you think? He was upset. Angry. But in a quiet way. He struck me as the quiet sort but who knows, it was hardly a normal situation."

Click.

I tried the number. Blocked. Returned to Milo's office.

CHAPTER

39

He typed away, finally pushed away from his keyboard.

"Mr. Flick does not live in Hollywood but he's close enough, near Fairfax and Pico. He was kind enough to legally register two weapons six years ago, a Pardini and a Hammerli, both super-expensive target pistols."

"No rifle."

"Big shock, huh? But owning weapons like that tells me he's a serious marksman who practices. Maybe we can find which range he uses. Not that I'd choose to nab him there, can you imagine? But it's possible someone's seen him with the rifle. So what were you just up to?"

I repeated what I'd learned.

He said, "But I'm not supposed to look into it."

"If it turns out the brother actually contracted Flick, look to your heart's content," I said. "If we're talking some sort of volunteer mission on Flick's part, I don't see the point."

He grunted. "So how'd Flick—or the brother—I.D. O'Brien with only a partial?"

"They're both math people. Don't imagine basic hacking with some algorithm is beyond either of them."

"Your Jane Doe was victimized a year ago. Why wait till now to shoot O'Brien?"

"Joy of the hunt," I said. "Planning, stalking, staking out. And now that I think about it, a lot of advanced math is like that. Problems that take a long time to solve."

"Maybe that or O'Brien will still come back to Boykins protecting Keisha."

"Either way, you've got Flick to focus on."

He faced his desk, spun around and looked at me again. "Ye olde anonymous informant, huh? That's actually not so bad, I can just list it that way in the murder book, we do it all the time. So okay, thanks. Meanwhile I've called another meeting."

"When?"

"An hour. Tell me you've got no patients."

"Not today."

"Perfect. Everyone's hyped and rarin' to go. Including ol' Buck but he won't be here. In South Dakota visiting a daughter."

He looked at his Timex. "Fifty-six minutes. Let's get nourished."

We left the station and walked north to Santa Monica Boulevard. Milo's a regular at most of the restaurants on a four-block westward stretch, leading to consistent VIP service and sometimes hero worship. But he turned east and stopped a few feet from Butler where a painted banner on a Technicolor food truck proclaimed

TASTEE BITES!!!

❤ ❤ ❤ ❤ ❤ ❤

A gorgeous young woman in a red Tastee Bites T-shirt worked the counter. A second beauty queen in matching tee, white shorts, and high-tops was outside the truck, taking orders from the half a dozen people lined up at eleven a.m. Including two uniformed officers who nodded at Milo.

The women also nodded and the one on the sidewalk hurried up, exultant. "The usual, Lieutenant?"

"You bet, Sasha."

"Great! And to drink?"

"Large Coke."

"Perfect! And for you, sir?"

I said, "Roast beef sandwich sounds good."

"Awesome! It *is* good! And to drink?"

"Iced tea."

"Sweetened?"

"No, thanks."

"Large?"

"Sure."

"Beautiful!"

This time Milo took the stairs with no complaint. This time we used the big interview room to polish off lunch.

Flex space given a new meaning.

No false promises about my sandwich; generously dimensioned, amply stuffed with rare roast beef, and augmented by some sort of hand-whipped horseradish sauce. All of which was appreciated because sloshing coffee was the only thing in my gut.

Milo's breakfast burrito was the size and shape of a lumbar cushion. He sized it up the way a coyote assesses a rabbit.

When we were through eating, he said, "Hold on, right back," and returned with an enlarged version of Cameron Flick's DMV photo. Wheeling one of the whiteboards to center stage, he taped the image dead center.

Nothing noteworthy about the face. On the bland side, really. Even the eyes were unremarkable. Medium brown, slightly down-slanted, neither angry nor kind. Just a pair of eyes, free of that cold forever-stare some witnesses report encountering when faced with evil.

People expect monsters and ogres but sometimes you just get terrifyingly ordinary.

40

As we finished our drinks, the door swung open and five detectives filed in looking stunned.

Ten eyes shot to Flick's face.

Petra, Raul, Alicia, Moe, and Sean continued to stare as they settled at the long tables.

Raul was the first to speak. "He drives a five-year-old Beemer that doesn't show up on our citation list from that night. Neither does his name so maybe he's the one who cut the chain. Or he found somewhere else to park."

Petra continued to study the image. "He looks like what he is, a grad student."

Moe said, "Majors in math, minors in evil."

Alicia turned to me. "You figured this out last night?"

"Hopefully."

"Hopefully? Sounds like a definite." She turned to Milo for confirmation.

He stepped up to the board. "It's looking promising, here's what we know so far."

———

His lecture was brief and informative, and left five pairs of eyes active and bright. If he'd been a professor at Oberlin or some similar place, five stars from the undergrads.

"Questions?"

Moe said, "Just the obvious one: What's the plan?"

Milo said, "There are two things we need to do simultaneously. Priority one is keeping a close eye on Mr. Flick with the dual purpose of making sure he doesn't shoot anyone else and learning as much as we can about him to build up the evidence."

Alicia said, "Are we sure he soloed?"

"We're not sure of anything, so exactly, checking out if he has pals is essential. Which will hopefully also come up on his phone. My gut, though—and Alex's—is that Flick has been soloing. Guy's a serious marksman, wouldn't need to hire out."

He told them about the target pistols.

Raul whistled. "Looked into a Hammerli. Two thousand bucks."

Sean said, "Explains the precision of the neck wounds."

Milo said, "He's gotta be practicing somewhere. If we get lucky, he'll bring the rifle to a range and we can photograph him with it and, more important, get hold of some bullets. Either way, we can't ever lose sight of him. Mr. Nguyen has dropped his usual tight-sphincter objections and authorized subpoenas on Flick's phone and finances. But he won't go along with taps and I don't want to breach Flick's residence yet because if we don't find anything and he's alerted, we could be in big trouble. So for the time being, I want a combo of stationary and mobile surveillance with shorter shifts and plenty of task-switching to avoid boredom and fatigue. Questions?"

Head shakes.

He said, "Okay, the second priority is learning if any of the parents did hire Flick for more than coaching their little geniuses or is Alex's instinct right and we're talking a self-justifying shooter."

Sean said, "Why do you feel that way, Doc?"

I said, "It's hard for me to imagine an easy transition from tutoring math to murder for hire. How would Flick approach the families? With the exception of Gerald Boykins, none of them have criminal records and Boykins's arrests were nonviolent and years ago. As Milo pointed out before you guys came in, even hinting about a paid hit ran the risk of horrifying at least one of them and getting ratted on. And Flick's risk-averse. Thinks, plans, takes his time."

"Foreplay," said Alicia.

Smiles from the others.

Alicia said, "So to speak."

I said, "That's actually a great choice of words. Given the time lag between the victims' perceived offenses and the shootings, it's clear that for him the planning process is as satisfying as the outcome. Maybe more so. If he was the Ohio shooter, he began killing in adolescence and may have incorporated hunting humans into his fantasy life. And that's likely to have included a sexual element."

Petra said, "Just another serial killer."

"One who requires justification."

"So do guys who murder prostitutes."

I said, "Good point, it's always about ego. In any event, he found his pattern early and sticks with it."

Alicia said, "If it ain't broke."

Milo said, "We'll fine-tooth as far back as we can for any interesting calls and texts and for money transfers that go beyond what he gets for tutoring. Which according to his website is a hundred and eighty an hour. If any of the family members come up dirty, we'll refocus on them. Now, let's talk division of labor."

CHAPTER

41

Milo's initial plan had been for three 8-hour surveillance shifts, two detectives per shift in separate cars with radio contact. All of the D's preferred twelve hours and he said, "Fine."

Moe and Alicia took the night shift because neither minded being up late. Petra and Raul began with days, Milo and Sean were on schedule for the following night.

I left them to their preparation and went home.

That didn't mean I put the case aside.

Cameron Flick listed himself as a doctoral candidate in math at the U. I pulled up the department's website, which obligingly included a list of graduate students.

Surprisingly long list: a hundred sixty-two names, some for terminal master's degrees, some for doctorates. None of them Flick's.

Had his enrollment been a total lie from the beginning or had he been asked to leave? I had no contacts at Math but I did know someone married to a possible source: a geology prof named Llewelyn Greenberg who taught at the old school crosstown where I had a faculty appointment.

I generally avoid faculty functions but Llewelyn and I had sat together at a Kappa Alpha Phi dinner where a student I'd mentored had merited membership in that graduate honor society. Sitting next to Llewelyn was a pleasant, quiet woman he'd introduced as "my considerably better half, Karen's an expert in topology over in the New World."

She'd blushed and spent the evening silently doodling formulas on her napkin, then running over to Llewelyn's, and finally to mine. Thanking me with a sweet smile.

Llewelyn was a bit more outgoing but not by much and by the end of the evening, they both looked exhausted.

More introverts. They don't make a lot of noise but they often create wonders.

I looked up Llewelyn's wife. Karen Salzman-Greenberg, Cratchett-Fillmore Professor of Mathematics.

I reached Llewelyn in his office and made my request. No need to explain because, as I'd expected, no curiosity on his part. That likely made asking for confidentiality unnecessary. But you have to be careful.

Llewelyn said, "Of course," as if I'd stated the obvious, hung up and called me back two hours later.

"That person was there but no longer as of two years and slightly over five months ago."

He recited the date.

I said, "Any idea why?"

"The usual," he said. "Floundering. Couldn't come up with anything original."

I thanked him and thought about a grad student, taken with his own brilliance, tossed from academia like a piece of detritus.

Shattered. Then angry. A few months later, he deals with it in a tried-and-true manner.

Go get the rifle.

I moved on to an image search on Cameron Flick and pulled up five photos of a smiling tutor next to even more broadly beaming high school seniors, each holding up a college acceptance letter.

Plugging in Flick's address on South Ogden Drive revealed a non-descript, off-white one-story bungalow, tagged by a real estate site at twelve hundred thirty-three square feet on an eighth-acre lot. Four years ago, the property had sold for just over a million and a half dollars. L.A. real estate psychosis.

Four years ago, Flick had still been a grad student and even with a host of clients paying a hundred eighty bucks an hour, that price was a stretch.

A second site included what the first hadn't: the presence of a three-hundred-square-foot guesthouse. Milo probably knew that already but I included it in my notes and switched to a ten-year-old shooting in Shelter Lake, Ohio.

Rainer Steckel's funeral had been memorialized in the same local paper that had listed his death one month prior. The ceremony had been "well-attended by family, friends, and Oberlin faculty members and students who remembered Rainer with great fondness."

The dead man's willingness to help others was emphasized, as were his "love of the outdoors and excellence in building birdhouses that he gave free of charge to neighbors and friends."

No spouse or children listed. I looked for Steckels in Ohio, found a heating, air-conditioning, and plumbing company in Dayton owned and run by William and Della Steckel.

Nearly five p.m. there but worth a try.

A man answered, "Steckel AC, this is Will, how can I help you?"

"My name's Alex Delaware and I'm calling from Los Angeles where I work with the police department."

"Work with? How?"

"Criminal analysis, I'll give you a phone number and if you'd like you can verify—"

"No, that's fine. What's this about?"

"We're looking into a ten-year-old murder that took place—"

"Rainer," said Will Steckel, his voice dropping. "I was hoping you'd say that. But why the devil would Los Angeles be interested?"

"It's possible that whoever shot Rainer committed a crime here."

"Huh. Crazy."

"He was your brother."

"Older brother," said Will Steckel. "Well, at least you're trying to do something. The yokels over in Shelter Lake. Do you know the details?"

"Your brother was shot while hunting deer."

"That was the claim but it was bullshit. I told the idiots, they ignored me."

"What did you tell them?"

"That it had to be one of those spoiled brats from the college— Oberlin, that's where Rain worked."

"Which brat in particular?"

"That's the problem," said Will Steckel. "I had no name, no description, nothing. Just what my brother told me like a month before it happened. So who's the bastard you're looking at over there?"

"Sorry, can't say at this point."

"You're claiming there'll be a point where you *can* say?"

I said, "The more we know, the better the odds of that. What did Rain tell you?"

"That he had a giant kerfuffle with one of the college brats. Sick kerfuffle, Rain was working at night cleaning the gym, went into a bathroom, put the lights on and caught some weirdo whipping his wienie. In full view, sitting in one of the stalls with the door wide open. Pervert shouldn'ta been there for any reason, the building was supposed to be closed up for the evening, but Rain said he was always finding doors unlocked when they weren't supposed to be. Windows, too. Coupla times he found raccoons wandering around eating garbage and once in a while there'd be a couple doing their thing. But never that. I mean, why? Use a dorm bathroom. Or just wait until dark and fool around in your bunk bed. So we're obviously talking sick puppy."

He laughed. "I'm not saying what happened was funny but picturing it is kinda funny, no? Rain walks in ready to mop and sees *that*? He said he told the kid, 'What the hell are you doing, boy? Stick it back in your pants and scram.' So what would you expect someone caught in the act to do?"

"Be embarrassed and leave."

"Exactly. You tuck your tail between your legs and get the hell out of there. Not this brat, he gets an attitude, starts yelling at Rain. Tells him he's intruding. That's the word he used. *Intruding.* Rain can't believe what he's hearing, says, 'Are you nuts, boy?' Then Rain cracks up and says, 'Speaking of nuts, yours are shrinkin',' and that *really* pisses the brat off. He pulls up his pants and comes at Rain like he's itchin' for a fight. Rain holds out his mop and says, 'Don't even think about it, boy.' The brat stops, tries to stare Rain down, then finally he leaves. But on the way out, he bumps into Rain's shoulder. Hard, on purpose. Rain shoulda reported it but that wasn't him, he was softhearted, give you the shirt off his back. So he let it ride and then a couple weeks later, he sees the same brat on campus giving him the stink-eye. That's when he told me about it, said the kid gave him the creeps. A couple weeks after that, Rain's dead. That sound like a hunting accident to you? Yokel fools."

"Did Rain give you any details about the creep?"

"No," said Will Steckel. "Just what I told you and that was supposedly the problem for the yokels. Insufficient details. But I think it was more than that. They'd never do anything to embarrass the college, place does a lot of hiring. So is your guy some sort of sex deviate?"

"Again, sorry, can't—"

"I'll take that as a yes," said Will Steckel, chuckling. "Didn't know beating your meat in public was even a problem in L.A."

———

Milo said, "Filling out subpoena forms and enjoying it. What's up?"

"Two things," I said. "Flick's no longer enrolled at the U. Dismissed due to lack of performance a little under two and a half years ago. That's not long before the shootings began. So it's likely career frustration played a role."

"Cammy-poo all upset? Don't tell Flick's defense attorney that, Alex. No, I get what you're saying. It could fill out the motive. Thanks. What's the second thing?"

"I may have found out why Rainer Steckel was shot."

He said, "I leave you alone for a few hours and you invent another wheel? Okay, go."

I recounted what Will Steckel had told me.

He said, "Brother's right, it is a weird story. You're saying Flick's got that short of a fuse?"

"Far from it," I said. "The picture I'm getting of Flick is he expends a lot of mental energy maintaining his self-image as smart. Which would be consistent with child abuse. He has no tolerance for being challenged and certainly not for being humiliated and registers rage immediately. But he controls it and doesn't act out impulsively. Instead, he takes a reasoned, step-wise, problem-solving approach to revenge."

"Mathematical approach."

"Exactly. And now that I think about it, just like the Unabomber. He murdered because he enjoyed it but he got as much gratification from stewing, mapping out a plan, choosing his time and place, then basking in self-congratulation and writing a manifesto."

"Jesus," he said. "Hope none of Flick's students have pissed him off."

"Now that you mention it," I said, "tutoring college applicants would be perfect for someone craving admiration. He enters the situation as an expert, his students are anxious and needy and grateful for every bit of edge he gives them and so are their parents. That's in sharp contrast with his experience as a grad student where he ultimately ended up failing."

"Haven't heard of any math profs at the U. reaching an untimely demise."

"So far, so good," I said. "But let Flick mull on it too long and who knows?"

"Don't even say that, Alex. Yeah, yeah, I need to catch him. So let me go back to his damn phone records and his moolah records and start to invent my own wheel."

42

The next couple of days were taken up by new court referrals and that was just fine because I'd adjusted my focus to what I'd learned in school and had nothing to offer Milo.

On the first day, he called me at eight p.m.

"Think of anything?"

"Nope."

"Keep trying. Here's our situation. Records haven't come in yet and nothing earth-shattering from the surveillance. Today was a yawner. Flick lives in a rented guesthouse, there doesn't seem to be anyone sharing the place. At eleven a.m. he drove to a Starbucks for coffee and a sandwich then on to five fancy houses. First Boykins in B.H., then two in Brentwood, one in Holmby, one in Santa Monica. Back home by five where he washed his car in the driveway, went inside, and hasn't shown himself since."

I said, "Westside clientele."

"Adoring clientele. Three of the kids walked him to his car hanging on his every word. Hero worship, like you said. One of them was Keisha who seemed a little frail according to Petra. Hope her family's innocent, not looking forward to bursting *that* bubble."

"Five clients adds up to nine hundred bucks for a brief day's work. Well compensated hero."

"Yeah, it's a nice setup, a helluva lot more than he'd make as a T.A. He's not spending it conspicuously. The place is a converted garage and his rent is six hundred a month."

"Who owns the house?"

"A nice old lady. Also smiling at Flick as he chatted with her then wheeled the garbage cans to the curb."

"Model tenant."

"Yeah," he said. "Hate that kind of thing."

On the second day, he called just after nine p.m. "More of the same except only four clients, all in Encino and Sherman Oaks."

"Consolidating his Valley shift. Very efficient."

"What a guy," he said. "He worked from two to six p.m. and raked in another seven hundred twenty bucks. It keeps up like that, he's making serious change. Good for the self-esteem, no?"

I said, "But not good enough."

"For what?"

"Keeping him away from his rifle."

Day Three, he called at two p.m. Different voice, brightened by a lilt.

"Finally something to report. I'll give you the minor-league news first. Did the day shift myself with Sean. No phone data yet but Flick's bank records came in late so I took them home and did my home-work. He uses Zelle so it's easy to pinpoint his deposits. Every single one of them is a hundred eighty bucks. His best week he put away close to four grand, his average is around twenty-five hundred."

I said, "What does he do with the money?"

"No investment schemes if that's what you're asking. He lets it sit there in an account that earns about one percent, withdraws the rent money on the dot plus another eight hundred for his living expenses.

He gets everything delivered—groceries, laundry, and all his restaurant tabs are takeout for one. Nothing gourmet: casual Italian, Thai, Mexican. The major-league news is that if anyone's ever paid him for more than teaching math, it's not showing up, though I'm sure he wouldn't use an online service. I suppose he could be stashing evil bucks under his mattress and maybe we'll learn something when we glom his phone. But I'm feeling more and more confident it's what you said: He took it upon himself to go hunting. So again, Sahib, you were right."

"Aw shucks."

"Indeed," he said. "Now for the all-star news. Flick started off the day with the usual—two clients in Bel Air. But then he got on the 405 and drove to a shooting range all the way up in Santa Clarita. Where wouldn't you know, he took a camo-patterned rifle case out of his car in which was a camo-patterned Featherweight Winchester .308 that he used to inflict lethal injuries on a bunch of paper bad-guy targets. The place is interesting, clientele's either off-duty cops or tatted-up gangbanger types."

"Brothers-in-arms."

"Hah. Fortunately the proprietor of the on-site gun shop's a former deputy. I gave him gloves, he went and pulled out the bullets from the hay bales behind the targets and also retrieved the targets. Don't need to tell you where the wounds were centered."

"The neck, slightly off center to the right."

"In a nice tight pattern. I'm driving everything straight to Hertzberg soon as I get off the phone with you."

Nice enough way to cut the conversation short.

I said, "Have fun."

"I just might."

The moment he clicked off, I thought of something.

A while back, Milo had mentioned an art show where Marissa French had spent her last night alive in the company of Paul O'Brien. Rather than call for details, I ran my own search, keywording *art gallery melrose* along with the date.

That pulled up an exhibit titled *Dots and Dashes* at the Hollow Eyes Gallery.

Truth in advertising. The works on display were large unframed canvases filled with black circles and clipped gray lines. No obvious meaning to any of it. The artist someone named Damien D'Aze, the listed prices comically crazy.

None of that interested me. Fifteen publicity shots taken at the party did, posted proudly on four photo sites. I found Marissa French and Paul O'Brien in numbers six and seven. The two of them, standing together. She looking confused, he self-satisfied.

I found what I was looking for in Number Twelve.

Cameron Flick had tucked himself into a corner, a glass of something clear in his hand. Crowded by shoulders and faces and clearly not enjoying it. Blond hair sheathed his forehead diagonally but he'd made no attempt to block his eyes and they were different from the unremarkable orbs on his driver's license.

Narrowed, focused, somehow darker.

The face below, tight with concentration.

The same look I'd seen on Paul O'Brien's face at the Chanel party as he studied Vicki Saucedo.

Hungry.

Hunting.

I downloaded the photo and emailed it to Milo along with a message: *Another brick.*

I got my answer forty minutes later: *Just got to H. Muchas gr. Keep at it. Eat fish, maybe? Supposed to be brain food.*

43

Day Four he called at eight fifty p.m. and said, "If it's too late to bop over, tell me."

Robin was back in her studio, French-polishing the top of another vintage classical guitar, a hundred-year-old Simplicio with a gorgeous carved headstock. More repetitive work with the pad and the spirit varnish. She finds it relaxing and sometimes saves it for quiet nights.

I returned to the house, called Milo, and said, "Bop."

He was at my door half an hour later.

This time he beelined to the fridge, peered inside as if examining a crime scene, then reached in and drew out half a turkey breast, roast beef nearing the end of its shelf-life, dry Genoa salami, tomatoes, lettuce, mustard, and mayo. Adding rye bread from the bin, he set about constructing a monumental sandwich.

Humming.

I said, "You got a ballistics match."

His feet performed a little shuffling dance as he built a tower of intemperance.

"Coupla hours ago. Fast-tracked the arrest warrant and a search warrant for Flick's house and his car. So why am I here?"

"Sharing good news with a pal."

He brought the sandwich to the table. "I want to take him into custody with minimal risk to us, his landlady, neighbors. Him, too. Figured you might have some wisdom on that. *If* you've been eating finny critters, as I suggested."

"Sorry, tonight was turkey. Where's Flick now?"

"Home. Petra and Raul have been on him since three, now they're sitting on his block since he got home at six ten after five tutoring gigs. Hopefully nearly a grand's worth of fees will keep him mellow for the night and we can grab him when he walks to his car tomorrow morning."

"Too many guns in his house to go frontal."

"And it's a tough layout, only one way to his door, way too much time for him to prepare."

He sat down, tucked a napkin under his collar, chomped, wiped his chin, took another bite. "Delicious. Especially the turkey."

Two bites later:

"He registered his pistols but not the rifle, so yeah, who knows what kind of arsenal he has in there. Also, your comment about the Unabomber got me thinking. What if he's also stockpiled lunatic stuff? Grenades, explosives, has the place booby-trapped. So the plan is to box him in the moment we see him. I'll be there with all the kids."

I said, "No SWAT guys. Too conspicuous and likely to set off a war."

"That was my thought. You agree?"

"I do."

"Any other suggestions?"

"If he's carrying his rifle or any other weapon, wait until he's inside the car and you can see that his hands are clear. Then move in as quickly as possible. He's a planner so maybe not great with surprises."

He thought about that. "Okay, then, it's set. I'll finish this repast and notify the troops about tomorrow."

———

He was enjoying a final bite of sandwich when his phone rang.

He listened for a while, gulped with effort, as if the food had de-hydrated. Frowned and said, "Okay, time for Tac Four, keep me posted."

Standing, he pocketed his phone, drew out his police radio, and set it on a tactical band. "That was Petra. Flick just left his house, got in his car, and is driving west on Venice."

I said, "Did he take the rifle with him?"

"She doesn't know, too dark. But even if he wasn't carrying, he could be keeping weapons in the trunk. I'm going to notify the troops then meet up with Petra and Raul."

"I'll tell Robin then we'll go."

"Forget the plural. You're staying put."

I was somewhat prepared for that.

A couple of cases ago I'd gone along on a surveillance and been attacked by a psychotic killer. My body had healed quicker than Milo's guilt but I thought he'd settled down. Then again, self-blame can be a chronic disease, going into remission then popping up without warn-ing.

I said, "Don't worry, not a comparable situation."

"Feels comparable to me. I thought I was being careful by having you stay behind. Who knew the asshole would be coming from the opposite direction."

"I was outside the car. This time I'll remain inside. With the doors locked."

"Forget it, Alex. What's the point?"

"I've been on this from the beginning. Kind of helped develop the suspect, wouldn't you say?"

"Oh, please."

"Also," I said, "you'll likely want me in on the interview so the more I can observe him, the better equipped I'll be."

Flimsy even to my ear, and a total lie. The real reason: I like the excitement.

Milo said, "What if he does have the rifle within arm's reach and it does turn into a war?"

"I'll duck."

"Not funny."

"Six cops on one suspect who has no idea he's under investigation? It'll go smoothly."

"You and your optimism."

"Let's go out to the studio. If Robin objects, I stay here."

"You're willing to take that bet?"

"Yup."

He said, "What if the pooch objects?"

"I'll risk that, too."

Fourteen minutes later I was in the passenger seat of the Impala as Milo idled the engine and radioed Petra for the third time.

She said, "This guy drives weirdly. He started off pretty briskly on Venice, then turned north onto Sepulveda and gradually slowed down. I thought he might be looking for something or preparing to stop but he just kept going and slowing, all the way to the Sepulveda Pass, which he just got onto . . . uh-oh, he *has* pulled over . . . just past that two-lane 405 on-ramp . . . nothing here, why would he—nope, wrong about that, just a momentary stop. He *is* different."

Milo said, "Maybe he prepped a weapon."

"God, I hope not . . . but you're right, that makes sense. Okay, I'm appropriately nervous and hanging back—you get that, Raul?"

Biro said, "Totally. I'm half a block behind you."

"Stay that way unless something changes," she said. "All right, he's back in motion. Crawling. The Pass is totally open but he's doing twenty. Wonder if that's good or bad."

Milo looked at me.

I said, "He could be in planning mode and getting closer to his goal."

He passed that along.

She said, "Okay, we'll be super-careful. Can you call everyone else and catch them up? I want to concentrate on every move Flick makes."

Milo said, "Will do, then we'll set out ourselves."

"You and Alex? Good. Flick's for sure not normal. He goes total-freakin'-psycho after we nab him, we could use the help."

I kept my smile to myself but Milo felt it.

Grinding his teeth, he said, "Don't gloat," then he texted Alicia, Sean, and Moe to go on Tac Four and radioed them to keep their phones active in order to stay aware of Petra's location.

They all lived in the Valley, which could turn out to be a bit of luck, cutting the drive-time if Flick's northward drive ended up in one of the bedroom communities on the other side of the Santa Monica Mountains.

Moe: "Copy, L.T."

Alicia: "Ditto, L.T."

Sean: "Ready, Loot."

CHAPTER

44

It was nearly eleven when we left.

The best way to access the Sepulveda Pass from my house is to climb up the Glen and hook westward on Mulholland. The trip winds through miles of S-curves and past high-priced housing developments unseen from the road. Beyond that, two churches and a synagogue and a couple of expensive prep schools.

Seeing the schools tensed Milo up even further. "Hope the bastard's not planning some ugly headline thing," but when he radioed Petra, she said, "Nope, he's beyond any access to Mulholland, still on Sepulveda and we just crossed Ventura. There's that stretch a few miles up where the hookers hang out so maybe this'll turn out to just be his night for dirty fun . . . oops, wrong again, he swung right onto a side street called . . . Green Briar Lane, is hurtling east at . . . fourteen miles per. Now eleven."

Milo said, "Sounds like he's looking for something. Maybe a place he hasn't been before."

"Makes sense," said Petra. "Street's hilly and curvy and not well lit, I turned off my headlights, am going by the moon and his brake lights."

Milo said, "All residential?"

"Nothing but. Decent houses, quiet even though Ventura's not far. One of those places you'd have to know about—okay, he's down to five miles per . . . has stopped and pulled over to the south and parked. Turned off his engine, no more brake lights, he's basically invisible. I'm too far to see the address but it's the eleven five hundred block of Green Briar Lane. Can someone map it and tell me if it can be approached from the opposite side?"

Alicia said, "On it, Sarge . . . yes it can but you'd need to exit Ventura on Haig Terrace then take two little short streets that discontinue . . . Escondido Drive, Ramsey Drive, Ramsey becomes Green Briar maybe a . . . third of a mile from where you are. You want me to take that position? I can be there in about ten."

Moe said, "Same here."

Sean said, "I'm closer . . . yeah, I see it. I can be there probably in five."

Petra said, "All three of you do it, Raul and Milo will back me up at this end."

Milo said, "What's Flick doing?"

Petra said, "Still just sitting there."

Moe said, "What Doc said, bastard likes the process."

Petra said, "Any ideas while we wait?"

Milo handed me the radio.

I said, "You could try to find out who he's studying."

"I would if I knew which house interested him."

I said, "He's likely parked right in front of it but you could expand it to one or two neighbors on each side then figure out the address spacing and make an educated guess."

Petra said, "Why not? We may be here for a while. Uh-oh, scratch that, he's moving again."

CHAPTER

45

Cameron Flick drove assuredly to where Green Briar turned into Ramsey Drive, then onward to Escondido Drive and Haig Terrace, where he glided to a smooth stop at Ventura Boulevard, made an easy right, crossed to the left-turn lane, paused for the light at Sepulveda, and was back on the Pass moments later.

Petra radioed: "Maybe he's going back home."

This time she was right.

By the time the BMW pulled onto Flick's street two blocks from its destination, Milo was waiting for it, concealed by the shadows of an obligingly massive deodar cedar tree sprouting from the front yard of Flick's landlady's house. Heavy branches hung nearly to the ground. Good cover in the darkness.

From where I sat in the Impala, he'd disappeared.

Alicia and Sean had also made it in time for Flick's arrival. She'd parked four car lengths north of Flick's residence, he the same distance south.

Petra and Raul had held back so Flick wouldn't notice them following, and Moe's drive took him a few extra minutes. All three were relegated to positions half a block north. Flick paid them no notice as he cruised by.

As the BMW swept onto the driveway, Alicia and Sean got out, armed themselves, and ran silently forward on rubber-soled feet.

Flick got out of the car, wearing sweatpants and a hoodie. Carrying nothing. He'd walked a couple of bouncy steps before Milo materialized, Glock pointing, shouting.

"Police hands on your head where I can see them on your head now now now!"

Flick stood there, disobedient hands remaining at his sides. Clenched. Sean came up from behind and tackled him and while he was down, Alicia cuffed him.

They both yanked him up. Milo faced him.

I got out of the car just in time to hear, "Cameron Flick, you're under arrest for four counts of murder. You have the right . . ."

If Flick remained stunned by capture, he wasn't showing it. He sagged but not from despair. Wanting to increase the burden of his weight on Sean and Alicia. As Milo recited, he raised an eyebrow. Not the predator's eyes from the art party. The blandness of his DMV photo.

He yawned.

". . . anything you say can and will be—"

Flick smirked. A drawling voice said, "Like I never heard that on stupid TV."

Milo said, "You're going to hear it again."

"That," said Flick, "is because you're a redundant moron."

Suddenly his shoulders rose.

Alicia said, "What's in your hands? Unclench them."

Flick stiffened. Ignored the command. Sean forced his left hand open.

Nothing.

On to the right hand. Something fell to the ground.

White, a loose blossom.

Gripping a flower? No, a wadded tissue, unfurling. Alicia gloved up and tweezed it between her fingers.

Sniffed.

"Gross," she said. "Talk about foreplay, Cammie."

Return of the hunter's eyes. Flick writhed and spat at her. Barely missed polluting her face.

Sean kicked Flick's legs out from under him. Flick pitched forward and Sean guided him facedown onto the driveway.

Milo turned to Alicia. "You okay?"

She said, "Yeah. He's good with a gun but his mouth is a joke."

"I've got masks in my trunk."

I went and fetched two.

Double-masked, cuffed, and prone, Flick seemed to wilt.

Milo called for a patrol car for transport.

Flick said, "You are all so incredibly *stupid*."

Milo said, "Let's start from the beginning. You have the right . . ."

"Lawyer," said Flick. *"Lawyerlawyerlawyerlawyerlawyer."*

46

Nothing of interest was found in Flick's car but for an amoebic stain near the front rim of the driver's seat and several smaller speckles on the *Oberlin* floor mat below. All of it fluoresced blue under UV light, the way organic material does. It didn't take long for the lab to get specific. Semen. Same for the tissue Alicia had retrieved.

Milo said, "Public bathroom, his car. What's that, a danger thing?"

I said, "Like I said, a sexual component. Also, a mastery thing. The rules don't apply to me."

We were in an Italian place two blocks from the station, drinking coffee and eating almond biscotti.

I said, "Maybe that's why he was driving slow. Timing it so he could finish in front of that house."

He said, "Everything's a production with this lunatic. Those people have no idea what they avoided."

Those people were a family named Streicher, who lived in *that* house. The parents, city-employed accountants, had a seventeen-year-old daughter and a fifteen-year-old son, both of whom were enrolled at a prep school in Sherman Oaks.

Neither of the kids was Flick's client but the girl had been cited as the ringleader of a *mean clique* that had tormented a junior at the same school named Shania Fellows. Who *was* a longtime client.

Self-described as *proudly introverted, quantitatively aroused, and cerebrally-active,* Shania had repeatedly posted about her oppressors on social media. Her parents had complained to the headmaster then griped online that *no one seems to care about oppression if you're suffi-ciently privileged.*

"No one except Sir Cameron," said Milo. "Someone files a com-plaint, he starts planning a permanent solution. While he rubs him-self. Crazy. *Is* he?"

"With his level of premeditation?" I said. "Not even close. And even if his lawyer wants to try diminished capacity, I doubt Flick's ego will allow him to go along with it. He's heavily invested in being men-tally superior."

He laughed. "How many times did he call me an idiot before the black-and-white arrived?"

I said, "Maybe a dozen. Interspersed with his *lawyer lawyer lawyer* mantra. Who's representing him?"

"Lance Guidot, court-appointed, not bad but not brilliant."

"Then it won't last long. Flick will downgrade him and want noth-ing to do with him."

"He can switch counsel as much as he wants. We've got more than enough."

That confidence came from the ballistics match and the treasure trove found at Flick's home.

The converted garage was an open space kept up neatly and fur-nished minimally with contemporary pieces, including two wire-framed bookcases filled with math and science books that ranged from junior high to grad school level.

One exception to the minimalistic décor: a seven-and-a-half-foot carved mahogany armoire, ungainly and Victorian, that nudged the ceiling.

The inside rear wall of the oversized cabinet was faced with pegboard and outfitted with movable hooks and braces that supported the two pricey target pistols Flick had registered along with a forty-year-old long-barreled Colt six-shooter, a Glock not unlike Milo's, a Benelli Super Black Eagle shotgun, and mounted dead center, a .308 Winchester Featherweight bolt-action rifle enhanced by a custom Cerakote camouflage finish. Next to the guns, heavy-duty bolt cutters.

Below the rifle, a matching bipod and carrying case and an infrared nightscope. On the bottom rung, five bladed weapons: a squared-off chopper, a leather-handled Buck, a curved Indonesian fighter, an all-black knuckle knife, and a stiletto. All appeared unused.

Milo said, "What's that all about?"

I said, "Maybe he takes them to shootings for moral support."

Flick's computer, unprotected by a password (my answer to Milo's question: "Overconfidence"), gave up a file on each of his L.A. victims, always headed *Ansatz.*

Milo said, "Sounds German."

I looked it up. "Good guess. It's a word mathematicians use to describe setting the framework for a proof."

"Wonderful."

We read the files. Each began with an exposition of "the necessary documentation of offenses" inflicted on Flick's "followers."

Rhiannon Sterling, "a crackerjack math-head, especially good with probability theory which will serve her well as a quant and probably make her rich," had wept to her tutor about the stress her dad was under due to "hateful and unreasonable demands" by his "vicious and asocial ex-girlfriend" and her fear that "never ever seeing baby boy Jarrod will tear my family utterly apart. Essentially cancel him and us."

Keisha Boykins had been "terrified to the point where her AP calc is suffering right when she needs it to be Harvard-shiny and her IBD is intensifying." The source of her fear: Jamarcus Parmenter's "vile, misogynistic doggerel" and the possibility Parmenter would "take out his rage at Mr. B for his quite reasonable dismissal on my brilliant girl K."

Michael Saucedo was "adjusting to Oberlin gradually (something I can relate to) but like me he'll triumph due to superior cognitive ability." Vicki's brother had expressed "justifiable despair at the unwillingness of law enforcement" to investigate his sister's "brutal" assault. "Mike admits that inertia on the part of his parents isn't helpful, either, but he is certain that if a serious attempt had been made to uncover the truth, they would have come around."

Errol Moffett "is extinct and that's an outrage and one that was eminently preventable. Remedial measures must and will be taken."

At the end of each account: *QED.*

That one I knew from a statistics prof who proclaimed it on the final day of every semester.

"Quod erat demonstrandum. Latin for 'what was to be demonstrated.'"

"What the hell does that mean?"

"The proof is complete."

47

The day after Lance Guidot Esq. began his court-appointed task of defending Cameron Flick, he was fired by his client.

Milo said, "I was over at the jail filing papers, met the guy leaving and looking kinda glum. I said what's up, he said Flick claimed he wasn't smart enough and gave him the boot. But that's not why I'm calling. Followed your advice and called Crystal Jo Wiebelhaus in Akron and yeah, she's Flick's older sister. Hasn't seen him since he moved to L.A. ten years ago but her voice still shakes when she talks about him."

I said, "She grew up with his unpredictable cold anger and his cruelty to animals, other kids, and her."

Silence.

"Why do I bother? Yeah, from the time he was little he terrified her and her mother. Who is indeed Felicia Sue in Vantage who is not taking my calls. Crystal's sure Cam murdered Wiebelhaus but not because she has evidence. She just said Leonard was strict, he and Cam didn't get along, and Cam hated his guts and smiled for days after Wiebelhaus's death."

"No abuse."

"Not according to her. Looks like Cam doesn't need much of a trigger to reach for his trigger."

48

The day after firing his first lawyer, Cameron Flick was assigned a second counsel from the court roster named Marcia Kendall.

That association lasted twenty-six hours, after which Flick fired Kendall for "insufficient attention to the gravity of my situation."

Milo called and told me. "Gonna be a while before we're rid of him. He's obviously playing games."

I said, "Is there a limit how far he can take it?"

"I asked Nguyen. He says when you pay your own way you can manipulate for a while but with court-appointed counsel it's up to the judge. Luckily for Flick he got one of the D.A.'s buddies on the bench, total moron, believes bad guys can do no wrong. So who the hell knows? I'll keep you posted if anything changes."

It did. But not the way either of us expected.

On the third day of his incarceration, Cameron Flick summoned a jail deputy and announced that he'd be serving as his own counsel. Then he said he wanted to talk to Milo.

I left my car at the station and the two of us drove east of down-
town to the Men's Central Jail on Bauchet Street. Forty-minute
ride from West L.A. Five minutes from the Coroner's on Mission
Road, which is efficient.

Before we got out, Milo said, "Anything else you want to tell me?"

"Nope."

"Just be aware that his world revolves around his self-image as brilliant."

"Exactly. He'll likely insult our intelligence and try to control the
situation with insults and erudite vocabulary."

"Got it," he said. "Duh."

It had been a while since I'd been at the jail but the procedure hadn't
changed.

Check in, leave your I.D., stash any weapons in a locker—in this
case, Milo's Glock.

That completed, a Sheriff's deputy named Ortiz met us on the
other side of a sally port and guided us up the elevator to a stale-
smelling hallway and finally to an interview room where a second
deputy named Coolidge stood guard.

Ortiz left and Coolidge let us into a stingy, windowless space that would never recover from decades of human stink.

Cameron Flick sat behind a small steel table screwed to the floor. His right hand was chained to a heavy eyebolt welded to the table's side.

His red uniform signaled *High Risk*. So did the *H* on his red wristband. Below that, *K1*, for "Keep him away from everyone else."

His free hand flicked the blood-colored fabric. "Not my best hue but good taste is in dire shortage here."

We sat down facing him. Coolidge said, "I'll be right outside."

"Superfluous announcement," said Cameron Flick. "If you know what that means."

Coolidge remained stoic and left, closing the door behind him.

Flick said, "Good riddance to maladaptive detritus."

He'd shaved off his beard, ended up with a pale, doughy, soft-around-the-edges baby face blotched in places by pink razor rash.

I thought about him wielding a razor in his cell as I studied him.

Just a face. Like his eyes, unremarkable.

Sometimes you see the same kind of countenance in old photos of young Nazi storm troopers making their way through the streets of Munich or Berlin.

The monster concealed within.

Camouflaged like the weapon Flick had used to slaughter half a dozen people.

Milo said, "You wanted to talk to us."

"To you. Who's he?"

"Alex Delaware."

He looked me up and down and shrugged. Eager to clarify how little my presence meant to him. Returned his attention to Milo.

"So," he said, "you must be quite pleased with yourself. With the erudition you acquired learning about me in the course of your so-called investigation."

"I'm pleased you're in here and not shooting people."

Flick nodded. "Of course you'd see it in a narrow perspective. I've summoned you here for some corrective education."

"You're going to tutor me."

Flick smiled. "The first thing you need to know is that I'll be representing myself in court. All the supposed experts say it's foolhardy but I've learned that following my own instincts works best."

Milo said, "The court will assign you a lawyer as backup."

"Whom I will utterly ignore."

Milo crossed his legs.

Flick said, "Relaxing your posture in order to tell me you're not concerned. Pathetic attempt at insouciance."

"What would I be concerned about, Cameron?"

"My getting acquitted."

I smiled. Milo laughed.

Flick said, "Expected response. Again, constricted by lack of imagination."

"You murdered a lot of people, Cameron."

"Expected response. Tell me, do you enjoy parades?"

"Not particularly."

Flick smirked. "Even *pride* parades?"

Winking. *I've done research on you.*

Milo's failure to react made Flick blink.

He repeated the question. Vocally twisting the word "pride."

Milo said, "Even them."

"I doubt that but now you're reaching for the *un*expected response," said Flick. "Well, putting that aside, a lot of people do enjoy parades. And who's often honored at a parade?"

"A hero."

"A military hero. And what did that military hero do to garner admiration?"

Milo said, "You want me to say he killed a lot of people."

"It's not a matter of what I want," said Flick. "It's a fact. Heroes are mass murderers who get to ride in parade floats."

"You see yourself as a war hero."

"Why wouldn't I? Just like good old G.I. Joe, I eliminate bad people."

"Whitney Killeen—"

"Was in danger of destroying a family."

"So it was time for cruel to be kind."

"Are you being dense to annoy me or have we simply reached the limits of your education-starved imagination? Pay attention: Nothing separates heinous from heroic other than intent."

"Leaving a two-year-old in a boat next to his mother's corpse was heroic."

Flick lifted a free index finger into the air and waved it. "The ultimate expected response. I don't need to explain myself to you but I will. That child was never in danger. I observed him closely and had, in fact, every intent to rescue him when a nosy neighbor showed up and simplified matters."

"Meanwhile, he's next to his mom's bloody corpse."

"Not an issue," said Flick. "Memories registered that early inevitably fade."

"Do they."

"If you knew your child psychology, you wouldn't even raise the issue."

"Thought you were a mathematician."

"I am, indeed," said Flick, "but that doesn't preclude my acquiring knowledge in other fields. In fact, it enhances it. Mathematics engenders an overall sense of intellectual inquisitiveness and creative problem solving and is the undisputed ruler of academia."

"You're interested in the world."

"In the meaningful aspects of the world."

"Ah."

"I don't expect you to fully grasp it," said Flick. "But once you're out of here, give it some thought and you may glean a bit of insight."

"Thanks for the encouragement," said Milo.

"So," said Flick, "you're undoubtedly wondering why I've summoned you."

Milo said nothing.

Flick said, "That's not going to work, you're curious and showing it. And let me emphasize that I use the term intentionally. Summoned. I called, you arrived, obedient as a trained poodle. With a sidekick so you can appear more authoritative but that does nothing to alter the basics."

Dismissive smile in my direction. I was ready for it and had looked away.

Flick frowned. "Would you care to ask?"

Milo said, "Ask what?"

"Why I've summoned you?"

"This isn't a game, Cameron. If you have something to say, say it. If not, see you at trial."

"Now that you mention it," said Flick. "*That's* why you're here. To become educated about the trial. I'm putting you on my list as a defense witness and thought it would be a gracious notion to inform you so that you can prepare your testimony."

"You want me to be on your side."

Flick said, "It's not a matter of what I want. It's what will transpire. You'll be on the defense list and that fact will be noted. Once you've parroted the prosecution case as their unsurprising pawn, I'll have my way with you and get to the core."

Licking his lips on "have my way."

Milo said, "Ah."

"Milo, Milo, Milo," said Flick, "you can posture all you like but you will help me, despite yourself. Here's why: A. You're more aware than any juror of my intentions and we will explore that in great detail.

Including the heroism/criminal dichotomy I've just cited. B. You're aware of the precision of my shots. A single, precisely placed bullet that managed to sever the carotid artery, the jugular vein, and the trachea. A triumph of marksmanship aimed—pun intended—on reducing needless pain."

Milo said, "You engaged in humane slaughter."

"If you must," said Cameron Flick. "But that's selling me short. Not far from where I grew up there was a slaughterhouse. Cows and bulls dispatched daily so the world could have burgers. When the wind was right, their lowing and moaning could be heard for miles. Traveling along with the stink."

Another lip-lick. Violence and sexuality melded early.

"As a child, I'd go over there to catch a glimpse of how the poor bovines were actually processed. Quite a mundane but nonetheless bloody routine. Hoisted, shackled, a shotgun shell to the skull, then the butchers would get busy with their long knives whether or not the animal's chest was still heaving."

Milo said, "Did that turn you into a vegetarian?"

Flick's lips pursed. Genuinely perplexed. "Why would it? I'm merely pointing out that my military mission was maximally humane, far beyond anything offered to animals or humans. And that the targeted enemy had in every case committed a heinous act."

"You think if you get me to say those things you'll be acquitted."

"If not acquitted, I'll be offered a brief, relatively benign sentence, which my good behavior will shorten further. In the meantime, a time-limited incarceration will be easier on me than on other inmates. I'll engage in my studies."

"Ph.D. in math."

"As I've pointed out, the apex of academia," said Flick. "There's no debate: Mathematicians have been shown to have the highest I.Q.'s. Higher, I might add, than the psychologists who design the I.Q. tests and undoubtedly give themselves a sizable advantage."

"You're a smart guy," said Milo. "Therefore, you'll beat the system."

Flick grinned. "If I was a lottery ticket, Milo, you'd be wise to buy me."

"Hmm. Parole, then finish your Ph.D."

"Followed by a post-doctoral fellowship and eventual welcome into the tenure track of a highly ranked institution."

"Your time behind bars—"

"Will not make a difference. Math is free of irrelevancies. That's the beauty of it."

"Hmm," said Milo. "Too bad it'll never happen."

"Your lack of faith is comical, Milo. A few years in some minimum security will not impact—"

"I'm not talking jail, Cameron. I'm talking the Ph.D. The U. booted you out two years five months ago because you could never come up with anything close to original."

Flick's pale skin turned gray, the pink rash, beige. His neck tendons—cords he'd severed in other people's necks—stood out in relief, stiff as pencils.

"You," he said, extruding words through taut lips, "are stupid and obtuse and ludicrously in error."

"Not claiming to be a genius, Cameron, but I'm totally on base. Not only were you kicked out of the department, you didn't make much of an impression while you were there. I've spoken to several of your professors. They barely remember you."

"That," said Flick, "is . . . is . . . you're *blaspheming.*"

"Now you're God?"

"God-*like.* The mentally gifted are. I was talking when I was ten months old. Taught myself to read at four and a half—"

"Great, Cameron. But looks like you front-loaded your smarts and reached *your* apex at the bachelor's degree level. Didn't even earn a master's. Even a dumb guy like me could do that. M.A. in American Literature. True, it's not math, but it's still one degree above you."

Flick stared. Gripped the table. Opened his mouth, clamped it shut. Produced a small oval aperture in the center of taut, nearly white lips.

"Session over!"

No response from outside the room.

Milo said, "Maybe Deputy Coolidge took your words to heart, Cameron. Superfluous, so why stick around?"

"You," said Cameron, "are a dolt. A taurine—no, too charitable, you're a *porcine* dolt. An obese, slavering, sweaty-faced porcine *saurine* admixture of scale and swine . . . and . . . and . . ."

His lips continued working but nothing came out. Something choking internally.

Unable to come up with more words, he began shaking. Banged a left fist on the table, so hard it had to hurt.

"Session over!"

Milo said, "So there you have it, Cameron. I may be a dolt but I'm a dolt with a master's. Which you don't have. But let's put that aside and talk about Alex here. *He's* got a Ph.D."

Flick gaped. "Right."

"This is *Dr.* Alex Delaware, our consulting psychologist. Didn't you get your Ph.D. from the U.?"

I nodded.

"Same place that had no use for you, Cameron. How old were you, Doc, when you earned your degree?"

"Twenty-four."

"Twenty-four, Cameron. Did you eventually get tenure, Doc?"

I nodded.

"How old were you when you got tenure?"

"Thirty-two."

"Hear that, Cameron? Tenure at thirty-two, which is just around your age, isn't that something. *Dr.* Delaware earns tenure and you can't even—"

Flick's body shot upward. His shackled hand yanked him down on his right side and he ended up standing in a lopsided, crab-like position.

"Smart is as smart does, Cam. You're here because you're stupid."

"Session over! Overoveroveroverover!"

The door opened. Slowly. Deputy Coolidge peeked in, then stood back for a second as Flick continued to pound and shriek.

"Everything okay?" he asked Milo.

"Someone's having a rough morning."

"Looks like it. Okay, you shut up or I'll call the medics and they'll inject something in you."

Cameron Flick shouted, "Sess—" then stopped himself and stared at each of us in turn.

"You fixin' to behave yourself?" said Coolidge. "The least bit of trouble and it's Thorazine or whatever."

Flick said nothing.

Coolidge said, "I need a response."

"Yes."

"Yes, what?"

"I'm fine."

"Better be," said Coolidge. To us: "Have a good one, Loo. You, too, Doc."

Milo said, "You as well, Twan."

"'Bout as good as it can be taking care of idiots."

Cameron Flick shuddered.

Coolidge said, "Don't start or you will get injected."

Flick's face seemed to melt.

As we left, he said, "Don't think it's over." But in a new, pitiful voice.

Outside the jail, Milo said, "What do you think he meant by that?"

"Empty threat," I said. "He's pretty much torn down."

"Think he will subpoena me?"

"Maybe. Doesn't matter. He's delusional."

"Hey," he said. "Keep your voice down, just in case his next lawyer's around here."

No one in sight but for two deputies returning to the jail. Fronting the building was a dirt patch in which a few gray-green shrubs struggled to survive. I went over and pretended to search behind them.

"Nope, coast is clear."

He laughed. "Time to ditch my own delusions, huh?"

50

No subpoenas or other communication arrived from Flick. Milo and Petra were busy refining their murder books pretrial.

Unnecessary, as it turned out.

Three days after our visit to Flick, he was found dead in his isolation cell by a deputy making her rounds, lying in a massive pool of blood. A pile of legal books and math texts that he'd requested were stacked neatly in a corner, unstained.

Milo called to tell me. I was at my desk, reviewing notes on a custody eval.

I said, "How'd he do it?"

"With a pen. They gave him a few to do his trial prep. Felt-tips to avoid problems with ballpoints. He snapped off one of the plastic clips, sharpened it, and tried to slice open his own neck. Big mess, from what the deputy told me, had to hurt but he lacked the gumption to dig deep enough. Even though he'd stockpiled and swallowed a whole bunch of extra-strength Tylenol they'd given him for headaches. After the neck didn't work out, he moved on to his wrist. Did it the right way—longitudinal."

"Sounds horrific."

"Sure does," he said. "And it makes me wonder."

"About what?"

"When we saw him he was so goddamn arrogant. Then to just toss it all in and destroy himself? Remember what you said when we left the jail? He was torn down. Did I rip him up to the point where he couldn't take it anymore?"

"No reason to think that," I said. "And spare yourself anything close to guilt."

"Why?"

"He was highly disturbed and unpredictable."

"Still—"

"No still," I said. "He murdered a lot of people in cold blood and would have kept doing it. Plus, this saves a bunch of families having to endure his antics at a trial."

"True," he said. "I need to keep that in mind. Actually was talking to Donna Batchelor when the message came in and for the first time she sounded kinda happy. Before that I'd informed Dr. Rosales and he started crying. I was about to call Hannah Gardener, then Shari Flores to thank her for alerting us to Whitney's case."

"There you go."

"Okay, thanks. Send me your bill."

After I hung up, I sat there, wondered why I felt uneasy.

A pen clip.

I wrote *at least six people* on a piece of paper and stared at it. When that wasn't enough, I downloaded the photos of Flick's victims. Studied them, one by one.

Woman in a boat. Little boy watching her die. Terrified by abandonment.

A gifted teacher slaughtered while taking out the garbage.

No need to go beyond that.

No reason to give any of it another moment of thought.

I went to get a cup of coffee.

About the Author

JONATHAN KELLERMAN has lived in two worlds: clinical psychologist and #1 *New York Times* bestselling author of more than fifty crime novels. His unique perspective on human behavior has led to the creation of the Alex Delaware series, *The Butcher's Theater, Billy Straight, The Conspiracy Club, Twisted, True Detectives,* and *The Murderer's Daughter.* With his wife, bestselling novelist Faye Kellerman, he co-authored *Double Homicide* and *Capital Crimes.* With his son, bestselling novelist Jesse Kellerman, he co-authored *The Lost Coast, The Burning, Half Moon Bay, A Measure of Darkness, Crime Scene, The Golem of Hollywood,* and *The Golem of Paris.* He is also the author of two children's books and numerous nonfiction works, including *Savage Spawn: Reflections on Violent Children* and *With Strings Attached: The Art and Beauty of Vintage Guitars.* He has won the Goldwyn, Edgar, and Anthony awards and the Lifetime Achievement Award from the American Psychological Association, and has been nominated for a Shamus Award. Jonathan and Faye Kellerman live in California.

jonathankellerman.com
Facebook.com/jonathankellerman

About the Type

This book was set in Garamond, a typeface originally designed by the Parisian type cutter Claude Garamond (c. 1500–61). This version of Garamond was modeled on a 1592 specimen sheet from the Egenolff-Berner foundry, which was produced from types assumed to have been brought to Frankfurt by the punch cutter Jacques Sabon (c. 1520–80).

Claude Garamond's distinguished romans and italics first appeared in *Opera Ciceronis* in 1543–44. The Garamond types are clear, open, and elegant.